Alicia Lawson is a pen name created by Relay Publishing for co-authored Detective Thriller projects. Relay Publishing works with incredible teams of writers and editors to collaboratively create the very best stories for our readers.

Book Cover Design by ebooklaunch.com

www.relaypub.com

ALICIA LAWSON

WHAT YOU DESERVE

FBI AGENT ERIN HASTINGS BOOK ONE

BLURB

When lives are on the line, failure is not an option…

FBI Special Agent Erin Hastings is driven by the pain of her past. Fifteen years ago, she could've stopped her twin brother from killing his sixth victim. All she wants now is a second chance at catching a killer.

Riding high after a media blitz over her latest arrest, Erin is plunged back to reality with her first serial killer case—in Erin's hometown. Reminders of her brother's murders plague her nightmares. Haunted by the similarities between the two cases, Erin vows she won't make the same rookie mistake again. This time, she'll stop the murderer before he can claim any more innocent lives.

But the race to catch this ruthless killer grows more desperate as the body count rises. And with every suspect her team clears, Erin's chances at redemption wither away. All while pressure for an arrest from higher-ups intensifies.

Erin won't quit until she gets her man. Not when history seeks to repeat itself. With another victim's life at stake, she'll risk going rogue before she gives up.

But will she jeopardize her own life, rather than let this killer strike again?

CONTENTS

1

E rin crouched in the damp leaves, the sunset in her eyes. The Kentucky mud sucked at her boots, stinking of wet rot and pregnant with gnats. Her socks were soaked through, but Erin barely noticed. The cabin stood due west, hulking in the gloom. Anderson was in there, a beast run to ground.

"Hannon in position." Catherine's voice came through tinny. Erin fiddled with her earpiece. A sharp burst of static nearly drowned Brody's response.

"Close in on my go."

Erin leaned forward, adrenaline surging. Fifty yards to the cabin, to the end of the chase. The place was a ruin, all sloped to one side. Its windows were red wounds, the sunset bleeding through.

"*Go.*" Brody crept forward, off to her right. He crouched low to the treeline, one shadow among many. Erin was moving as well, cutting smoothly through the brush. An hour ago, she'd been dead tired, eyes drooping shut. Now she was focused, a hunter on the prowl. She closed in through clouds of bugs, eyes slit against the sun.

"Hold positions."

She hissed through her teeth. Brody had gone stiff, head cocked to one side. Erin listened intently, but all she heard was the forest, the whisper of leaves.

"What's the holdup? I—"

"*Shh.*"

Erin shut her mouth. The sun clouded over, and a chill walked down her spine. Somewhere, a bird trilled, and then she heard it—a low metal *chunk,* a sputtering roar. The cabin door flew open and Anderson surged out, hunched over the handlebars of a ridiculous green dirt bike. He caught sight of Erin and buttonhooked right, aiming between her and Brody.

"What the actual—" Brody charged like a quarterback, head down, shoulders bunched. He slammed into Anderson with an agonized grunt.

Anderson skidded sideways. His bike dipped like a dancer, churning up leaves.

"Erin! Get down!"

Erin tore after him, leaves in her face. He swerved in a half-circle and accelerated past the cabin. Erin ran faster, pulse pounding in her ears. Her breath came fast and ragged. Her heels squelched in the mud. Anderson hit a root and went flying, headlong over the handlebars. His bike careened out and Erin launched herself over it.

"Erin! Fall back!"

Her vision narrowed to Anderson, his stringy black hair, his faded blue shirt. He scrambled upright, flailing in the mud, then tripped, found his feet, and took off like a jackrabbit. Erin thundered after him.

She was close now, and gaining. Twenty feet and she'd have him face down in the dirt. Fifteen feet, almost there.

She pushed herself harder, drawing on fumes. The ground inclined upward, sudden and steep. Anderson's breath came in loud, rasping bursts. He'd tire before she did, and—

Anderson launched himself into the sunset and vanished from sight. Erin lurched after him with a shout. The sun glared in her eyes, bright red and gold. Up ahead, the ground gave out, a steep, crumbling slope descending into darkness. Anderson's blue shirt gleamed palely from the bottom, maybe a five-foot drop, maybe ten or fifteen. He was moving, turning over. Rising on his knees.

"Erin!"

Erin plunged after him. She fell blind, stomach dropping, and came down on his back. Anderson made a whoofing sound, like a punctured tire. He pitched forward, boneless, and she had him at last.

———

"I thought the earth swallowed you up." Catherine plucked a leaf from Erin's collar. "You were running, then *poof.* There and gone, just like that."

Erin made a huffing sound, half-laugh, half-wheeze. Her head was all foggy, her stomach tight and sour—an adrenaline hangover in the making.

"You should sit down." Mo Mirza, their profiler, was sitting cross-legged in the back of the evidence van. He moved to make space. "Come on, before you fall down."

"Can't sit. Too wired." Erin bit back a yelp as someone clapped her on the shoulder. Her nerves were still jangling, primed for a fight. "Gonna walk the scene," she said. "In case, y'know..." She left the thought unfinished. Her work was done here, but she needed to move. To walk off her willies, as Brody would say.

Brody fell in beside her as she headed back up the slope. His elbow bumped hers, a companionable nudge.

"You did good," he said. "One more scumbag off the streets."

"But?" Erin could feel it coming, her team leader's reproach.

"But, see for yourself." Brody pushed through the trees, up to the embankment. He stood on the edge, peering into the gloom. "Go on. What's down there?"

Erin squinted past him. The sun had dipped below the horizon, leaving a thin line of red. "I don't know. Leaves, I guess? It's too dark to see."

"Over there, past that bush. Take a good look."

Erin took a good look, and then looked some more. Had she seen it before, the dull gleam of train tracks threading through the woods?

"I'd have heard a train coming," she said.

"Would you?" Brody pulled her back from the drop. "Do you remember me yelling? Ordering you back?"

Erin said nothing. She remembered Anderson's blue shirt, the chuff of his breath. She remembered him flying, plunging over the edge. *Had* Brody called to her? She touched her earpiece—still there.

"You lost situational awareness," said Brody. "You jumped ten feet into God knows what, and never stopped to look. Forget the trains for a minute. What if he'd had his knife?"

Erin closed her eyes. That, she could picture, Anderson twisting as she dropped, the flash of his Bowie as it found her throat. A shudder ran through her, and she swallowed hard.

"Hasty Hastings strikes again." Brody made a disgusted sound. "You need to retire her ass before she gets you killed."

Erin just nodded. She didn't trust her voice. If Brody had yelled at her, she'd have been fine. She could've got mad then, armored herself in resentment. But Brody's shoulders were slumped, his arms loose at his sides. When he raised his head, all she saw was exhaustion.

"Say it hadn't gone well. Say he'd had backup waiting down on those tracks. We'd have had to go after you—me and Cat, everyone. Say we'd got gunned down right there on the tracks. What would you tell our families? You gonna tell Cat's kids Mom's not coming home?"

Erin's mouth tasted of copper. She'd bitten her cheek. "Guess I screwed up pretty bad."

"Only at the end." Brody blew out a long breath. "I was all set to tell you how far you'd come. How you'd finally learned some patience, worked up some restraint. Then you get one whiff of him, and you're off like a hound with a squirrel in your sights. Why'd you go and do that? You were doing so well."

Erin looked away. "You going to write me up?"

"Maybe I should." Brody's tone had gone sharp. "I need to be able to trust you, not nine times out of ten, but *every damn time*. I need to know you've got my back, or I don't see how—"

"Brody? Erin? You out there?" Catherine's voice drifted up, eerie in the dark.

"Coming," called Brody. He turned to Erin. "Look, you need to get past this, this need to rush in. I don't care how you do it, but you get squared away."

"Yes, sir."

"And I'm going to be on you until I see that it's done."

5

"Yes, sir."

"Now, let's get out of here before we're eaten alive." Brody swatted the gnats away and headed back down the hill. Erin followed more slowly, a lump in her throat. She couldn't stop picturing Catherine laid out on the tracks, eyes wide and glassy, a bullet through her skull. How *would* her kids cope, if the unthinkable came to pass? And who'd mourn Brody? For all she'd come to trust him, she hardly knew him at all.

Erin slept on the plane, mud drying on her boots. The sandman had claimed her the moment she closed her eyes. She'd crashed hard, as she always did, wide awake one minute, snoring the next.

"Erin."

She grunted, dove deeper into the syrup of sleep. She'd been dreaming, something pleasant—something she might still get back.

"*Erin.*"

"Go 'way Brody. I'm off the clock."

"Not for me, you're not."

"Sir!" Erin jerked upright. Sometime in the night, her boss had plopped down next to her, Special Agent in Charge Randy Cho. He sat regarding her with amusement, thin lips turned up.

"Had a nice nap, I trust?"

"Yes, sir. Sorry. I—"

"Don't be." Randy waved her off. "I wouldn't disturb you, but I'm afraid this can't wait."

6

"What can't?" Erin scrubbed at her eyes, bleary with sleep. Randy rose, straightened his tie.

"Come up to the galley. We need to talk."

Erin stood up and followed him, half in a daze. The cabin was dim, Catherine stretched out sleeping, Mo reading a book. He nodded as Erin passed, and tipped her a *don't worry* wink. Erin tried to smile back and yawned widely instead.

Brody was waiting in the galley, his mouth a grim line. Erin straightened at the sight of him, and her stomach turned over. So this was a reprimand—a suspension, maybe. Brody had gone to Randy, and her goose was cooked. She couldn't blame him, she guessed, but—

"I'm sorry to do this," said Randy. "I know you're both exhausted, but this can't wait. You may have noticed we're heading west, away from Atlanta."

Brody's brows shot up. Clearly, he hadn't. Erin caught his eye, but saw only confusion.

"The LA field office has requested our presence. They've got a potential serial killer operating across California and Nevada, but..." He looked away, frowning. "There's no easy way to say this, so I'll just spit it out. Victims one and two died in Lancaster. That's where we're headed. That going to be a problem?"

Erin's insides went cold. She clutched at the counter, missed, and nearly staggered. Brody twigged a moment later. Erin caught the moment it happened, the hitch in his breath, the tightening of his fists.

"You can't drag Erin back there. Not after—"

"Yes, he can." Erin's voice cracked, and she cleared her throat. "I'm fine. I'll be fine."

"Why's it got to be us?" Brody's Texas drawl deepened, the way it did when he got pissed, or when he hadn't slept. "Seems to me LA could handle this themselves."

"Not this time." Randy frowned. "They've got their hands full heading off a major gang war. If they don't get ahead of that, they could be looking at another Golden Dragon massacre." He folded his hands, almost primly. "This team *will* assist them. That's not up for debate. But, given Erin's special circumstances—"

"My brother. You can say it." Erin scowled at Randy, mostly to avoid Brody's eye. She couldn't take his sympathy, or worse still, his doubt. She'd screwed up at the cabin, but that was done, in the past. And so was Eric, her infamous twin. "He's not involved, is he?"

Randy made a choking sound. "No. Of course not."

"Then he's not a problem. Not for me, anyway." She crossed her arms over her chest. "How many bodies? And when did they drop?"

Randy's gaze was skeptical, but Erin met it square and true. After a moment, he sighed, and he reached for his tablet.

"Three so far," he said. "The first two died in Lancaster. The third was in Nevada, in Indian Springs. All three victims were women, and similarities at the crime scenes suggest a single killer. I don't have all the details, but I'm expecting, any minute—"

Erin's head swam. Randy's words washed over her, losing all meaning. Lancaster—*Lancaster!* What were the odds? Even the thought of it had her stomach in knots. She'd fled fifteen years ago and never looked back, and now she was hurtling there at five hundred miles an hour. Panic surged sickly, and she swallowed it down.

"You should sit," said Brody. "This could take a while."

Erin didn't move. Couldn't. Jagged snapshots burst forth, one after another—Eric cuffed in a cop car, his gaze blank and vacant. Dad on

8

his knees, hands clasped to his chest. Eric's victims, all six of them, dead eyes glaring crimson in the cops' cherry lights. Erin hadn't seen them that way, not in real life. But in her dreams, they'd accused her, night after night. She'd left them in Lancaster, but—

"Erin. If I'm not mistaken, this'll be your first serial case." Randy's voice cut through her nightmare. Erin blinked, nodded twice.

"Yes, sir. It will."

Randy frowned. "The first one's always the hardest, but we've got your back. Keep your eyes open, and you'll learn a lot." He turned to Brody. "And you—this'll be a good chance to collaborate with LA. Check out how they do things and see what you think."

Erin felt Brody's eyes on her, but she didn't turn his way. Her guts were all curdled, her throat sore and tight. One hint of pity, she might just scream.

"You two should get some rest," said Randy. "While you still can. And good work, both of you, on the Anderson case."

Erin stood and let Brody go by. Her eyes felt dry and scratchy, like she needed to cry but she'd run out of tears. Randy set his hand on her shoulder, and Erin felt weak. If he asked again, she might just bow out.

"I'm proud of you," he said instead. "Keep going like you have been, you might make team leader inside five years."

Erin blinked. She heard herself thank him, perfectly calm. Then she was moving, headed back to her seat. A deep numbness had settled over her, much as it had the day she'd left Lancaster. She'd left her whole life behind her, all she'd ever known, but all she'd felt flying out was a vague sense of relief.

She sank down, limbs heavy, and let her eyes drift shut. She could run from this, too, tell Randy she couldn't hack it and catch the first flight back. No one would think less of her, all things considered. She could run—but Brody's words still haunted her, a miserable refrain. *What would you tell our families? You gonna tell Cat's kids Mom's not coming home?* She'd got lucky today. She'd got her collar, and life would go on. But she knew, and Brody knew, she'd let down her team. She'd dropped the ball hard, and she had to make it right.

"Make it *right*," she muttered, through gritted teeth. The words came out angry, half-apology, half-curse.

The desert wind blew his hair back as he flew down the highway. The stars shone above him, bright as diamonds. He was on top of the world and nothing could stop him. Nothing, unless...

He goosed the gas and surged forward. The speedometer jumped to eighty, eighty-five, ninety. His doubts dwindled behind him, behind a rising plume of dust. In a fast enough car, you *could* outrun fear. You could outrun a lot of things—your past, your crimes, yourself.

He turned the radio up and exhaled gusty laughter. Tonight had been a triumph, his first in...what did it matter? He'd been a victim once, miserable, downtrodden. But those days were behind him, over and done. Now was his time. His just reward. He leaned back in his seat, basking in the satisfaction of a job well done. Mile markers flashed by and vanished. The wind sang in his ears, and he sucked in its tang of hot tarmac and freedom. Every dog had its day, but he wasn't a dog. Tonight had been glorious, but it was only the beginning.

He slowed down reluctantly, approaching a speed trap. He dialed the music down too. Best to keep a low profile. Tonight was his night, but this party was *private*. He coasted through the danger zone at a sedate sixty, past the midnight blue cruiser parked just offroad. The cop turned to watch him, maybe jealous of his ride.

"Yeah. You like that." A sharp thrill ran through him, a strange, heady mixture of triumph and fear—almost like nausea, but he knew he wouldn't puke. He almost had the first time, but only from nerves. From too much excitement, roller-coaster butterflies.

A smirk spread across his face as the cruiser dropped from his rearview. How long would it be, he wondered, before the police fingered him as the killer? Maybe they wouldn't. Maybe they *would*, and they'd look the other way. What he'd done wasn't murder, not by any sane definition. He'd committed *justice*, and who'd blame him for that?

The radio DJ's voice cut through his thoughts. "And that was 'What You Deserve,' by No Resolve. Up next—"

The killer burst out laughing, a deep, merry bark. He pumped the gas and sped on, an arrow through the night.

2

E rin sprawled across three plastic chairs in the cramped laundromat. She should be sleeping, she knew, ahead of her briefing at noon. Instead, she'd come here, and she guessed she knew why. She needed routine, something normal and dull. Something to ground her in her here and now.

She watched her clothes tumble, blue and beige, blue again. Her thoughts tumbled with them, present jumbled with past. How was she back here? How? How? *How?*

She'd been mostly a kid, the summer it all happened—eighteen years old, a senior in high school. She and Eric had come here, not to the laundromat, but the Dairy Queen across the street. He'd had a burger. She'd had a banana split. She'd pointed at the newsstand just outside.

"Who do you think it is?"

"Hm?" Eric had followed her gaze. Had he frowned at the headline— LANCASTER SLASHER STRIKES AGAIN? She thought he had, but maybe he'd smiled. "Probably some old perv," he'd said. "It's always some old perv."

She'd laughed at that, but the summer taste of ice cream had curdled on her tongue. She'd known those girls, at least to say hi. She'd had classes with most of them, sometimes sat with them at lunch. Had she suspected, even then, Eric might be—not the killer, not then—but *enjoying* this, somehow?

She sat up, swallowing nausea. She'd never forget the moment the truth had clicked home. She'd pushed it away then, refusing to believe it could be her own brother. She'd denied what she knew, and Eric had struck again. He'd claimed his sixth victim, one victim too far. The cops had descended, bubble-lights flashing red and blue. Dad had dropped to his knees, pleading *no, no*—pleading with no one, and no one answered his prayers. The papers screamed the truth, all the grisly details. Eric was tried and found guilty, and Erin's heart turned hard.

The washer stopped spinning. Erin got up, stone-faced, and transferred her clothes to the dryer. She could've saved that last girl—Althea Morris, nineteen years old. She could've spared her a dog's death, if she'd only found her voice.

A sob caught in her throat, caught her by surprise. She could still see Althea's mom, the way she'd sat at that trial, gray-faced with heartbreak, eyes flat and stunned. She hadn't said a word, but she might as well have been screaming, her pain shone so bright. Erin liked to tell herself that's when she'd chosen her path, there in that courthouse, drowning in guilt. She hadn't run from Lancaster. She'd run here, to this—to a life where she'd end that grief, curb it at its source.

Her phone buzzed in her pocket and she fished it out. Brody had texted, two lines, quick and curt. *Went by your room. You never checked in.*

She fired off a short reply—*no clean clothes. Doing laundry.*

She thought Brody might admonish her, but he sent back a poo emoji, and the letters *P-U.* Erin laughed, but her eyes stung. She felt raw as a

13

wound, inside and out. A few moments later, Brody texted again. *Chin up, okay? Got a feeling about this one: open & shut.*

Erin sent back a thumbs-up, but she didn't share Brody's optimism. She'd been on enough manhunts to know they rarely went as planned. There'd be evidence to gather, leads to run down, witnesses, family members, forensic reports. Three bodies in two states, that meant a mess. With the LA office chasing their gang war, her team would be swamped. Worst-case scenario, she'd be stuck here for months.

Erin lay down again, flat across the chairs. She stared at her phone, but Brody didn't text back. She should call Dad, she knew, let him know she was in town. The thought made her tired, and she closed her eyes. Dad would want to see her, but what was the point? They'd meet up for coffee, exchange howdy-dos. He'd update her on his work; she'd update him on hers. That'd eat ten minutes, then the well would run dry.

She jammed her phone in her pocket. Dad could wait one more day. Erin closed her eyes and let Lancaster wash over her—the stale smell of laundry soap mixed with Dairy Queen burgers; the soft hush of traffic; the patter of rain. It had rained that day, too, the day she'd stumbled on the truth. It had rained all morning, then the sun had come out.

***

The sun had come out just after lunch. It got hot after that, late July hot, the sky turning surf-postcard California blue—perfect pool weather, or so she'd thought. She'd gone to the linen closet and found it picked bare.

"Eric? Hey, Eric? Where's all the towels?"

No answer. She scowled.

"Eric, I mean it. It's your turn to do laundry, so..." She trailed off with a sigh. If Eric was home, he'd have yelled out by now. Besides, the house felt empty, that broody way houses get, left to themselves.

"I'm taking your fleece, okay? To dry off from my swim."

Eric didn't answer, so she barged into his room. It stunk like a locker room, and like old grilled cheese. She kicked her way through piles of laundry and crumpled magazines, toed his hamper aside to get to his closet. Crap fell out when she opened it, his red Razor scooter, a ketchup-smeared plate.

"Seriously? Slob much?"

Eric still didn't answer. She raked through his clothes, shunting summer wear to one side in search of his fleece. His closet smelled better than the rest of his room, like the herbal shampoo he'd switched to last year. She'd tried it too at first, but it'd dried out her hair.

"Damn it. Where's...?" Erin felt for his fleece and hit canvas instead, some kind of rough jacket, worn at the seams. She pulled it out, frowning, and held it up to the light—an old camo bomber, covered in Air Force patches. It struck her as familiar in a vague sort of way, like something from a movie, or an old photograph. She shrugged into it and turned to admire herself in the mirror. She looked pretty good, she thought, deeply badass. Especially with—with—

The breath caught in her throat. Erin made a wounded sound, a small, strangled whine.

"Eric?"

The jacket was slashed open, all down one sleeve. The collar was brownish, and damp to the touch. Damp at her throat, like—

Erin shrieked, high and breathless. She did a half-spin, caught in the jacket. Its lining had torn, and her arm was stuck. She panicked and

15

thrashed, blundered into the wall. She sobbed, thrashed some more, and the jacket slid off. Erin ran, then stopped dead, heart pounding in her throat.

"Eric..."

She did a slow turn. The jacket lay crumpled, an awful gray heap. She lifted it gingerly and held it up to the light. When she closed her eyes, she felt sick, like she might pass out. Last night on the news—that witness, the little kid—

"I saw him run away from where they found that girl. He ran down by the Metrolink and I thought he missed his train. But then he kept running, into the park. He had on, like, an army jacket, torn down one sleeve. And his face was all bloody, so I ran away."

Erin swallowed. "Like an army jacket. Torn down one sleeve." She stuffed it in the closet, all the way in the back. It was some sick joke, had to be. Or he'd borrowed the jacket, or someone had stashed it here. Eric wasn't a killer. He wasn't because she wasn't. Because they were twins. Because if he could snap like that—

She turned and ran, straight out of the house. She didn't stop running until the sidewalk ran out.

Erin checked into her hotel with time to spare. She didn't bother to unpack, just dug out a shirt and skirt, still warm from the wash. She slung them across the bed and headed for the shower. The showerhead was old and the pressure was weak, but the water was hot and it got the job done. Erin watched the black Kentucky mud swirl down the drain with something like dismay—like in washing off Kentucky, she'd arrived in Lancaster for real.

She scrubbed herself clean with gritty hotel soap, sudsed up her hair with thin green shampoo. When she was done, she felt fresh enough, but her eyes had a bruised look, circled in black. She splashed her face with cold water and set the coffee pot to brew.

"I'm good," she said, and she *did* sound good. Firm and steady, as she should be. "I've got this. I'm good. Just need my armor."

She pulled on her turtleneck, a deep earthy brown to bring out her green eyes. Her skirt came next, knee-length, no-nonsense, a heavy gray knit. Catherine had helped her pick it, her first week on the job. *Got to dress like you mean business, like "hey. FBI."* She'd chuckled at that, but it helped to look the part. When she looked it, she felt it. She felt like herself.

She strapped on her holster and felt herself relax, the weight of her weapon reassuring at her side. She stared at it for a moment, then shrugged into her jacket and took a deep breath. First impressions mattered. She needed to get it together, to start out right in Lancaster. She'd go in full-bore, by the book all the way. Make it right with her team, and right with the world.

"I'll find you," she whispered, "whoever you are." She went to the window and watched the rain fall—washing away evidence, like as not. But that wouldn't stop her. She wouldn't hesitate this time, not like with Eric. She'd bring down the killer before he claimed another life.

3

"Where's Brody?" Erin scanned the lobby, brow knit in a frown.

"He went on ahead," said Catherine. "To deal with the press."

"Already?" Erin shook her head. "I hoped we'd get a day, at least, before the vultures descended."

"Come on. I'm parked out front." Catherine led the way, ponytail swinging. She got into the driver's seat, and Erin piled in beside her.

"How's the coverage looking?"

"Too early to say." Catherine eased into traffic, relaxed at the wheel. "Listen, Brody's set up a press conference outside the police station. We'll head in the back way, avoid the whole scene."

Erin nodded. "Fine with me."

"They don't know you're here yet, but they're about to find out. And we need to prepare for the possibility they'll know who you are."

"The *possibility*." Erin covered a snort. "I still hear from them sometimes, scrounging for comments. Mostly on the anniversary of Eric's arrest—but sometimes, just for fun, they'll call on our birthday."

Catherine flinched. "I'm sorry," she said. She hung a right, heading downtown. "Hey, on a brighter note, it's almost Thanksgiving. If you're not doing anything, we could—"

"I'll be seeing my dad." The words sprang out unbidden, to Erin's surprise. She hadn't called her dad yet, hadn't made any plans. She sank down in her seat, color rising in her cheeks. This place, this case had her feeling exposed. Embarrassed, even, like she had something to hide. Catherine's sympathy only made it worse. So did slinking into the cop shop through its cruddy side door.

Randy met them inside, along with a red-faced detective who introduced himself as Robson.

"I've got you set up in briefing room B." Robson gestured down the hall. "I can come in with you, get you all caught up."

"It'll be just us for this part." Randy smiled warmly to soften the snub. "But we'll need you right after, to walk us through that first crime scene."

"Guess I'll wait out here, then." Robson's face darkened to a new shade of red, somewhere between brick dust and a side of salami. Erin nodded politely as she passed him by.

Mo was waiting in the briefing room, tapping on his laptop. Sasha, their tech wizard, was still en route, sipping tomato juice at forty thousand feet. Her head filled the big screen, in a giant Zoom window. She spotted Erin and lit up with glee.

"So *that's* where my bags went."

"Excuse me?"

"My luggage. That's it right there, isn't it, under your eyes?"

Erin flipped her the bird. Sasha snickered, delighted. Randy motioned for silence, sliding into his seat.

"First of all, let me apologize for the rush. I'd have let you all sleep a while, but Mo flies back at three. I need you to hear his profile before you dive in."

"What about Brody?" Erin glanced at the door.

"He'll be here any minute. In the meantime, let me recap." Randy thumbed on his tablet. "We've got three potential victims, two here, one in Nevada. Our killer's moving fast, and he's crossed state lines, so we can't discount the possibility he's done more we don't know about." He swiped at his tablet, a quick, angry gesture. "We have two women, mother and daughter, killed in Lancaster last Friday. Our third victim, also female, died in Indian Springs. That was on Tuesday, just four days' cooldown."

The door swung open behind him and Brody slipped in. Randy waited while he sat down, and then he forged on.

"The bodies were posed post-mortem, two on their knees, one in her bed. The two on their knees had their wrists bound, their hands stretched out in front of them with their palms turned up. That's why we're thinking they're all the same unsub. Mo?"

Mo perked up, features coming to life. "So, we're looking for a white male—"

"—late twenties to mid-forties. Kind of a loner, a mom's basement type." Sasha smirked from the big screen. Mo pulled a face.

"Knock it off, Sasha. I *will* pull your plug."

Sasha poked her tongue out, but she zipped her lip. Mo smiled, a little sheepishly, and flipped through his notes.

"Sasha's snide, but she's not wrong. I'd say he *is* in that age range, and a mild, quiet type. He may not live in Mom's basement, but his life won't have turned out the way he hoped. He's had a lot of disappointment, a lot of setbacks. He's felt powerless, even victimized, and his resentment runs deep."

Brody shifted in his seat. "Where're you getting all that?"

Mo got up and began to pace. "His kills are up close and personal: one strangled, one smothered, one bashed in the head. He's *angry* with his victims, blames them for his life. Then there's the posing, down on their knees."

"What about that third one?" said Brody. "The one found in bed?"

Mo frowned. "She's an anomaly. Her body *was* moved from the living room to the bedroom, but she was tucked in almost tenderly, and her hands weren't bound. Her posing suggests remorse on the part of the killer. It's possible he wasn't expecting her—she surprised him mid-kill and he hit her to shut her up. But the other two, those are different. The posing's highly specific. He's made them vulnerable. Submissive. He's asserting his power."

Erin leaned forward. "How about a religious angle?"

"I was getting to that." Mo glanced at his laptop. "The posing *might* imply penitence, a position of prayer. But there's no evidence so far to back up that assumption. No Bibles, no rosaries, no evidence of religious ritual. Right now, I'd focus on the victimhood angle—someone feeling hard done by. Someone out for revenge, maybe on someone specific, maybe on victims who fit a certain profile."

"Thanks, Mo," said Randy. He checked his watch and frowned. "I'll be heading back to Atlanta along with Agent Mirza. But we'll both be available, anything you need."

Mo sat down again, and Erin thought he looked tired. "I'll get you a victim profile this afternoon. I just got their background files, so I'll read them on the plane."

"Good. Good, then." Randy massaged his forehead. "We've got a lot of pressure on this one—not just from the locals, but from up the chain. Chief Hannady wants it cleared, the quicker the better. And it goes without saying, a killer moving this fast..."

"We're on it," said Brody. Randy barely glanced his way.

"Erin and Catherine, I want you on the crime scene—and make nice with Robson. We need him on our side. Sasha, you're on evidence, and Brody, you're in charge. You're on press duty too, keep the lime-light off Erin."

Brody straightened in his seat. Erin shot him an apologetic look. He hated the press, she knew, though he handled them well.

Randy got to his feet. "Everyone clear?"

A murmur of agreement went around the table. Randy signaled to Mo, and the two headed out. Sasha's Zoom window collapsed, leaving the screen dark and empty.

"We should head out," said Catherine. "Robson looked antsy."

Erin made to head out, but Brody caught her arm.

"Hey. You get some sleep?"

"A few hours," she lied.

"Well, get some more soon. This is a marathon, not a sprint."

Erin shook him off and jogged out to join Catherine. They piled into her car and set out after Robson. Catherine's mouth quirked up as they stopped at a light.

"Reach in my bag and pull out my phone."

Erin frowned. "Why?"

"Just do it. And open my camera roll."

Erin did as she said, keying in Catherine's password to bypass the lock. She tapped on the camera roll and burst out laughing.

"Is that—is that a hamster in a tutu?"

Catherine grinned. "I thought you'd like that."

"But *why?*"

"Noah adopted his class hamster." Catherine's grin faded, turned soft and fond. "Izzy's been sewing it costumes. Don't ask me why."

"Your kids are the best." Erin smiled. For the first time since they'd landed, she felt almost optimistic. Shit happened, no doubt, but life wasn't all bad.

Erin stood in the driveway, adrenaline surging. The crime scene wasn't sinister, or even unusual—a regular house on a regular street, gnomes in the garden, welcome mat out front—but still her blood sang with the start of the hunt. This was it, her first whiff of the battle to come.

"Agent Hastings?"

She realized Robson was talking, droning on in her ear. She nodded— *I'm listening*—and headed up the drive.

"So, as I was saying, November fourth. Two officers responded to a possible break-in. That was around noon, uh...yeah, twelve-oh-four. A neighbor saw a broken window and called it in. Upon responding, the officers found..."

Erin circled the house, around to the back door. It was closed now, but they'd found it ajar. Had the killer left it that way? Or had one of the victims made a break for it, a desperate dash?

"The victims were identified as Rayna Cook and her daughter, uh, Valerie. Rayna was forty, Valerie just nineteen."

Just nineteen. Eric's last victim had been the same age. Had she tried to run when she saw what was coming? A vision flashed through her head, Valerie bolting for the back door, only her face was Althea's, and spattered with blood. She was screaming, teeth bared in a rictus of fear. She pounded on the door, fists battering, bruising—

"It's fine to head in. We're done with the scene." Robson went in first, Catherine on his heels. Erin brought up the rear, recoiling at the rich smell of overripe fruit. A bowl of bananas sat on the counter, all black and bruised and swarming with flies. Robson swatted at them, but the flies just came back.

"They were killed between eleven PM and two AM, the night of the third. Rayna was suffocated. Valerie died of blunt force trauma to the head. I sent the reports to your...Sasha, I think."

Erin nodded again. She drifted through the kitchen, not much to see there. Beyond lay the hallway where Rayna was found.

"Right there," said Robson. He pointed at a shadowed patch just shy of the stairs. Erin had spotted it already, knew it from the photos. The killer had used the banisters to bind Rayna's wrists, her arms outstretched in a gesture of supplication. He'd posed her on her knees, with her back to the—

"Oh." Erin made a low sound, sick and dismayed. Robson didn't seem to notice, but Catherine cocked a brow.

"Found something?"

"Not really. Just, look." She gestured at the long wall across from the stairs. A line of family photos stretched down the hall—Valerie's christening, a birthday party, her graduation. Rayna on a boat, holding up a big fish. Rayna and Valerie together, draped in pink bridesmaid's gowns. "You think that's deliberate? Putting that all behind her, her life, all those moments?"

Catherine frowned. "Maybe. Or maybe he needed the banister to hold her up."

"Right. Probably that." Erin swallowed hard. She was spinning, off her game. Identifying with the victims when she needed to focus.

"They'd just moved here," said Robson. "We talked to their neighbors, and they'd settled in fine. They hadn't made many friends, but no enemies either."

Erin turned to face him. "What about the ex-husband?"

"Allen Cook, currently residing in Pahrump, Nevada. He's not a suspect."

"Why not?"

"He works as a night guard at the children's museum. He was at work at the time of the murders. We've got a co-worker's statement, plus surveillance footage of his car parked out front."

Erin scowled. She'd liked Allen for the crime, the scorned ex-husband, discarded, pushed aside. He fit Mo Mirza's profile, and then there was Valerie. Her body hadn't been posed, at least not like Rayna's. She'd been tucked into bed, covers snugged to her chin. Like a father might do, a father who'd loved her.

"This co-worker, are they close? Enough so he'd lie for him?"

"Don't think so," said Robson. "They'd only been working together four or five months. Plus, he didn't seem nervous, no sign of deceit."

Erin stared at the floorboards. Rayna's nose had been bleeding, and a few drops remained. She resisted the compulsion to kneel down beside them, where Rayna'd been found.

"We should head back," said Catherine. "Brody's just texted. Captain Woods is on his way."

"Oh, from Indian Springs." Robson's expression brightened. "I should sit in on that, so I'll keep up to date."

Erin opened her mouth to tell him that wouldn't be necessary, but Catherine smiled at him. "That would be great."

Brody was waiting back at the station, shooting the breeze with Captain Woods. They both rose to greet Erin and Catherine, and Woods tipped his hat.

"Ma'am—ma'am. Detective Robson. Good to meet you, and see you again."

Brody made an impatient sound. "So, now we all know each other, on to our third victim. Woods, you have the floor."

Woods cleared his throat. "Please, call me Marcus. Let's not stand on ceremony." He shot Brody a grin. Brody didn't smile back. "Anyway, our third victim is Jessica VanRijn, thirty-five years old. She was discovered early Tuesday morning when she didn't show up for breakfast with her folks."

"Peter and Miranda Michaels," said Robson. Nobody paid him any mind.

"She'd moved back to Indian Springs to be near them," said Woods. "She'd had a nasty divorce, and she needed her family. Coroner puts cause of death as manual strangulation, time of death between eleven

26

and midnight the night before. Detective Dahlia Givens was working the case, and she's the one noticed it matched up with yours."

Erin frowned. "I'm sorry, but how'd she make that connection? Rayna was suffocated, Valerie died of blunt force trauma, and Jessica was strangled. They're from different states, different economic brackets —other than the posing, what ties them together?"

"The posing's a big thing." Woods drew himself up. "Both women were found on their knees, their hands stretched out in front of them like they were begging for their lives. But the other thing is, they were both bound with items found in their homes—Jessica with her scarves, Rayna with gardening twine. That's unusual, the improvised nature of their bonds. Most killers, they'd bring something, zip ties, duct tape. Pair that with the posing, and it's too much coincidence not to follow up."

Brody pinched the bridge of his nose. "You could've led with that."

"You don't have our reports?"

"Just got 'em an hour ago. I've only skimmed."

An uncomfortable silence descended, and Erin steamed in. "Captain...uh, Marcus, how are you on suspect leads? We're drawing a blank out in Lancaster, so anything would help."

Marcus shook his head. "We interviewed her parents, and her husband as well. Warren VanRijn. He got sick in the interview, had to run for the head. The parents were distraught, too, kept asking why."

Erin blinked. "Wait, the husband. Did you finish his interview?"

"He was in shock. His lawyer took him home."

"What about his alibi?" Erin's voice rose, and she cleared her throat. "You did get one, right? Where was VanRijn at the time of the murder?"

Woods turned purplish. He shifted in his seat. "No way he did it. The man was a mess. No one can fake that kind of emotion."

Erin surged to her feet, but Brody cut in smoothly. "We'll do our own interview," he said. "For now, I'd like to go over your reports. Erin and Catherine, go catch up with Sasha."

"But—"

"Go on. She's waiting." Brody's smile hadn't faltered, but his tone had gone stern.

Erin waited until the door swung shut, then started in. "Can you believe that guy? How naïve can you *be?*"

Catherine stopped, set her hand on Erin's arm. "You need to relax," she said. "I swear, standing next to you feels like standing by a live wire. You've got this hum going, like *warning. High voltage.*"

"I do not."

"You do. Come on—breathe with me." Catherine drew a deep breath, and Erin did the same. She felt mildly silly, parked in the hallway, huffing like a horse. Still, when she breathed out, her tension ebbed away. She shook out her arms, let her shoulders go loose.

"*There* you go. Better?"

Erin managed a nod.

"Okay. Let's do this." Catherine headed back to the briefing room. Sasha was waiting, laptop at the ready. She smirked at the sight of them, eyes bright with mischief.

"What were you doing, all that shaking around?" She did a quick shake herself, like a wet dog. "I saw you on the security cam. I thought you were having a seizure."

"Mind your own business," said Catherine. "Or better, mind our killer's. What have you got?"

"Got some tidbits on your victims." Sasha spun her laptop to show off the screen. "Jessica VanRijn was filing for divorce. The motion was filed a few days before her death. According to Facebook, she had quite the party that night. A divorce party, maybe, happily never after."

Erin nodded slowly, assimilating the new information. "I'm sure *Warren* VanRijn loved that."

Sasha chuckled. "I'd say he hated it. He flubbed a hearing the next day, blew up at the judge."

"He's a lawyer? That explains a lot." Catherine shook her head. "We need to pull him back in, sooner rather than later."

"This afternoon." Erin peered at the monitor. "You got anything else, or is that it for now?"

"I've got more, but nothing urgent. I'll forward it to your tablets."

Erin nodded her thanks. She liked VanRijn for the killer, maybe more than Cook. A lawyer, that fit—ego-driven, image-conscious, always up for a fight. Jessica hadn't just left him. She'd humiliated him as well. She'd clearly unbalanced him, if he'd screamed at a judge.

"Let's go find Brody. I want to head out right now."

"Head out where?" Brody poked his head in, as though summoned to the scene.

"To interview Warren. No time like the present."

Brody shook his head. "Normally I'd agree, but you're dead on your feet. No, no, don't argue. I need you on your game when you square off with Warren."

Erin sagged, all the fight draining out of her in a rush. Much as she hated to admit it, Brody was right. Her eyes were glazed over, all gritty and raw. Her body felt heavy, ready to drop.

"Okay," she said. "But we're going first thing."

"Fine by me." Brody turned to go, then stopped in his tracks. "I probably don't need to tell you this, but watch out for the press. Keep your heads down, and avoid the siren-chasers."

"Will do, boss." Catherine sketched a mock-salute. Erin just stood there, too tired to react. The mention of sleep had brought her exhaustion to the fore, and her eyelids were drooping, already half-mast.

"I wish I had two of me. Myself and a spare." She stumbled into Catherine, heading out to the car. "So I'm still catching killers, even in my sleep."

"Round-the-clock Erin. Sounds like a lot." Catherine bundled her into her seat. "We'll get him, don't worry. But first, a good night's sleep."

Erin rose before dawn for the drive to Pahrump. She drove out in high spirits, but the trip proved in vain. Warren had run out last-minute to meet a client in Vegas, and hadn't thought to send word.

"Or he wasted our morning on purpose," groused Erin. "Just to show us who's boss."

"He can't avoid us forever," said Catherine. Her voice was low and soothing, but Erin wasn't soothed.

"It has to be him, right? It's *always* the husband."

Catherine chuckled, playing along. "What about Rayna and Valerie? Why'd he go after them?"

"I don't know, practice? I'm still working that out." She dug out her phone. "I'm going to text Sasha and have her set up surveillance. Sooner or later, he's bound to slip up."

"Uh-oh. What's this?" Catherine slowed down, closing in on the police station. A news van was parked outside, and another down the street. Reporters were swarming, print and TV. Brody stood stone-faced, shaking his head. His hands were raised in negation—*uh-uh. Not today.*

"I'll pull around the side," Catherine offered. Erin didn't respond. A blonde anchor had caught her eye, a familiar face. She was older now, face tight with Botox, but Erin remembered her from Eric's trial. She'd come every day with her miserable crew, steamed in on Erin as she'd trudged up the steps. *Did you ever suspect? You must have that twin bond—did you know? Did you guess?*

"Bitch."

Catherine's brows rose. "Excuse me?"

"Not you. Never mind." Erin hopped out of the car and hurried inside. Brody was waiting, and he pulled her aside. "Have you seen today's papers?"

Erin shook her head. "No. We've been on the road."

"I think you need to see this." He held out his tablet, open to the *Ledger-Gazette.* Erin flinched at the sight of her own grainy photo, the same one they'd used during Eric's trial. Above it, the headline screamed—LANCASTER'S OWN RETURNS TO SEEK JUSTICE.

Erin's stomach did a slow roll. "Does it mention Eric?"

"Just a line at the end. It's mostly about our case—someone leaked we've got a serial, and that's their big scoop. But you need to prepare yourself. You're on their radar."

Erin stood frozen, counting her breaths. She'd thought she *had* been prepared, but time had crunched up somehow, present colliding with past. The tears she'd choked back fifteen years ago welled up anew. She blinked them back now, as she'd done then.

"I should go," she croaked. "I've got... I should go."

"Erin?" Brody reached for her, but Erin barreled past him. VanRijn—he was it. She just had to nail him, and this would all be a memory. This, Eric's trial, the whole sorry mess.

The killer let out a chuckle. *The killer,* that was him. The anchor had called him that last night on the news. She'd done it again today, and this time, it'd felt right.

"Did you see it too?" He leaned down and kissed her, just a peck on the cheek—and recoiled, almost gagging. He hadn't meant to do that. Then his good mood returned, and he grinned ear to ear. "They've brought in the FBI, those *Criminal Minds* types, all looking for me." A frisson ran through him, dread mixed with glee. "You did see it, didn't you? Everyone watches the news."

He paused and regarded her. Her hair was a mess, matted to her cheek. He peeled it away, combed it through with his fingers. "Of course, it's one thing to *see* the news and another to be part of it. I've watched them, you know, the police at work. Not everyone gets to see that, not in real life." He chuckled again. It came out sort of nervous, and he bit his lip. "You'll get to see, too. The police, I mean. You're not going to talk, are you?" He pressed his finger to her lips.

Outside, a siren wailed, headed back toward town. The killer paused to listen, head cocked to one side. "I don't suppose it matters," he said, once the sound had died down. "Talk, don't talk, those cops won't care. You know what their problem is? No pride in their work.

The FBI, on the other hand..." He rocked back on his heels to survey his handiwork. "Maybe they're more like me. *I* pay attention, take pride in my work."

He flicked a stray hair from his victim's unseeing eyes. Smiled at the way she stared back, beseeching.

"Well, this has been lovely, but I need to get home. I'll see *you* on the news, so, uh, ta-ta for now."

His knees popped like gunshots as he got to his feet. The killer jumped, then he burst out laughing. He walked away cackling, grinning up at the sky. Today was shaping up to be a very good day.

4

"DB's down there." The patrolman jerked his thumb over his shoulder and kept walking away. His face had gone grayish, shiny with sweat.

"Did you catch her name? Any details, or...?"

"Let him go." Brody's voice was subdued, rough from lack of sleep. "Let's just head over and see for ourselves."

Erin obeyed, half on autopilot. A sense of unreality had settled over her, getting out of the car. The sky was clear overhead, a crisp, pale fall blue. The breeze smelled of dried leaves, bonfires, and damp. It was a perfect November day, just shy of Thanksgiving—a day for warm jackets and leaf piles, walking the dog.

"What was she doing out here?" Brody peered down the hill, at the gray line of storage lockers. The cops had gathered at the corner, three cruisers on the tarmac. Erin clenched her fists. If she'd gone straight for VanRijn, hadn't stopped to sleep—

"FBI, right?" A patrolman jogged up to meet them. "I'm Blunt. My partner's...still down there, I guess. I thought—"

"What's the story?"

Blunt snapped to attention as Brody cut through his chatter. "We're still securing the scene. A dogwalker reported the body, and we came out to check. She's tied up like the other ones, so we called you. Oh, and she's also, uh..."

"What?"

Blunt looked away, lips pursed in disgust. "Warm to the touch, sir. She's still warm to the touch."

Erin's skin crawled. She brushed past Blunt without comment and squeezed between the cruisers. One of the cops raised the police tape to let her inside. Erin ducked under it and turned her attention to the body.

"Do you have her name yet?"

"Alice Newman," said Blunt. "Her ID was in her purse."

Erin nodded, said nothing. The sun was warm on her back and Alice Newman was dead—strangled, from the look of her, eyes bulging from her head. The killer had propped her on a sawhorse, up on her knees. Her arms were stretched out, palms to the sky.

"We kept that from the press, right?" Erin glanced at Brody. "The bound hands, I mean?"

"*We* didn't tell them, but it's hard to say with the leak. We can't rule out anything, at least not yet."

"She worked here in Victorville," said Blunt. "At Highgate, Inc."

"Highgate..." Erin turned the name over in her head. She'd heard it somewhere before, not long ago.

"Rayna worked there as well," said Brody.

"So this is our guy?" Blunt's tone was almost eager. Erin shot him a scowl.

"Too soon to say," said Brody. "This might be connected, or it might not. Might even be a copycat, trying to use our case to throw you off his scent." He bent to inspect Alice's body.

"She looks young," said Erin, and cleared her throat. Her head buzzed with sickness, a thick nausea. Death had stripped Alice of her defenses, left her vulnerable and small. Her mouth hung open in a silent gasp. She was probably in her forties—her skirt had slipped down and a faded Cesarean scar bisected her belly—but her face was unlined, her hands smooth and delicate.

"It looks almost sexual," said someone, "the way he's got her set up. On her knees, mouth open..."

Erin swallowed bile. The idea of taking pleasure from something so sad—

"No signs of sexual assault," said Brody. "The coroner'll need to confirm, but the others were the same."

Erin's head hurt, a dull, throbbing ache. Her eyes felt wet and full, and she blinked twice, hard. Alice gazed up at her, her dead eyes clouded over. *Pleading,* thought Erin, and a shudder ran through her. Had Eric's victims knelt that way? Begged for their lives? Had he stood over them, as she stood right now? She blinked one more time and Althea stared up at her, eyes black with accusation.

"I'm heading back," she said. Brody looked up, surprised.

"You don't want to stick around?"

"I've got a lead to run down." She spun on her heel and headed back up the hill. Brody trotted after her and caught her by the arm.

"Hey. What's so urgent? You know we're a team."

Erin sucked in a deep breath, but she couldn't quite keep the anger from her voice. "We know who the killer is. It's Warren VanRijn. He has no alibi, and he's been ducking us for days. And Sasha says he and Jessica never signed a prenup. From where I'm standing, he's guilty as sin."

Brody frowned. "That's a theory. Where's your evidence?"

"I'm going to get it before he strikes again."

"Don't get ahead of yourself. Hey—Erin, *hey.*" Brody darted in front of her, blocking her path. He took her by the shoulders and held her in place. "This is what I'm talking about: you do great for a while, smart work, methodical. Then you do your greyhound thing, off like a shot."

"Don't compare me to a dog."

Brody made a snorting sound, not quite a laugh. "I'm just saying, you can't twist the evidence to fit your theory. You've got to go where it leads you, one step at a time."

Erin bit her tongue. "Are you through?"

"Not quite." Brody let go of her, but he didn't move aside. "Warren had motive to kill his wife, but what about the Cooks? How about Alice? Why'd he kill her? You need to find a connection, or all you've got is a hunch."

"So let me go find one." Erin dodged past him and hurried up the hill. She thought Brody might follow, but he stayed where he was. After a while, he called after her, his voice sharp with warning.

"You have until I get back to chase down your hunch. After that, you're with me, no ifs, ands, or buts."

Erin waved a vague affirmation, already lunging for the SUV. VanRijn was her man. She could feel it in her guts. Her phone buzzed in her pocket, Catherine checking in, but she swiped the text aside and pinged Sasha instead.

Need timeline on WVR's movements since murders began. ASAP.

She hit SEND, frowned, and added a *please.* Sasha's reply popped up almost immediately.

Already on it. How was the crime scene?

Erin stared at her screen, outraged, disbelieving. Sasha was a friend, but she could be such a *ghoul.* Like those medical examiners on TV, joking over their tables—*guess he just...lost his head. Hyuk-hyuk-hyuk.*

It was sad, she sent back. *Just get my report.* She jammed her phone in her pocket and threw the SUV into gear.

Brody rode back with Catherine, just before sunset. Erin's temper had cooled by then, and she offered a wave.

"Hey, how'd it go? Any new leads?"

Brody shrugged. "Maybe, maybe not. But first, what'd you find?"

She slid a fat file his way, over her desk. "It took some digging, but I think I've got him." She flipped the file open and tapped on the first page. "Warren stayed in Victorville last night, charged a room to his Visa. And he was still there this morning, just hours before the murder. He swiped his card at a café, and here, he got gas. Not only that, but he called in sick to work today, and no one saw him at home. His assistant went to check on him, but his car wasn't there."

Brody leaned forward, his eyes lighting up. He skimmed through the file, then passed it to Catherine. "This is good work, Hastings. Let's bring him in for questioning, see what shakes loose."

Erin leaned back, weak with relief. "So, what about Alice? What did you find?"

Brody sat down, eyes narrowed, appraising. Catherine stayed standing, watching the traffic outside. "Alice was forty-five, married, a mother of two," said Brody. "She was murdered this morning, just before noon. She'd just stopped for lunch—she still had the receipt."

"Forensics will tell us more," said Catherine, but Erin was glowering at Brody.

"What's with the face? I followed the evidence, just like you said."

"This isn't about your work." Brody shifted where he sat. He opened his mouth, then closed it again. Catherine sat down next to him, shaking her head.

"We're worried, okay?" She laughed, soft and rueful. "I know you don't want to talk about it, and I'm not here to make you. But you've got history here, and if it all gets too much—"

"I need you to tell me before it gets out of hand."

Erin stood up so fast her chair hit the wall. "Nice ambush, you guys."

"We're just saying we're here for you." Brody hurried after her as she stalked down the hall. "I've never seen you look at a victim like you looked at Alice today. I actually thought you might know her, the way your eyes welled up."

"It was bright out, was all." Erin brushed at her eyes, though they'd dried long ago. She huffed out a long breath and let her shoulders go lax. "Okay, she got to me. I got sad, okay? It's this beautiful day, not a cloud in the sky—the kind of day you'd write home about, and she... She probably had plans. She probably felt *good,* and then..."

"Okay. Okay." Brody clasped her shoulder, a quick, firm squeeze. "You're human. I get it. I felt bad too."

"You did?" Erin looked up, surprised.

"'Course I did." Brody met her gaze squarely. "I'll be open with you if you'll be open with me. We got a deal?"

Erin stuck out her hand and he shook it. She couldn't be open with Brody, not about Eric. Not about what she'd seen, standing over Alice. But she'd give him enough to keep him off her back.

Brody stepped out of his SUV, tucking his phone in his pocket. He jammed it in with some force, and Erin raised a brow.

"Bad news?"

"Huh?" Brody glanced at his pocket. "Oh, no. Just Hannady wanting to know why our case isn't closed. Wanting to know rather *forcefully,* if you must know."

Erin flashed him a grin. "Wait'll we tell her we've got our killer in custody."

"He's not in custody yet," said Brody.

"He will be once I'm done with him." Erin picked up her pace, heading inside. Warren awaited, and an end to this case. Her adrenaline was back, that thrum in her veins that told her she was close. Her predator's instinct, Eric had called it, when they'd fished off the pier at Granddad's lake house. She pushed that thought aside, and the chill that came with it. She was here for Warren's confession, not a trip down memory lane.

"All ready?" Catherine joined them outside interrogation room 2, pale in the fluorescent light. Erin nodded tightly, her pulse ticking up.

"Don't forget to breathe," said Brody.

Erin took a deep breath and headed inside. Warren glanced up at the sight of her, or maybe rolled his eyes. He wasn't a large man, but he took up a lot of space, legs spread, elbows out, leaning back in his chair. He sized up Erin, then Catherine, and let out a snort.

"Which one of you's good cop and which one's playing bad?"

Erin smiled, sweet and pleasant. "I'm playing stood up cop. You're a hard man to pin down."

Warren's expression didn't change. "I'm a busy attorney. My schedule is full."

"Not yesterday, it wasn't." Catherine sat down across from him, consulted her tablet. "You weren't feeling well?"

"A touch of the flu. It's that time of year."

"Flu, yeah, I had that." Catherine poked at her screen, random jabs on the glass. She pretended to study it with growing puzzlement. Warren checked his watch.

"Cheap tricks won't work on me," he said. "Just ask what you want to ask, and we'll all be on our way."

Erin had anticipated his reaction. She met his eye, deadpan. "It's not a trick," she said. "She's checking on a warrant. To trace your GPS."

"Excuse me?" Warren's brows drew together. A faint flush colored his cheeks, the first hint of anger. "You won't get that warrant. My privacy is—"

"You could spare us the trouble," said Catherine. "Your assistant stopped by to check on you yesterday morning at ten-thirty. Your car wasn't in your driveway, and you didn't answer your door. Tell us where you were and your private life is safe."

"It's safe already," said Warren. "It's not a crime to take a sick day, or even play hooky. Unless you're a client, I—"

"We don't need the sordid details," said Erin. "Just walk us through the basics, where you were, who saw you, what you can prove." She consulted her own tablet, mostly to annoy Warren. "The night before last, where'd you say you were?"

"I was home with the game on, same as everyone else."

Erin's blood surged, a flush of heat down her neck. A lie—he was lying. She had him dead to rights. "So, you were home," she said. "Then I'm guessing your credit card went to Victorville without you?"

Warren's expression didn't change, but Erin heard his foot scuff under the table. She pressed her advantage.

"Looks like your Visa had quite the night out—treated itself to a hotel room, and breakfast, and gas." She smirked. "What do you drive? A Jaguar, right? That's got to stand out, a neighborhood like that. I've got uniforms out there already, canvassing the—"

"Okay, fine, you've got me." Warren's lip twitched, a quick moue of disgust. "Yeah, I went to Victorville. I stayed at the Hilton and ate at Bernardine's. I could refer you to a witness, but..."

"But?" Erin leaned forward. "As of this moment, you're our number one suspect. If you've got an alibi, now's the time to speak up. If you don't, we're going to turn your life upside-down. Whatever you're hiding—"

"Did you look at my order?"

Erin blinked. "What?"

"At Bernardine's Café. Did you check what I ordered, or just confirm the charge?"

Erin glanced at Catherine. Something was wrong. Warren didn't look scared or defensive, or even resigned. He took off his glasses and polished them on his sleeve. His eyes were small and peevish, the color of slate. He eyed Erin, then Catherine, and seemed to come to some decision. "Let's say I were to co-operate," he said. "I could eliminate myself as a suspect and save you some time. In return, might I expect a modicum of discretion?"

"That depends," said Erin. "Were you breaking the law?"

"God's law, maybe. California law, no."

Catherine regarded him flatly. "You were with someone."

"I'm not saying that," said Warren. He replaced his glasses and pushed them up his nose. "I'm saying I went to Victorville to meet a colleague, one Ruthanne Green. We spent the night at the Hilton, then we ate at Bernardine's. I had bacon and eggs, and the chocolate crois-sant. She had the fruit salad and a plate of French toast. After that, we drove to Beverly Hills and checked out rings at Harry Winston. Ruth suggested, and I agreed, it was too soon to buy one—in poor taste, to say the least—but I'm sure they'd remember us. She tried on half their stock."

Erin searched his face for the hint of a lie. He could've bribed the clerk—but a place like Harry Winston, they'd have cameras all over. He could've sped to LA straight after breakfast, then sped straight back after checking out rings, but LA to Victorville was two hours' drive. Alice would've been dead by the time he hit Rancho Cuca-monga. A sick feeling gathered in the pit of her stomach.

"This Ruthanne Green, she'll confirm your affair?"

"She'll confirm our *meeting*, and that it ran late." He tipped her a wink. Erin wanted to kick him. Instead, she forced a smile.

"Sit tight," she said. "An agent will investigate your alibi. If what you say is true, our business is done."

"I think we're done now." Warren stood up and stretched, all gangly limbs. "If I'm not under arrest...?"

Erin fumed, apoplectic. She wanted to grab him, shake him by his lapels. "We need to clear you," she said, but Catherine shook her head.

"It's fine. He can go," she said. "You hear that? Shoo." Catherine made a *get lost* gesture. Warren smirked meanly, and Erin sagged where she stood. She'd been convinced, certain she'd got her man. She watched him strut out, and something in her broke.

"Wait. Wait—why Victorville?" She took a step forward. "You could've met up anywhere, so why Victorville?"

"Convenient for her; discreet for me. She's from Hesperia, so..." Warren cocked a brow. "Was there anything else, or am I free to go?"

Erin waved him off, fuming. Catherine caught her arm.

"He's still a piece of work," she said. "*Meeting*, my ass."

Erin leaned in the doorway, watching him march out. If he started whistling—

Catherine bumped her shoulder, heading out the door. "Now we know, right? Time to move on."

Erin nodded tightly, her voice caught in her throat. She should've seen this coming, should've seen from the start. A quick resolution was a pipe dream—this town was a trap, a grim Escher maze, every road a circle wending back to the start. Escaping the first time had cost everything she had. What would it cost her to break free again?

Warren's alibi checked out.

Erin waited for Brody, hoping he'd yell. She'd gone off half-cocked again, convinced herself black was white. Classic Hasty Hastings— she deserved his disdain.

"That's one lead cleared," he said. "And, here. Got you lunch." He tossed a sub on her desk, ham and cheese, extra mustard. Erin couldn't look at him. She wanted to scream. Brody plopped down across from her, unwrapping his own sub.

"You're not beating yourself up, are you? You know how this works: we chase every lead. They can't all work out."

Erin swallowed thickly. Her mouth tasted bad. "He's out there right now," she said. "The killer I *didn't* flag, stalking his next victim." She sank into her shame like a toad into a mud bath. Brody's kid gloves hurt worse than any lecture—like she'd sunk so low his frustration had turned to pity. She wished he'd pile on the guilt. Maybe then she'd want to fight him. Maybe she'd find the strength to keep forging on.

"Eat your lunch," he said instead. "You're about to be busy."

"I am? How so?"

"While you were with Warren, I dug up a new lead." He slapped down a folder next to her sub. "Here you go, Cecil Fromm. He does deliveries for Highgate, and here's the good part: his route puts him in the area for *every single murder*."

Erin's heart leaped. "And you couldn't have led with that?"

"I led with lunch. Be grateful." Brody shoved her sub at her. "Take a bite and I'll tell you where to find him right now."

Erin clawed at the cellophane, clumsy in her haste. "What's his motive, this Fromm?"

"We don't have one yet, but he had access and opportunity. Two out of three, that's not a bad start." He tapped on her tablet. "He's doing a pickup at Highgate's LA depot tonight at five. Sasha's sent you the address."

45

"Wait an hour and I'll go with you," said Catherine. "I need to finish this press release, and then we can go."

"Can't I go on ahead? Start interviewing his co-workers?" Erin turned to Brody, eyes bright with appeal. He regarded her a moment, considering, then gave a slow nod.

"All right," he said. "Erin, go ahead, but don't approach Fromm on your own. Catherine, you'll go when you're done here, and meet up by five."

Erin tossed her sub in the trash on her way out the door. She hated to drive and eat, and besides, ham and cheese wasn't what she craved. She was hungry for Dairy Queen, a big banana split. She hadn't had one in years, not since high school. Eric had showed her how to eat them—a bite of iced banana, then a slurp of Coke, so the carbonation would prick her cold tongue. He'd showed her a lot of things: how to get two plays for one quarter at the arcade; how to pop a wheelie on her red Raleigh. How to fake Dad's signature to sneak a day off school. She'd followed him without question from one game to the next, right up until...when *had* she stopped?

She pulled up at a red light. Would things have been different if she'd told him *no* sooner? In eighth grade, maybe, when he'd got the idea to egg Mr. Hoff's house? A couple of months later, when he stole a case of Dad's beer?

The light changed. Erin slammed the gas pedal so hard her tires squealed. Eric wasn't her fault. If Mom hadn't died so young, if Dad had remarried—if he'd had the slightest clue, when it came to raising kids. She couldn't think of anyone less qualified to bring up twin toddlers. Erin had been the easy one, so she'd gone unnoticed. Eric had been *fun*, so he'd been Dad's pet. Had that been what twisted her brother into the killer he became? Growing up without *no* ever entering his vocabulary?

46

Erin got on the freeway, the same route she'd taken heading out to Victorville. To Alice's crime scene. Her stomach boiled and churned. What she hadn't told Brody—what she'd hardly admitted, even to herself—was standing over Alice, a sick thought had crossed her mind. She'd looked down and seen Althea, and in her head she'd heard Eric: *go on. It'll be fun.* And just for a moment, she'd seen *herself* strangling Alice, choking the life out of her while she struggled and thrashed.

Why *hadn't* she told, when she'd found that bloodied coat? That sickness in Eric—was she sick as well? Was she still following two steps behind, and one day, one day—

She swung onto the shoulder. Braked hard. Red dust rose up, and the smell of hot rubber. She couldn't go on like this, not knowing *why*. She'd never asked, hadn't dared. Hadn't spoken to Eric since he'd gone away. But she could if she wanted. She could do it *right now*. The state prison was close, just back up the road. Half an hour tops, and she could—

"I need answers, that's all." She pulled a screaming U-turn, knuckles white on the wheel. Her throat had gone tight again, and she sucked air through her teeth. Ten minutes with Eric, and she'd put her demons to bed. She'd face him down, her twisted other half—face him down, demand answers. He owed her that much. He owed her for her shame, half a lifetime of guilt. He owed her for leaving her, ditching out on their plans. He owed her for all of it, and it was time to collect.

5

E rin sat fidgeting, leg jiggling under the table. She'd forgotten about prison time, how everything moved slower on the inside. How every task came with checklists—gates to open, gates to lock, cuffs and pat downs, protocol. Had she been waiting ten minutes, or had it been half an hour?

She studied the room to settle her nerves, a regular visitation room, same as any prison. The walls were concrete, the floor old, scratched tile. A moldy drop ceiling hung overhead. Erin closed her eyes and let the quiet wash over her. The walls were thick, nearly soundproof, admitting only murmurs. Buzzing fluorescents thrummed in her ears. She bent her head forward to knead her aching neck.

A thump at the door cut through her idle musings. Erin stood as a guard walked in, followed by her twin. She tried to swallow, but her mouth had gone dry. Eric still looked like her, maybe more than ever. His brown hair, once close-cropped, straggled over his shoulders. His green eyes mirrored hers, crinkling just as hers did as he flashed her a smile. He'd got thin, prison-lean, all angles and lines. Erin scowled to keep from flinching as the guard cuffed him to the table.

"I'll be outside if you need anything."

Erin nodded. The door slammed behind her. She studied Eric, and he studied her back. At last, his smile widened, and he said "Hello, Erin." He said it all creepy, like Anthony Hopkins in *Silence of the Lambs*. Erin didn't laugh.

"You look well," said Eric, but now he sounded uncertain. "Are you going to sit down?"

"I guess so." She sat. Eric leaned forward, then leaned back again. He shifted and his cuffs rattled, and he let out a chuckle.

"So, this is awkward."

"You had to lead off with *Hello, Clarice?*"

"I didn't call you Clarice." Eric's lips quirked up, and Erin's did the same. She clapped her hand to her mouth, but her laughter broke through—loud, nervous laughter, but laughter all the same. Eric laughed with her, shoulders jerking up and down. Then they both sighed and shook their heads side to side.

"I missed you," said Eric.

"I—" Erin cleared her throat. "I came to ask you a question."

"About your case?"

Erin nearly choked. "What?"

"You're here for those women, right? The ones on the news?"

Erin stared at him, baffled. "Why would I ask you about them? You've been here the whole time."

Eric leaned forward, cuffs chinking. "I could help you find their killer."

"Help me?" Erin nearly choked. He thought she'd come for the *case?* To—to, what? Make him her Hannibal Lecter? She wanted to smack him, a good *knock it off* whap.

"I've been here a long time," he said. "I know killers, all kinds of them. I know what makes them tick. I could tell you what *I* think, and if my leads pay off—"

Erin stood up, nerves jangling. "I can't discuss an open case with you. Why would you even think that?"

"Why *wouldn't* I?" Eric half-stood as well, gripping the table. His voice had gone rough—angry, maybe hurt. "Thirteen years, Erin. I've been here thirteen years, and you don't call, don't visit. My letters bounce back RETURN TO SENDER. Now you're hunting a killer, and just like that, here you are." He flopped back in his chair. "Wouldn't you think the same, if our positions were reversed?"

Erin made a fist. She'd been wrong to come here.

"Wait—please don't go."

Erin frowned. "What?"

"You're about to knock for the guard. But I wish you'd sit down."

Erin relaxed her fist, but she didn't turn around. "I came to ask why— why you did what you did."

Eric didn't respond. His breathing got louder, long, heavy breaths like he was trying to stay calm. Erin stood and listened, and after a while, she realized she was breathing with him. She closed her eyes and breathed deeper, and her shoulders went loose.

"Hey, Erin?"

"Yeah?"

"Remember that time Dad set the sink on fire?"

Erin barked laughter. "Ninth grade, Thanksgiving. The great turkey inferno."

"He tossed it in the sink, but the pipes were full of oil."

"From that nasty salad dressing he'd just poured down there—what was *in* that, anchovy juice? And the whole thing went up like the Fourth of July." Erin shook her head. "Then he threw in the table-cloth, and the cranberry sauce over that. Our Thanksgiving dinner was...gravy and leeks?"

"And whipped cream from the can." Eric scratched at his chin, *scrape-scrape* on the stubble. "Now, there's a good memory. One I don't mind reliving."

Erin's smile faded. "You mean..."

"Don't you have things you'd rather forget? Things you've done or not done, and going back would just...hurt?"

Things you've done or not done. Erin felt cold. Did Eric know, some-how, what *she'd* failed to do?

"I should go," she said. "I've got to be in LA."

"But you'll come again, right?"

"I don't know, Eric. I..." She bit back a glib excuse. If she didn't come back, it wouldn't be because she was busy, or because Brody wouldn't approve. It would be a rejection, plain and simple.

"I'm *not* Hannibal Lecter," said Eric. "If I ever got out of here, I wouldn't do it again."

"Would you take it back if you could?"

For a long time, Eric said nothing. Then he let out a snort. "If I said I would, would you believe me? *Sorry*'s just a word. Let me give you something better. Something you can use."

"If this is about my case—"

"Don't get hung up on what's different from one scene to the next. That's just a distraction. Look at what *doesn't* change, what your killer can't help. Figure out what he *needs* to do, and you'll get to your *why*."

Erin rolled her eyes—*thanks, Captain Obvious*. "Does the same go for you? What did *you* need to do?"

Eric made a hissing sound, a sharp intake of breath. "Guard."

"Eric—"

"*Guard!*"

The steel door swung open, and the visit was over.

———

Erin thumbed on her recorder and cleared her throat. "Tuesday, November fourteenth, Agents Erin Hastings and Catherine Hannon interviewing Cecil Fromm. Please state your name and occupation for the record."

Cecil pulled a sour face. "Is this going to take long? I've got deliveries to make."

"The sooner you answer our questions, the sooner we'll be done. So, name and occupation?"

"Cecil Angus Fromm. Truck driver. Obviously."

"Thank you." Erin set down her recorder. "Now, can you account for your whereabouts on the nights of November third and seventh, and the morning and afternoon of November thirteenth?"

He snorted. "Nope. Can you?"

Erin studied his face. She read irritation there, resentment, but not guilt. "Let's start with the thirteenth," she said. "That was just yesterday. What'd you do then?"

"I don't know, worked?" He tilted his head, considering. "Yup. I worked, then I worked some more, then I went to the Red Tie and got me a lap dance. You can ask her, uh, Treasure. She'd remember me."

Catherine regarded him blandly. "What time was that?"

"Five o'clock, maybe six. I don't know. After work."

"And what were you doing between eleven and noon?"

"I told you, I was—" Cecil broke off abruptly, mouth hanging open. "Wait, is this about that body? The one by the U-Store?"

Erin leaned forward, keeping her tone carefully neutral. "What makes you think that?"

"'Cause I drove right by that, all those cops in the street. You'd better not be thinking *I* did it, because—okay, the third? The Lakers played on the third, so I'd have been home. The seventh, uh—oh! I was up in Sacramento. I stopped at the Chick-Fil-A, probably around eight. You can check on that, right?"

"You got a receipt?"

Cecil slapped at his pockets, slack-jawed with dismay. Then, his face lit up. "Wait—I got weighed. My truck, at the Antelope Station. They'd have a record of that."

Erin fired a text Sasha's way—*Antelope weigh station, Nov 7—confirm Fromm weigh-in?*

"Which brings us to yesterday." Catherine frowned. "You *were* in the area, is that correct?"

"Yeah, but not *killing* anyone. I didn't even have time to stop for lunch, just grabbed some candy bars and a soda when I stopped to gas up. I know I've got *that* receipt, 'cause I wrote my lottery numbers on it."

Erin glanced at her phone—nothing from Sasha. She ran through the standard questions, but though she found Cecil unpleasant, he didn't strike her as guilty. His outrage felt genuine, and his story never changed.

"You can't hold me without proof. That's how it works, right? You gotta have proof, or—"

Erin's phone beeped. She held up one finger.

"What? That your boyfriend?"

"Better. It's your walking papers. Our tech just confirmed you weighed in at Antelope Station just before nine. It's eight hours from Sacramento to Indian Springs, so—"

"*Told* you."

Erin shut off her recorder and stowed it in her pocket. "Thank you for your time, Mr. Fromm. At this point, you're not a person of interest, but I'll ask that you don't speak with anyone about the case—no friends or family, and especially not the media. The FBI appreciates your cooperation on this matter."

Fromm made a *tch* sound and stalked off without a word. Erin watched him go, deflated.

"So, where does this leave us?"

Catherine shrugged. "His alibi's shaky for the Cook murders, but no. I don't like him." She got to her feet. "Oh, and Hannady called. Chewed Brody a new one for letting VanRijn off the hook."

"VanRijn?" Erin blinked, surprised. "His mistress checked out."

"Brody said she was pitching some murder-for-hire angle. Kind of unlikely, but he said he'd run it down."

Erin stifled a snort. "What's with the chief lately? She was all over us on Anderson too."

"She always gets like this when her close rate is down." Catherine shook her head. "Anyway, forget her. She can badger all she wants, but the evidence is the evidence."

And precious little of that. Erin heaved a deep sigh. If something didn't turn up soon, she might just lose her mind.

———

"I found your lunch in the trash."

Erin stopped in her tracks, one foot out the door. "Excuse me?"

Brody nodded at the trash can. "One ham and cheese on rye, extra mustard. Going to pretend that wasn't yours?"

"I didn't want to get crumbs in the SUV."

"Right." Brody drew out the word, long and sarcastic. "I know you haven't had dinner, so come on. Let's go eat."

Erin opened her mouth to protest, then inspiration struck. "Can we get Dairy Queen?"

Brody shrugged. "Not quite what I had in mind, but I don't see why not."

Brody turned up the radio on the ride over, some soft rock station still stuck in the oughties. Bland autotune ditties drifted from the speakers, one running into the next. Erin caught herself wondering what Brody *really* listened to, what he put on when he wanted more than to fill the silence.

"So, Fromm's out," he said, as he parked outside Dairy Queen. "We've confirmed his alibis for the seventh and thirteenth. The third, we're not sure, but that's two out of three."

Erin waited for him to say something else, but he just killed the engine and got out of the car. He seemed to perk up heading into the restaurant, an odd little smile tugging at the corner of his mouth.

"What made you pick this place?"

"I don't know. A craving?"

Brody gazed at the cake display, still smiling that strange half-smile. "What are you getting?"

"Chicken strip basket. And a Sprite." All the way over, she'd been salivating for that banana split, but now she was here, she didn't want it at all. She wasn't sure she'd ever want one again. She felt kind of sick, just seeing it on the menu.

"I'll have the flamethrower combo," said Brody. "Double fries, double ketchup."

They got their food and sat down, and Brody bit into his burger. He leaned back and sighed, licked mustard off his lip.

"You look tired," said Erin."

"It's been a long day." He took a sip of his Coke and crunched on the ice. "We got our forensic reports for the Cooks and VanRijn."

"And?"

"We've got foreign fingerprints at the Cook scene, but they're not a match to any of our suspects. Apart from that, it's just confirming what we know. Rayna was suffocated with her pillow. Valerie died from blunt force trauma, and Jessica was strangled." Brody licked salt off his thumb. "Nice dinner conversation."

"He's getting away with it, isn't he?"

"Is that why you're not eating?" Brody's eyes had gone sharp. "Listen, he's slipped up somewhere, and we're going to find where. We got Anderson, didn't we? Come on, try a fry."

Erin took a fry and nibbled it down. It tasted of grease and summer, and she reached for another. "The Anderson case," she said.

"Hm?"

"The way I ran in back there, it felt like..." She tried another fry, but this one stuck in her throat. "It felt like a thrill ride. Like I came alive. I felt powerful, unstoppable, like...I guess what I'm saying is, I got carried away."

Brody made a snorting sound, his mouth full of beef. Erin sat nervously, waiting for him to respond. Back then, she'd felt powerful, but looking back on the chase, her stomach felt sour. Had Eric got that same thrill, stalking his victims? Was that what he'd needed, that power? That high?

Brody finished chewing and reached for his Coke. "You're thinking that's weird," he said, a statement, not a question. "Well, I'll tell you it's not. I've been there too. I'm pretty sure we all have. The trick is, you've got to harness it. You use that rush, that passion, but you keep your brain online." He tapped his temple. "Situational awareness. Never let it go."

Erin let out a long breath. What Brody said made sense. Eric, on the other hand—she pushed the thought aside. She'd let this place get to her, let it get in her head.

"I used to come here a lot," she said. "But I never tried the chicken."

"Yeah? And how is it?"

She took a bite and crunched it. Grease squirted on her tongue. "Pretty good, actually. I needed something new."

6

Erin woke with a start to find Catherine standing over her, hands on her hips.

"What gives? Did you sleep here?"

"No—maybe..." Erin peeled a straw wrapper off her face and dropped it in the trash. Brody had dropped her off after dinner, back at the hotel, but she'd been restless, unable to sleep. She'd made her way back here, to her makeshift workspace at Lancaster PD, and...

"Coffee. Extra strong." Catherine set a mug down in front of her. "So, you make any progress?"

Erin took a deep swig of coffee. It burned going down, and she pulled a face. "I might've found something," she said. "A pattern. A fixation."

"A fixation?"

"Something the killer needs. How he picks his victims." She reached for her tablet. "Rayna Cook divorced Allen Cook less than five months ago. She took her daughter and moved halfway across the country. She told her friends it was for work, but if you ask me, she wanted a fresh start." She swiped Rayna's file away and tapped on the VanRijns'. "Jessica filed for divorce right before she was killed."

Catherine cocked her head. "Mo said the same in his victim profiles—he likes 'em white, middle-aged, newly divorced. But what about Alice? She doesn't fit the pattern."

"That's where you're wrong." She sat up a little straighter, a sense of excitement gathering in her gut. She was onto something—she could feel it. "Alice was on her *second* marriage. Her first husband divorced her three years ago. They're both remarried now, and he's living in Florida. But the divorce was rough on them both, especially the custody battle."

"That could be something," said Catherine. "Valerie doesn't fit either, but Mo's got her pegged as collateral damage."

"Collateral damage." Erin bit her lip. The words tasted bad in her mouth. "Assuming that's true—assuming Valerie wasn't a target—we've got two constants: posing and divorce. Rayna and Alice worked at Highgate, but not Jessica. Rayna was smothered, Jessica and Alice were strangled. Alice died by daylight, the rest were killed at night."

Catherine rocked back on her heels. "Not bad," she said. "So, he's targeting divorcées. What's your next move?"

"With a grudge against divorcées, our killer's probably divorced. His kills are brutal and personal, which suggests a history of violence, maybe domestic abuse?" Erin gulped more coffee. "I thought I'd check the police database for local residents, divorced, with a history of DV."

"Good work." Catherine turned to go, then paused. "You want a donut? I saw some in the break room."

Erin shook her head, already firing up her PC. She'd found it, she thought, what the killer *had to have.* With the *why* in her grasp, the *who* couldn't be far off. She dove into her task with gusto, but as the morning wore on, her enthusiasm turned to frustration. Suspect after suspect proved a dead end—locked up already; six feet underground. Some had moved, some were too old. One was in traction, both legs smashed to flinders.

She got up around noon, mostly to stretch her legs, and when she got back, Brody was thumbing through her files.

"I like this one," he said. "Long rap sheet, divorced, lives near the state line. This one as well, though his divorce isn't final."

Erin took the files from him, swallowing irritation. All morning she'd toiled, squinting through file after file, and Brody'd breezed in and picked two juicy plums?

"We should check these two out," he said. "You'll come with me and we'll get Vernon Hayes. Catherine can take an officer and check out Danny Wickenheiser."

Erin's mood brightened at the prospect of action. This felt like a break, maybe the big one—and a feather in her cap, if it closed the case.

Or, let's be honest, a feather in both our caps—mine and Eric's.

Erin shoved the thought aside. She'd done the legwork. This was *her* breakthrough.

———

Vernon Hayes lived in Tecopa, nearly three hours out. Erin spent the drive digging into his rap sheet, picking through court records and police reports. He'd done two stints for assault, one on his wife, one on a waitress who'd "made his drink wrong." He had two ex-wives—

both with restraining orders against him—and a whole slew of complaints from...the Catholic church?

Erin turned to Brody. "Didn't Mo say there might be a religious angle? You know, with the posing?"

Brody frowned. "I think *you* said that. But he didn't rule it out. Why?"

"Our guy's been running a harassment campaign against his local clergy. It's a pretty long list—stalking, death threats, destruction of property. Two priests and ten nuns have restraining orders against him."

"That many? You serious?"

Erin nodded. "He lit some nun's car on fire while she was in it. She beat it out with her...wimple? But the seat got pretty scorched."

"You should interrogate him," said Brody. "Since he has a problem with women."

Erin just grunted, but she felt her pulse pick up. This was her chance to prove she could keep a cool head. Keep *situational awareness* in the heat of the hunt. She forced herself to breathe deep, focus on procedure. One step at a time, no rushing ahead.

Brody pulled up outside Hayes's residence. Erin wrinkled her nose. The place was a mess, all weeds and peeling paint. A faint smell of rotting leaves drifted from the back yard. Hayes obviously didn't care what his neighbors thought of him.

Brody leaned close as they headed up the drive. "Remember, he's dangerous. Push hard, but stay alert."

She nodded, but didn't respond, adrenaline singing. She ignored the doorbell and pounded on the door, an aggressive move, designed to rattle Hayes's cage. When he didn't answer, she pounded twice as hard.

Heavy footsteps approached, storming down the hall. Vernon Hayes flung the door open, a vision of fury in dirty sweats.

"What?"

Erin held up her badge, and he did a double take.

"FBI? What the—?"

"I'm Agent Hastings, and this is Agent Innis. Are you Vernon Hayes?"

His gaze flicked between them, almost childishly surprised. He hitched up his pants, a quick, nervous gesture.

"Vernon Hayes?"

"Yes. Yes, I'm Hayes."

Erin advanced on him, crowding him back inside. "We need to ask you some questions," she said. "Mind if we come in?"

She'd expected resistance, but Hayes only stared. He bit his lip, as though uncertain, and his hand gave a twitch. Erin thought he might try to slam the door in their faces. Instead, he stepped back. "Living room's down the hall," he said. "C'mon in, I guess."

Erin followed him in, down a damp, mildewed hall. Behind her, Brody sneezed. Hayes scurried ahead of them and half-collapsed on a dust-gray recliner. His flush of anger had faded and his color was off, an odd sickly yellow that made him look ill. Erin saw his hands were trembling and tried not to smirk. She pulled up a high-backed chair and sat looming over him.

"First, let me ask you, can you account for your whereabouts on the night of November third?"

"The third?" His eyes darted left and right. *Cornered,* thought Erin —*like a little scared rabbit.* Hayes wrung his hands. "The third, that was...I think I was home."

"You *think?*"

He bobbed his head quickly, avoiding her eyes. Erin frowned. She'd expected aggression, maybe even violence. Instead, Hayes seemed submissive, ready to fold. She pulled out a notebook and flipped it open, and ruffled the pages until she reached a blank sheet. Hayes watched her dully, flinching at every sound.

"I notice you haven't asked us what this is about." Erin leaned forward. "Do you know why we're here?"

"The..." His head snapped up suddenly, and he shot her a glare. "No. You're trying to trick me."

"Trick you how?"

"Make me guess, so I'll tell you—so I'll confess...look, if this is Sister Anne, I told the officer already. I never went near her, and if I did, I didn't mean to."

Erin straightened suddenly, and Hayes jerked back. She raised her voice without warning, to a drill sergeant bark. "Mr. Hayes, are you acquainted with Rayna Cook, Valerie Cook, Jessica VanRijn, or Alice Newman?"

He hunched his shoulders. "No, ma'am."

"Are you sure, Mr. Hayes? That was a very quick answer. I want you to think carefully, and I'll go through the list again to make sure. Do you know Rayna Cook? Valerie Cook? Jessica VanRijn? Alice Newman?" With each name she edged forward, until her knees brushed his. Hayes shrank into his chair, mumbling, "No, ma'am; no, ma'am."

"And the night of November third? Do you remember where you were?"

Hayes glanced at Brody, then back at the floor. "Home. I was home."

"Home." Erin noted his fist opening and closing. "Can anyone confirm that?"

He shook his head. "No. I was alone."

"And you've never heard of Valerie or Rayna Cook?"

His voice dropped to a whisper. "No, ma'am."

Erin flipped through her notebook, pretending to read. "I *see*," she said, voice heavy with doubt. "And where were you Monday, right before noon?"

"Work?"

"You don't sound so sure." She set down her notebook. "And, Mr. Hayes, according to your parole officer, you've been unemployed for six months."

He shifted in his seat. "I do odd jobs around the neighborhood. I might've been...I was cleaning—painting a garage."

Erin grinned wolfishly as he stumbled over his words. Hayes was about to crack. One more push and she'd have him.

"I need to use the bathroom." He stood up abruptly, nearly tripping over his feet. "If you'll excuse me, I—" He turned and fled, shuffling back down the hall. Erin started after him, and Hayes took off like a jackrabbit.

"Brody! He's running!"

"I got your back."

Erin took off sprinting, Brody in hot pursuit. Hayes plunged through the screen door and flung himself off the porch. He sprinted across the yard and dove for his van. Erin drew her weapon, and heard Brody do the same.

"Freeze! Not one more step!"

Hayes didn't listen. He scrambled into his van and slammed the door behind him. Brody grabbed for the handle, but Hayes was too fast. He reversed out of the drive like a bat out of hell, bent low over the wheel. Erin dropped to one knee, lining up for the shot.

"No." Brody laid his hand on her arm. "This is a residential area. And you don't have the shot."

"I know. I just..." Erin holstered her weapon. "I was aiming for his wheel."

Brody ignored her and pulled out his phone. "This is Special Agent Brody Innis. I need a BOLO out *now* on a gray 2017 Cadillac Escalade. Owner is Vernon Hayes of Tecopa, California. Another agent and I were interrogating him when he fled his residence. We need to get roadblocks up right away." He listened for several moments, then gave a stiff nod. "I'll be there in five," he said, and he hung up the phone. "I'm heading to the sheriff's office to coordinate the roadblock. If we move fast, we should be able to cut him off."

Erin wanted to go with him, still high on the hunt. Instead, she fell back, pulling out her own phone. "I'll stay here, secure the scene."

Brody flashed her a half-smile, a faint look of approval. Then he was gone, speeding off down the street. Erin watched until his dust settled, then called for backup. Her stomach felt queasy, her head hot and sore. She'd had Hayes in her grasp, and she'd let him slip away. She ached to go after him, ached to her bones, but instead she sat down to wait for CSI.

The killer paced restlessly, his TV dinner congealing on the table. The evening news played in the background, some puff piece on the local soup kitchen. They'd collected fifty turkeys for Thanksgiving, and still wanted more.

He pounded the floor in an agitated rhythm, three steps from table to fridge, five from fridge to counter. Four steps back to the table, and around we go again. The walls were closing in on him, driving the air from the room. His fingers twitched with the urge to take a slender throat and *squeeze,* dig in his thumbs until he felt calm again.

He hadn't set out to be a killer. Probably, no one did. But the peace that came with the kill, that blue, floating cool—that floating serenity was its own reward. It was more than just calm, more than a feeling. It suffused his whole body, from his scalp to his toes. He basked in it, glowed with it, and he knew what it was: a sign he'd done well. No, a sign he'd done *right.*

He flexed his hands, felt the strength in them. She'd deserved what she got. She'd *needed* to die, to atone for her sins. Sometimes killing was justice, like in the gas chamber, or the electric chair. He was an agent of rectitude, bringing punishment to the guilty. All those guilty women, going about their days without a care in the world. Going about their *wickedness,* ruining the lives of the very men who'd cared for them. Those men deserved justice, and he had it for them. He had the courage of his convictions, the strength to right wrongs.

He'd be out there now, but the feds were still prowling, snooping around. For one ugly moment, he thought they'd flagged him. But nothing had happened, and really, why would it? He hadn't left any breadcrumbs, not a trace of himself. Nothing to lead them here. All he had to do was wait, and the heat would die down.

He switched direction, table to counter, counter to fridge. Fridge to table, and back to the start. Waiting was *torture*, watching sinners roam free, married in God's eyes and free in their own, making eyes, fornicating... He shuddered. They were everywhere, when you looked —shopping malls, nail salons, conspiring on benches at the dog park. He'd seen one on the bus, smiling a secret smile that betrayed her black heart.

He stopped and leaned on the counter. The trouble was choosing one. Who was most sinful? Most deserving of death? That bottle-blonde news anchor from Channel 5? She'd had a wedding ring, and now it was gone. Or maybe that cab driver with her kids' art on her dash. No ring there, either, but had she had one to start?

He glanced at the TV and froze where he stood. A familiar face filled the screen, a small, birdlike woman with a thin, pointy nose. The chyron identified her as *Sandy Morrison, Highgate Inc.*. Another friend of Rayna's, just like Alice. He turned up the volume to hear what she had to say.

"I can't sleep at night," she said. She clasped her little sparrow hands under her chin. "I keep thinking he's out there, and nobody's safe."

"The virtuous ones are," said the killer. "The ones who know their place."

Sandy bowed her head. "I knew Rayna Cook. She was just the sweetest person. If this could happen to her...it doesn't seem fair, does it? Alice, as well. She had two little kids. And there's so many rumors—"

The interviewer cut in, another bottle-blonde. "What kinds of rumors?"

"First, they were saying he's stalking divorcées. Now it's Highgate employees, and look at me. I'm both!" She laughed, high and shrill.

"How can I close my eyes, knowing I could wake up with his—with his hands on my throat?"

The picture cut away. He flicked off the TV, the blood singing in his veins. Sandy was *perfect*, the sort of brazen sinner who'd squawk her crimes on TV. Who'd broadcast her shame without a hint of embarrassment. She was the one, and the universe had delivered her on a silver platter. What more confirmation could he need that his mission was righteous?

He pulled a tiny notebook from his pocket and wrote down her name: *Sandy Morrison*.

7

The CSI team arrived within twenty minutes of Vernon's flight, piling from their van and descending on the house. Their supervisor made a beeline for Erin.

"Elena Marks. Have you disturbed the scene?"

"We interrogated our suspect in the living room. Apart from that, no." The words had barely left her mouth when Elena gestured to her team.

"Jones, you're on photos. Vern, prints. Lyon, trace. Tullis, you're with me." The techs obediently scattered, and Elena studied Erin. She stared for several moments, apparently taking her measure, then gave a curt nod. "Staying or going?"

"Staying," she said. "The contents of his home might give me some insight into how the man thinks."

Elena pressed her lips together. "Suit yourself," she said. "Just don't touch anything until my techs have cleared it."

Erin bit back a peevish response. Elena was just doing her job. Erin left her on the doorstep and followed Jones inside. Jones was a small woman with a big camera, and she cataloged Hayes's house with ruthless efficiency, snapping every surface in turn, every nook and crevice. She didn't acknowledge Erin until they got to the kitchen, and she crouched down to photograph a gruesome mousetrap.

"Maid's year off, huh?"

Erin snorted. "Just a year?"

"Believe it or not, I've seen worse. We did this hoarder house last year, and a bum had snuck in and died in the piles. By the time we dug him out, he'd gone full-on mummy."

Erin pulled a face. "Mind if I check the drawers?"

"You've got your gloves, right?"

Erin waggled her fingers to show she did. She dug through Hayes's junk drawer, then his...other junk drawers. Every one was the same, filled to overflowing with flyers and junk mail and stacks of coupons. She hadn't expected to find much of interest in the kitchen, but still she let out a sigh.

"Agent Hastings, you in there?" Elena's voice drifted down the hall. "I think you'd better come see this."

Erin nodded at Jones—*thanks for the tour*—and strode down the hall to the master bedroom. Half the tech team were there, bunched around the closet. Erin craned to see past them.

"What've you got?"

Vern stepped aside. Erin choked back a whoop of triumph. If she'd ever doubted Hayes's guilt, those doubts were no more. There in the closet hung a disturbing collage, an old-fashioned pinboard crowded with women's faces. She counted two dozen at least, probably more. All of them were smiling, big Magic Marker smiles, the color of wounds. Their eyes had been cut out—*torn* out, rough and ragged. Erin suppressed a shudder.

"Creepy," she said.

Elena snorted. "Yeah. That's one word for it."

Erin leaned closer, tapped her nail on a picture pinned near the top. "That's Rayna Cook," she said. "And I think that's Alice beside her." She scanned the rest and found Jessica, and Valerie as well. She wasn't sure of the others, but a few had on nun's habits, and one was clutching a rosary.

"Did you see this?" Elena pointed at a statue on the closet floor, about a foot tall and surrounded by candles. Erin gaped at it, chilled to her core. The statue was of a nun, posed as though for prayer, hands raised in supplication. Her eyes were open, her lips parted in ecstasy.

Like Alice. Like Rayna.

Erin snapped a photo. "My team needs to see this."

"No problem." Elena knelt to examine the statue. "We'll have a detailed report for you by end of day."

"Thanks." Erin stalked out to the hall and shot a text to the team: *found THIS in his closet. What's the status on Hayes?*

Brody's text came back a few seconds later. *Not in custody yet. Stay with the scene.* Erin grunted, frustrated. One road out of Tecopa, and Hayes had slipped their net. How had he managed that, with almost no head start?

Brody was restless on the drive back, drumming his fingers, clicking his tongue. About an hour out of Lancaster, he slapped the radio off.

"Let's hear it. What've we got?"

Erin drew a deep breath. "We found twenty-five pictures. Four were our victims. Of the other twenty-one, we've identified ten, all still alive, all involved with the Catholic church. All of them had restraining orders against Vernon Hayes." She rubbed at her temples, staving off her headache. "I swear, it's like doing a puzzle blindfolded. So, okay, he hates nuns—but where do our victims fit in? None of them were religious, or not that you'd notice."

"Catholics don't much like divorce," said Brody, but he didn't sound convinced. He gave the wheel a good thump. "How the hell did he get past us? We had him, then—" His phone buzzed in his pocket and he scrambled it out. "Innis."

Erin stiffened as his face fell. A vein throbbed in his neck.

"Yes, I'm aware," he said. "*Yes,* we're still—we've got a BOLO out, troopers on the ground. We're doing everything we—" Brody's lip curled back. Erin could hear Hannady on the other end, her flat, waspish voice droning down the line. She talked for a long time, punctuating her monologue with sharp, exclamatory shouts. When Brody hung up, his face had gone red.

"Bad?"

"The worst." He tossed his phone on the dash. "She heard about Hayes. She wants him caught *now.*"

"Yeah. Don't we all?" Erin leaned back in her seat. "At least we're building our case. When we do bring him down, he'll be sewn up tight." A thought occurred to her, and she jerked upright. "Hey, those fingerprints at the Cook scene, the ones we couldn't account for. Has anyone run Hayes's prints against those? If he's a match—"

"He won't be." Brody laughed without humor. "Hayes has a rap sheet as long as my arm. He's been in the system. If he was a match, we'd have caught it already." He glanced over at Erin. "You feeling all right? That's 101 stuff."

"I'm fine." Erin stifled a groan. She was tired, beyond tired, running on fumes. But a brainfart like that—she felt her face go hot.

"You should try to nap," said Brody. "Even just half an hour."

Erin closed her eyes, already going under. She dropped into a dreamless sleep and woke dazed and blinking, hands flying up to fend off the sun.

"What—what the—?"

Bright light engulfed her, not the sun but a flashbulb. Cameras, floodlights—a swarm of press. She counted three vans, at least thirty reporters, crowded up on the sidewalk outside Lancaster PD. Something bumped her window, a fluffy boom mic. Brody honked his horn, two short, sharp blasts.

"What is it? What's happened?"

"Let's just get inside." He swung his door open and stepped into the street. Erin waited until he'd cleared a path, then she got out too.

"No comment," bellowed Brody, over the yammer of the crowd. "That's a blanket *no comment,* so—"

"How about you?" A microphone popped up, nearly bopping her on the nose. Erin batted it aside. The reporter trotted along beside her, his crew trailing along. "Will you comment on the parallels between this case and your brother's?"

"My brother's?" Erin paused, nearly stumbled, and shook her head. She felt heavy and sleep-logged, full of cobwebs.

"Agent Hastings has no comment," said Brody. He set his hand on her shoulder, but Erin shrugged him off. She didn't need his protection. She could fend for herself.

"Is this survivor's guilt? Is that why you're here?"

Erin lowered her head, raised her shoulders, and bulled through the crowd. She swatted a boom mic and feedback whined overhead. Anger roiled in her guts, and a hot sense of shame.

"Have you ever asked yourself, if they never caught him, would you have been next?"

Erin gasped harshly, choked on sour spit. She spun on her heel, light-headed with rage. "Who said that? Who *said* that?"

A woman in red squirmed out from the crowd. "It's a fair question," she said. "All his victims were brunettes, thin just like you. They were all about your age—and he never said why he did it. Could it be he picked his victims thinking of—"

Erin swung without thinking, a whistling roundhouse. The reporter jerked back and she missed by an inch. She hit a camera instead, sent it hurtling through the air. It came down hard on the steps and smashed like fine china.

"What the hell? Get inside." Brody had her by the arm, his grip tight and bruising. He muscled her up the stairs, nearly dragging her off her feet. He didn't let go until the door slammed behind them. Erin stood trembling, fists clenched at her sides.

"Brody—"

"What *was* that? You want to come up on charges?"

"Did you hear what she said?"

"I don't care what she said, and neither should you." Brody thumped the wall, rattling a bulletin board on its hooks. "You lost it out there. Assaulted a member of the press. Did you win some lottery I don't know about? Because that camera must've cost—"

"Brody." Catherine came up beside him, laid her hand on his arm. She nodded down the hall, where a knot of cops had gathered. Brody saw them and frowned, and he exhaled through his teeth.

"Catherine, go work on...something. Erin, with me." He strode off stiff-backed, not waiting to see if she followed. Erin trailed after him, a lump in her throat. All the fight had drained out of her, and she felt small and tired, like a kid up past her bedtime, all tantrummed out. She wanted to lie down, maybe for days.

"Sit down," said Brody. He ushered her into a cramped office and shut the door behind them. Erin sat down. She couldn't meet his eye.

"I know you visited your brother," he said. "Why didn't you tell me?"

Erin said nothing.

"Look, we're a team. If a case gets too much for you, you come to us. You don't go off on your own, pushing and—"

"We didn't discuss the case. I went to Eric for..." Erin trailed off, feeling sick. How to explain what had brought her to Eric?

"I'm not talking about that," said Brody. "I'm talking about—it's all symptoms of the same thing. The way you ran off on the Anderson arrest, the way you're acting now, don't you see it's the same? You're pushing yourself to your limits, not eating, not sleeping. You're jumping out onto train tracks, and you can't even see it."

"So, what? Am I reprimanded?" Erin winced at her own sulky tone. Brody just sighed.

"Give me one reason I shouldn't send you home."

Erin jumped where she sat, as though doused with cold water. "Send me home?"

"I've been thinking about it," said Brody. "I'm worried about you. So's Catherine, even Sasha."

"You've been talking about me? Behind my back?"

Brody leaned back, rubbed the bridge of his nose. "This isn't high school. We've been discussing you *as a team*. If you'd have opened up to us—what happened to our deal?"

Erin blinked. "Our deal?"

"Don't you remember? We shook on it. You were supposed to come to me if it all got too much."

Erin's stomach roiled sickly. She *did* remember that, and Brody was right. She'd been pushing herself hard, wearing herself to a nub. Her nerves felt raw, exposed, her skin too thin to contain them. Her eyes were full of grit, her guts a pool of acid.

"I lost situational awareness," she said. Brody snorted, nearly smiled.

"Take the rest of the night off," he said. "Hit the hot tub. Get some rest."

"But I'm not off the case?"

"I'm still deciding."

Erin stood stiffly, joints full of glass. She turned to go, but Brody cleared his throat.

"Your brother, uh...are you going to see him again?"

"I don't know. Maybe."

"Will you tell me if you do?"

"Yeah, Brody. I'll tell you." She thought she probably *would* tell him —bottling it up wasn't working.

8

Erin came in the next morning rested and fed, her purple-black eyebags faded to blue. Brody stuck her on desk duty.

"You're lucky," said Catherine, as she passed by her desk. "I thought you were done here when you came in last night."

Erin just nodded, heat rising in her cheeks. She'd blown it big time, no arguing that. "He's got me on cleanup," she said. "Tying up what we've got so it looks good for Hannady."

"Hey, someone's got to do it." Catherine flashed her a grin. "Besides, you never know. Maybe you'll turn up something new."

Erin bent to her task as Catherine strode off. Most days she hated paperwork, but today it felt soothing, sifting and organizing, filtering wheat from chaff. She found Fromm on a traffic cam the night of the third, speeding home for the game with a car full of snacks. That cleared him on all three crimes, striking him off the list.

Sasha dropped by around lunchtime and dropped a bag on her desk. "Brody said to feed you. Hope you like Taco Bell."

Erin didn't, but she was hungry. She grabbed a taco from the bag. "Those fingerprints at the Cook scene—any joy on those yet?"

"Well, we know they're not *Allen* Cook's, or Valerie's or Rayna's. Other than that..." She made a farting sound.

Erin nodded slowly, gears spinning in her head. "What do you think of Hayes? You think he's our guy?"

Sasha hopped up on an empty desk and sat swinging her legs. She had on red stockings that went strangely with her starched gray suit. "I'm not sure," she said. "But you might find out soon. I just talked to Catherine, and he's been spotted in Nevada. They haven't got him yet, but they're closing in."

Erin picked up a pen and marched it absently across her knuckles. "I liked him at first. But now I'm not sure. He's got means and opportunity, but his motive, I'm confused. Some of those nuns on his kill board, he's been harassing them for years. He's never been violent, never crossed that line."

"That, and he's *stupid*." Sasha stuck out her tongue. "I listened to his interview. He's got the IQ of an onion. How does *he* kill four people without leaving a trace? We should have DNA, maybe prints. Maybe a witness."

"That nun statue, though..." Erin shuddered at the memory. "You should've seen that thing. The way it was kneeling, I flashed right back to Alice."

"I should get back," said Sasha. "Unless you need me to feed you?" She grabbed a crispy-looking churro and poked it at Erin's head. Erin waved her off, laughing, and turned back to her work. She delved into Hayes's background, but her focus was off. Sasha could've put it more tactfully, but the man was a dolt. Or, was that an act? He'd slipped Brody's roadblock and made it to Nevada. His motive was shaky, but that statue. That *statue!*

Erin stood up abruptly. She needed a push, and she had an idea where she could get one.

———

Erin waited in the visiting room, breathing deep lungfuls of its cool concrete calm. Now she was here, she wasn't sure why she'd come. Last time had helped, but it'd been a fluke. Eric wasn't some oracle, or even her informant. He'd focused her, was all, reminded her where her attention should be.

The door swung open. Eric kept his head down as the guard secured him to the table. He didn't look up until they were alone.

"I didn't think you'd be back," he said.

"Well, surprise. Here I am."

A stiff silence ensued. Eric sat sizing her up, his expression tight and strained. When he spoke, his voice caught.

"You weren't, you know."

Erin frowned. "I wasn't what?"

"Going to be my last victim." His features contorted in something like pain. "Did you think that? Is that why—?"

"*No.*"

They stared at each other across the table, Eric's eyes searching, Erin's thunderstruck. A sharp pain jabbed at her, just under her ribs. The fluorescents buzzed dully, suddenly oppressive.

"I talked to Dad," said Eric. "He said you never called him. He only heard you were here when you showed up on the news."

Erin's guts lurched. "What's with the guilt trip?"

"What's with not calling?"

Erin bit her lip. Dad hadn't crossed her mind since...she wasn't sure when. "I'm going to call him," she said. "I just need...I'm going to call." She pinched herself under the table. She'd let Eric get to her, throw her off track. "About last time..."

"Hm?"

"You never answered my question."

"About why I did it?" Eric scratched his chin. His nail caught a razor cut and a drop of blood welled up. "The same reason we all do. I couldn't *not*."

Erin recoiled, disgusted. "What, like eating chips? You couldn't have just one?"

"Not like eating chips." Eric studied the backs of his hands. "The thing is, with killing, it's the biggest thing you can do. It's an ending. It's *the* end. You can't take it back. To do it, to *mean* it—premeditated murder, not the heat of the moment—you have to be sure. Not just sure, but *obsessed.* You have to...*have* to."

"What are you saying? You had to do it? It wasn't your fault?"

"No, it was my fault." Eric picked at his thumbnail. "It's not like you have to pee, and if you don't find a bathroom, you'll wet your pants. It's like you get focused, stuck on one thing. You think of it all the time, like a fixation. It could be something you want, something you hate. Something you don't know why, but you know you have to do it. It just grows and grows until nothing else matters. Until there's no 'if you don't', just when and how."

Erin swallowed. Her throat clicked. "Which was it for you? Something you wanted, or...?"

Eric looked up. His eyes had gone distant, a thousand-yard stare. He gazed through her into nothing, and she thought he wouldn't answer.

"This was a mistake," she said. "I shouldn't have—"

"Something that hurt." Eric closed his eyes. "Something that hurt so bad, I had to make it stop."

Erin's skin crawled. For a moment, she'd felt pity, even sympathy. She'd almost reached for his hand, almost offered him comfort. She pulled her hand back and balled it into a fist. She was here for Hayes, not for her brother. If Hayes had an obsession, what would that be? What choked his head until his thoughts couldn't breathe?

"You're not here for me, are you?" Eric's voice was small and hurt. "This is about that case. You're picking my brain."

Erin just looked at him. She couldn't bring herself to lie. Eric made a weary sound, part groan, part laugh.

"Remember in high school, Mr. Dorff's English class?"

Erin snorted. "I remember you putting a Whoopee cushion on his chair. Filling it with egg yolks so it actually smelled."

"That was you," said Eric. "And I didn't mean that. I meant how he'd make you rewrite your essay if your thesis wasn't clear. If you couldn't sum up, in one line, what you wanted to say. Your motive's like that. It's got to be clear. If you asked him, why'd you do it, what would he say?"

"I can't discuss the case with you."

"You mean you don't know."

Erin made a *tch* sound. In truth, she didn't. Why were the nuns all fine, and the victims dead as dirt? How did the church connect to Rayna, Jessica, and Alice?

"You should trust yourself," said Eric. "What do you *know*, deep down in your gut?"

"My gut's a traitor. It throws me on train tracks."

Eric shook his head. He glanced down at the table, then met her gaze squarely. "You knew about me," he said. "Back then, you knew. About the four women I killed."

Erin's stomach turned over. Acid rose in her throat. She gagged, swallowed convulsively, and shut her eyes tight. After a moment, the urge to puke passed, but a cold weight remained, heavy in her chest.

"You killed six women," she said. "Six women, not four." She gripped her knees under the table, so hard her eyes watered. For a moment, she saw double, two Erics frowning in tandem.

"It was four," said the Erics. "I only killed four."

Erin stared, disbelieving, until she counted just one of him. He'd almost had her with his sad eyes and slumped shoulders, that catch in his voice when he realized why she'd come. She'd thought she'd seen growth in him, even remorse.

"You're not sorry at all," she said. "You can't even acknowledge them. You can't, or you won't." She got to her feet. "I sat through your trial. I watched those families suffer—six of them, not four. And that last one—" She shut her mouth with a snap. She wouldn't confess her guilt, not here, to Eric. She wouldn't give him the satisfaction of admitting he was right.

"Erin?"

"I'm going." She went to the door and knocked for the guard. She'd got what she'd come for, and the rest was just noise.

Erin flung herself into the driver's seat and slammed the door hard. She dialed Catherine and waited impatiently for her to answer. She did on the fifth ring.

"Erin. What's up?"

A car honked on Catherine's end, and Erin flinched. "You driving?"

"Stuck in traffic. I'm headed back to Tecopa."

"Good, then you've got a minute." Erin switched her phone to her other ear. "Off the top of your head, Vernon Hayes—why do you think he did it?"

Catherine made a humming sound. "Well, he's angry, for one. He has issues with women, and a history of violence. And Sasha's been doing some digging, and wait'll you read up on his Catholic school days. They shut the place down, where he went to school—allegations of verbal abuse, corporal punishment. Indoctrination techniques verging on torture. I'd hate nuns too, if I'd—"

"But why'd he kill Rayna and Jessica and Alice?"

"Fear, maybe?" Catherine clucked her tongue. "I mean, picture it. He grows up with these nuns, thinking they've got God on their side. Their authority isn't just absolute. It's *divine*. I think he's been working up to killing them for a long time, and then it occurred to him, why not start small? Why not start with a sinner and work up to a nun?"

Erin thought about that. Catherine's argument made sense, but... "That's more than one line."

"Excuse me?"

"It's kind of convoluted," she said. "Kind of a long way from point A to point B."

"You met Vernon Hayes. You expect him to think straight?" Catherine huffed laughter. "Besides, he ran. If that doesn't scream *guilty*, I don't know what does."

Erin took a deep breath, ordering her thoughts. "He did run," she said. "And you're right, he looks guilty. But our evidence is shaky."

"What are you talking about? We've got his shrine, his statue. Photos of our victims. What more do you need, a gold-plated confession?"

"What about those fingerprints from the Cook scene? They're not his, so whose are they? And why'd he pick victims so far from his home? He has no connection to Highgate, none to Lancaster or Indian Springs, so why drive for hours, just to—"

"To put some distance between himself and his kills?" Catherine slid into the role of devil's advocate, just as she often did when they chewed over a case. "And he fits Mo's profile—disappointed, downtrodden."

"But does he have the patience to stalk his victims and wait for his chance? What about self-control? We didn't even have a warrant, and he ran like a rabbit. I think he's guilty of *something,* but four ritualistic murders, one in broad daylight? I'm not sure he could do it."

Catherine made a frustrated sound. "Erin, where is this coming from?"

Erin stared through the windshield at the high prison walls. "I went to see Eric," she said. "I asked why he did it, and..."

"What were you thinking?" Catherine's voice rose an octave. Somewhere in the distance, a truck horn blared. "Look, I don't know what he said to you, but your brother's not—the profile's not the same. Whatever pushed him to do it, Hayes is a different beast."

"Maybe. Yeah." Erin let her gaze drift up to the gray November sky. "I didn't discuss our case with him, if that's what you're thinking."

"It isn't. I know you better than that." Catherine's tone warmed, soft with understanding. "I'm worried, is all. This case is getting to you, and you've closed yourself off. Brody said he's had to practically force you to eat."

"I just housed four tacos," said Erin. "And a bag of churros, to boot." Her stomach rolled uneasily, and she stretched out in her seat. "Brody read me the riot act. I'm taking care of myself, okay?"

"You'd better be." Catherine cleared her throat. "Speaking of Brody, does he know you saw Eric?"

"I told him I was going," said Erin. "I promised I would."

"Okay. Well, if he approves... No, I don't like this."

Erin said nothing. She had nothing to say. She hung up and let her head loll back on the headrest. That unreal feeling was back, like outside the cop shop, when she'd swung at the reporter. Eric had made a good point, she'd thought—but who knew how honest he'd even been? With Catherine, at least, she could always count on the truth.

She pulled out of the parking lot no wiser than she'd come.

9

Vernon Hayes proved more slippery than anyone could've anticipated. The manhunt dragged on, three days, four, then a week. Brody kept Erin chained to her desk. She bore up as best she could, but some time around day three, boredom set in. By the end of the week, she was climbing the walls.

She swallowed an aspirin as she thumbed through Jessica VanRijn's autopsy report. Apparently, she'd had a tumor on one of her kidneys —a benign tumor, of no relevance to the case. She made a note of it anyway and set the report aside. She needed to be out there with Brody, hunting Vernon Hayes. Out where she was needed, where her predator's instinct might be of some use.

She poured herself a cup of coffee and tossed her swizzle stick in the trash. Maybe she'd go find Sasha, toss theories back and forth. Sasha goofed off too much, but she was sharp. She had a good eye for detail, and an instinct for the macabre. Erin thought she'd missed her calling, not training as a profiler.

"Hey. You done with those?" An officer was hovering over her desk, pointing at the stack of files threatening to spill over the edge. Erin shook her head no.

"Thought I'd give them one more pass. You never know what'll pop out on the, uh...tenth read."

The officer chuckled. Erin reached for the top folder—Allen Cook. She'd liked him first, she remembered. He'd fit Mo's profile, and Rayna and Valerie had been the first victims. The way Valerie'd been tucked in, a father would do that. A father who'd killed his wife and caught his daughter looking on. He'd lunged for her, grabbed her, tried to make her see reason. She'd struggled and fallen, and hit her head. Erin could see that—a crime of passion, then he'd got a taste for it. It happened that way sometimes, an addiction to the thrill.

She frowned, sipped her coffee. Cook's alibi was strong. He'd been on duty at the museum at the time of the murders, not just Rayna and Valerie's, but Jessica's as well.

"Anything new?"

Erin nearly jumped, startled from her thoughts. "Brody! Sneak much?"

"Sorry. Any progress?"

"Not really." She set Cook's file down, then frowned. "Did anyone follow up with Allen Cook, after his initial interview? I'm not seeing anything, but maybe—"

"I don't think so," said Brody. "I was going to have you do it, but then we locked on VanRijn."

Erin sat up, hopeful. "Want to do it right now? We can get to Pahrump before he leaves for work."

Brody gave her a long look, his lips a tight line. Then, he relaxed. "I don't see why not. You had breakfast, right?"

She jerked her head at the trash, at the greasy Denny's bag crumpled on top. Brody clapped his hands together and broke out in a grin.

"Okay, let's go. You're off probation."

Erin watched Allen Cook as he settled himself on the couch. If she had one word to describe him, she'd have to pick *ordinary*. Nothing about him stood out at all, not his short brown hair, not his flat brown eyes. Not his pale skin, with its dull, sunless pallor. His height was average, about five foot nine, his build somewhere between slender and plump. He was bland, non-threatening, boring as they came.

"Please sit," he said. Even his voice was perfectly mundane. Erin sat across from him, Brody at her side. Cook eyed them a moment, then cleared his throat. "Would it be rude if I asked you what brings you to my home?"

"Just following up," said Brody. "Now you're past your initial shock, we thought you might recall some more details surrounding the murders."

Cook let out a tired sound. "So, you haven't caught...Hayes, was it? He did it, right?"

"He's a person of interest," said Erin. "Hayes is still at large, but I promise you, Mr. Cook, we're doing everything we can to bring him in. And, in the meantime, we're pursuing other leads. We *will* get justice for your wife and daughter."

Cook seemed to deflate. He glanced at his watch. "Chasing every lead. I get it. But could we keep this brief? I'm on shift tonight, and I need to get some sleep."

"We'll be as quick as we can." Erin flipped through her notepad. "It says here you work at the children's museum as a night guard?"

He nodded. "I started a few months ago, when I moved out this way."

Brody leaned forward, just slightly. "You couldn't get time off? Bereavement leave?"

"They offered," said Cook. "But I need to keep busy. It keeps me from..." He trailed off mid-thought, as if he'd lost interest. Grief could do that to a person, drain their will to live. Erin offered a small smile, but Cook looked away.

"I hate to ask you this," said Brody, "but where were you on the nights of the third and seventh, and during lunchtime on the thirteenth?"

Cook's eyes narrowed a moment, but he only sighed. "The third, I was working, and the seventh as well. On the thirteenth, let me check." He got up and headed for the kitchen. Brody followed close behind him, but Cook didn't bolt. He just dug through a wicker box and came up with a receipt. "Here. I dropped my car at the garage for its yearly tune-up. I left it there and went home to get some sleep before work."

Brody took the receipt and examined it, and snapped a picture with his phone. Cook drifted back to the couch and sat with his head bowed.

"I know this is hard for you," said Erin. "But are you familiar with Jessica VanRijn or Alice Newman?"

"Only what I've seen on the news. I know one of them worked with Rayna, but we hadn't met." He wiped at his mouth. "To think someone would do this..."

Erin gave him a moment to compose himself, and then she switched tack. "I see you lived in Rochester before moving here last year. What made you relocate?"

Cook made a choked sound. He was shaking all over, his hands clasped together. "My wife..." He coughed loudly.

"It's okay. Take your time."

He sat up straight, squared his shoulders. "My wife and I were divorced. She got a job out here, so I found one close by. I wanted to stay close to Valerie, maybe work things out with Rayna. We actually —we— We were making some headway when..." Cook's face crumpled. Erin shifted uncomfortably. She hadn't meant to traumatize him, only run through his story and make sure it checked out.

Brody hadn't sat back down, and now he cleared his throat. "I think that about covers it," he said. "Agent Hastings, if you're through?"

"Yep. That'll do it." She got to her feet, then paused where she stood. Cook peered up at her, eyes pink and wet.

"Is something the matter?"

"Not at all." She smiled, wide and warm. "Thanks again for your time, Mr. Cook, and condolences on your loss."

Brody waited until they were on the road before he bumped her elbow. "So? What'd you see?"

"Hm?"

"On our way out. Why did you stop?"

Erin glanced back at the house. She wasn't sure she'd seen anything, at least nothing that mattered. "It's just, he didn't have any pictures, not on his mantel, not on his walls. Could be it's too painful, seeing their faces every day. But don't you think most folks would keep at least one?"

"I'd keep mine in my wallet," said Brody. "Close to my heart. But then, I'm never home, so..."

Erin hummed her agreement. Cook's home wasn't a home, not in any real sense—just a place to hang his hat until he got back with Rayna. Why decorate, if he planned to move on?

"I heard you and Brody struck out yesterday in Pahrump," said Catherine. She leaned over Erin's desk and snatched her tablet.

"Hey! I was using that."

"And now you're not." Catherine snapped her fingers. "Come on, get your jacket. I want to take you somewhere."

"Where?" Erin grabbed for her tablet and missed by a mile. Catherine stuffed it in her bag, out of Erin's reach.

"Just somewhere I found. Are you coming, or aren't you?"

Erin went. Her eyes were glazed anyway, from a long afternoon nose-deep in crime scene reports. A break sounded good, a chance to clear her head. They slipped out the side door and piled in the car. Erin rolled her window down and let the crisp November breeze blow her hair off her face. Catherine drove up past downtown, past the park where Eric had once found a wounded squirrel. Its leg had been broken, its tail squashed flat. Eric had wrapped it in his jacket and taken it to the vet. Had it survived? Erin didn't remember. She frowned and turned her head away—she didn't *want* to remember.

Catherine pulled off at the next block, into a crowded parking lot. Erin burst out laughing when she realized where they'd stopped.

"Laser tag? Are you serious?"

"You've been stuck at your desk all week. Tell me you don't want to."

Erin thought about it, but she had to be honest. She wanted to, a lot. "I guess I *could* kick your ass," she said.

"Yeah. In your dreams."

Catherine herded her inside, and they scrambled into their vests. The kid on the counter favored them with a bored look.

"Free-for-all's starting now, or you can wait for the tournament."

Catherine cocked a brow. "What's the difference?"

"We'll do the free-for-all," said Erin. "Twenty people go in, last one standing's the winner."

"Just fifteen," said the kid. "It's a slow night."

Erin headed into the arena, vision already sharpening. The place was a maze, full of runways and platforms, what looked like a trampoline smack in the center. She skirted the trampoline and vaulted up a level. She'd get up high, she'd decided, and pick off the civvies. Then she and Catherine could duke it out.

"And three...two...one..." The lights went out. Bright neon beams sparked up to take their place. A ribbon of excitement coiled in her gut. She raced up the runway and shimmied up a glowing ladder, flew over a barricade in a storm of laser fire. Someone yelled out, excited—

"D'you get her?"

"I don't know."

Erin smirked. No, they hadn't. She crouched behind the barricade, scuttled to one side. Her pulse pounded hard and steady, music to her ears. Whispers rose from the shadows, and she cocked her head to listen.

"Where'd she go? Is she up there?" *One by the trampoline, up against the wall.*

"You got her. Don't worry. Get the redhead. Get—" *One just below her, under the ladder.*

Erin slipped past the barricade, keeping to the shadows. She dropped down a level, firing as she went. The guy by the ladder yelped in dismay. His pimply face lit up violet as his vest flashed a hit. Erin slid down the platform and fired off the side, taking down the girl by the trampoline and a guy in red jeans. This was almost too easy, fish in a barrel.

"Hey, soldier! Up here!"

Erin rolled to the side as a bolt flashed from above. She dove for cover, blood singing, the fight thrumming in her veins. *This* was more like it, the hunt, the kill. She could see the guy who'd shot at her, peering out smugly from a forest of hanging barrels. His shoes gleamed bright white, and she focused on them, working her way behind him in a wide circle. Below her, someone shouted. Catherine laughed. Erin could've pegged her then, but she held her fire. Catherine was the big prize. She was saving her for last.

White Shoes froze in place, maybe sensing her behind him. Erin smirked—*too late*—and shot him in the back. He groaned, clutched his chest, and dropped dramatically to the floor. His white shoes drummed on the crash mat, and then he was still.

"Nice try," she told him. "But you never stood a chance." She picked off two more stragglers, shooting between the barrels, and then it was her and Catherine, pistols at dawn.

"Quick draw," called Catherine. "Ten paces, then bang."

Erin jumped down behind her, and grinned to hear her gasp. "Got you rattled," she said, but Catherine just smirked. They lined up back to back, and the duel was on.

"On my go," said Catherine. Erin did a tight nod.

"*Go.* One...two..."

Sasha jumped out from nowhere and shot Catherine in the back. Erin dropped to one knee, but Sasha was faster. She spun on her heel and fired off three bolts. Erin's vest lit up red, violet, then pink. She dropped to the mat, firing into the air.

"Where the hell'd *you* come from?"

"I was here all along." Sasha blew on her pistol and twirled it around her finger. "Oh, and Brody has a message: *situational awareness.*"

"Oh, screw you. Not funny."

"You know it is." Catherine got to her feet. "So, we going again?"

"All night, if we have to." Erin reset her vest and headed back for the start. This was just what she'd needed, a good jolt to the system. For the first time all week, she felt fully awake. Awake and ready for whatever came next.

10

A light frost had settled some time before dawn. It lent the world a dead look, lonely and gray. Erin's breath puffed white as she cut across the lawn.

"Hey." Catherine stopped her with a hand on her shoulder. "I can take the inside, if you want. You can talk to the neighbors."

Erin glanced at the rubberneckers trying to make like they weren't—two old men clutching garbage bags, gawping at the crime scene from the ends of their driveways. A woman in her window seat, sipping coffee and staring.

"I'd rather go in," she said. "Let them get their gossiping out of their systems."

"Suit yourself." Catherine led the way up the steps, heels crunching in the frost. Sandy Morrison's house was a sweet and neat faux-Victorian, big windows, sloping roofs. The front door was bright pink, with a heart-shaped wreath in place of a knocker. Inside was the same, all pink and knickknacks, up until the living room. Inside the living room was pink and knickknacks and blood. Catherine let out a low whistle.

"That's a whole lot of claret."

"Arterial spray." One of the crime scene techs stood up. "He cut her throat where you're standing. She struggled *hard.*"

Erin took in the mess with something like admiration. A wide fan of blood spread over the rear wall, and a high shelf full of Swarovski figurines. A blood-soaked ballerina sparkled in the sunrise. A turtle at her feet sipped from a pool of gore. A family of hummingbirds dripped red from their beaks.

"Even the ceiling, the chandelier..." Catherine shielded her eyes against the crystal dazzle, but Erin's gaze had settled, at last, on the victim. She stood, jaw clenched, anger rising in her chest. Sandy Morrison was a tiny woman, and only twenty-four. She'd liked fat pink throw pillows and crystal figurines, glittery lacquer that made her nails gleam like jewels. She'd liked little fluffy dogs, like the one yipping anxiously in the back yard. What the killer had done to her—

"It feels hateful," said Catherine.

"I was thinking obscene." Erin made her way across the carpet, stepping carefully to avoid the spattered blood. "Is that the *David?*"

Sandy was up on her knees, just like the other victims, lashed to a six-foot replica of Michelangelo's *David.* Her head was tipped back, dead eyes fixed on its cock. Her hands were stretched, palms up, between its marble legs. Her throat gaped open in a sick scarlet grin.

"All the way to the bone," said Catherine. "He nearly took her head off."

"He's escalating."

"I'll say." Catherine stooped to examine Sandy's bindings. "What is that? A jump rope?"

"No, a resistance band. I'm guessing it's hers, going by the color." Bright pink, now stained red. "Fits his pattern, though. He binds them with items found on the scene."

Catherine straightened up. "I'm going to talk to the detectives. Let me know when you're ready, and we'll start canvassing the neighbors."

Erin nodded vaguely, her gaze still locked on Sandy. Her clothes were a mess, blouse torn, skirt askew. She'd lost a shoe in the struggle, and her sole lay exposed, all pink and vulnerable in the cold light of day. Her hair, by contrast, hung in a smooth golden fall, tucked neatly behind her ears.

"Hey, uh..." Erin snapped her fingers to catch the tech's attention. "Can you get prints off skin?"

"In theory, sure. In practice, almost never."

Erin hissed through her teeth. "You should try anyway. Especially her ears, and up around her hairline."

The tech made a grunting sound. Erin went to the window and looked out across the street. Hayes would've stuck out here, a neighborhood like this. Like a turd in a flower arrangement, wholly out of place. Someone should've seen him, some busybody on their porch—an insomniac up reading, a shift worker coming home. She peered at the neighbors still angling for a look. *Which of you clocked him? Who's got the goods?*

She turned away from the window. She felt sharp today, focused, her windshield free of bugs. Somewhere here was the detail that'd blow the case wide open. All she had to do was spot it, and the killer was hers.

Brody straightened his tie and stepped up to the podium. Erin recognized his strained smile, the stiff set of his shoulders. She'd be the same in his shoes—inwardly seething, wanting to wrap up the press conference and get back to the hunt.

Brody took a deep breath, and his smile smoothed out. He drew himself up to address the crowd. "Ladies and gentlemen of the press, thank you for making time in your schedule to attend this briefing." He paused briefly, then went on. "As I'm sure you're aware, Sandy Morrison was discovered early this morning, deceased in her home. The FBI is investigating, in conjunction with the Lancaster PD, and we'll share more information as it becomes available. We ask for your patience until that time."

Erin edged closer, keeping the SUV between her and the press. She didn't need a repeat of last week's fiasco.

"Is this the Crusader?" A scrawny reporter pushed his way to the front. "Is that why the FBI are working the case?"

Erin grimaced—the *Crusader?* When had that started? Brody just shook his head.

"It's too early to draw that conclusion. Our team is gathering evidence, and our tip line is open. We'll let you know more as information becomes available."

A tall woman spoke up. "Have there been any developments with the Vernon Hayes manhunt?"

Brody's lips tightened. "We're running down every lead. It's only a matter of time before Vernon Hayes is in custody. If anyone has information regarding his current whereabouts, I repeat, our tip line is open. You should see the number at the bottom of your screen."

"Is it true your team took this case because of Agent Hastings? Because of her personal connection with Lancaster?"

Brody scowled into the crowd, searching for who'd spoken. When he responded, his tone was curt. "I'm not taking questions on the agents working this case." He held up his hands. "No—no further questions. That will be all." He turned abruptly and made his way back inside. Erin circled the building and slipped in the side door. She caught up with Brody at the water cooler and nudged him in the side.

"You okay?"

"Vultures. They're all vultures." He filled a Dixie cup with water and drained it in one gulp. "We've got a woman slaughtered in the prime of her life, and all they care about is making a meal of an agent with a killer for a twin."

Erin flinched, and so did Brody.

"Sorry," he said. "That came out wrong."

"It's this case," said Erin. "It's got us all up in knots."

Brody filled up his cup again, and seemed to relax. "How'd it go with the neighbors? You get anything there?"

Erin's lip peeled back. "Bunch of ghouls, every one. All they wanted to do was pump us for details. A few of them had doorbell cams, but none of the houses directly facing Sandy's. Plus there's trees everywhere. Our sightline's not good. Still, we grabbed all their footage, so you never know."

"Okay. Good work." Brody exhaled through his nose. "I need you to track down the whereabouts of all the suspects in this case, just to make sure there are no surprises. Also, when you get a moment, I need you to reach out to the California and Nevada state police. See how they're doing on Vernon Hayes."

Erin gave a curt nod and headed back to her desk. The optimism she'd felt in Sandy's living room had wilted around the edges. In her head, she knew this was the job—gather the evidence, sift through the pile.

In her guts, she was antsy, straining at her leash. The killer was out there, maybe plotting his next hit. Gloating, maybe, watching her chase her tail.

She flopped down at her desk and bent her back to her task. Allen Cook checked out easy: he'd been on duty at the children's museum. Warren VanRijn gave her the runaround, but the Hilton confirmed he'd been with his paramour, as evidenced by hotel surveillance and their hefty room service bill. Cecil Fromm had spent the night with his family and in-laws, who'd driven up early to celebrate Thanksgiving.

Only Vernon Hayes remained unaccounted-for. Erin spent nearly three hours on hold, bouncing from department to department, only to meet with disappointment at every turn. Vernon had been spotted at a Vegas casino, winning at blackjack—only "Vernon," in that case, proved to be one John Mahowny. Sightings popped up in Paradise, in Henderson, in San Jose. Every tip led to bupkis, another dead end.

She rubbed at her temples as she set the phone down at last. Hayes had been in the wind more than a week, and not one verified sighting. He could be halfway to China by now—unless he was the killer. If he was, he was close, and thumbing his nose.

She stood up and stretched, and headed over to Brody.

"Got the alibis for our suspects. Everyone checks out." She dropped the files on his desk. "As for the manhunt, *pfft.* No joy there."

"I'm not surprised," said Brody. "If Hayes had surfaced, we'd have heard by now."

"So...what now?" Erin twisted side to side, cracking the kinks from her back. Brody watched her a moment, distracted, then pursed his lips.

"Catch up with Catherine," he said. "Go over the victims—anything we might have missed, anything they have in common. Anything with the latest one that ties to the rest."

Erin nodded and strode off, already reviewing evidence in her head. She was halfway out the door before it occurred to her she'd never thanked Brody for defending her from the press.

Erin found Catherine just down the street, eating her bag lunch at a picnic table in a small, grubby park. She plopped down across from her and slid her a soda she'd grabbed from the vending machine on her way out of the station. "Brody wanted us to review what we've got on the victims."

Catherine cracked her soda and took a big gulp. "I thought he might. I've been digging into Sandy."

"Anything good?"

"Good? No. It's *awful*." Catherine scrubbed at her face, and for the first time, Erin noticed the faint puffiness around her eyes. She reached across the table and squeezed her hand.

"You okay?"

Catherine laughed, soft and brittle. "Oh, you know me. I'll be fine, always am. It's just, this one was so young. I keep picturing Izzy, not so far down the road. She likes pink too, and nail art, and poodles. She's even got one of those little glass dancers."

Erin cringed inwardly. She hadn't stopped to think this case might hit close to home for Catherine, too. "Did you call her yet? Izzy, I mean?"

"You bet your ass I did." Catherine managed a smile. "Caught her at the skating rink, her and her friends. She learned to do something called a...backward swizzle?"

Erin chuckled. "Sounds fun."

"Fun, yep." Catherine straightened up, suddenly all business. "And the sooner we wrap this up, the sooner I can join her." She reached for her tablet and powered it on. "So, Sandy Morrison, twenty-four. Married her sweetheart almost straight out of high school. He was her one and only; she wasn't his. She filed for divorce when she caught him in bed with—cue banjos—his cousin. She worked at Highgate, same department as Rayna."

"Who, the cousin?"

"No, Sandy."

Erin hummed thoughtfully. "So, Highgate, divorced. She fits the pattern, except for her age."

"And except for the way she died. But, even there, he still went for her throat." Catherine drummed her fingers on the table. "Forensics is still going over the scene. Hopefully, they'll turn up something."

"He fixed her hair," said Erin. "I told the techs to check her face for prints. Maybe we'll get some that match that first scene."

"From skin? Wouldn't bet on it."

"Still, worth a try."

Catherine frowned. "I don't like that he's escalating. The blood, the mess—he's losing control. He'll be less cautious now. Less time between kills."

"But more chance he'll slip up."

"We should get Mo on this," said Catherine. "He might pick up on something that doesn't jump out at us." Her phone rang, a loud burr. She glanced at the screen and broke out in a smile. "That's my kids. I need to take this. I missed our Thanksgiving, so I promised we'd Skype. Tell Brody I'll have my report on his desk by tonight."

Erin waved at the kids as they crowded the screen. Izzy waved back. Noah made bunny ears behind her head. Erin kept waving until Catherine retreated to the privacy of her SUV. Left alone in the empty park, she felt a touch of yearning. She was home for the holidays— technically, at least—but she'd yet to call Dad, and Eric was...Eric. She missed how it used to be, exploding turkeys and all.

"Nessun maggior dolore," she muttered. She'd forgotten the rest of the quote, but she knew its meaning just fine. *Nothing hurts more than looking back on happy days from the depths of despair.*

She pulled out her own phone, scrolled through her contacts. Dad wasn't there, not under *Dad,* not under *Graham Hastings.* When had she called him last? Not since she'd got this phone, but surely this year. Surely on his birthday.

Catherine's laughter bubbled up, muffled behind glass. Erin glanced at her, frowned, and jammed her phone in her pocket. She couldn't call Dad, but she knew where he lived, still in the same place she'd grown up. She could swing by if she wanted, swing by right now. Catherine didn't need her, and neither did Brody. An hour wouldn't hurt, and it might even—

She snorted out loud. Going home wouldn't fix anything, but it might make Dad happy. And, what the hell. It might be good to see him.

11

Erin hadn't been home in more than fifteen years. She parked at the curb and stared through the windshield, her stomach in knots. To all outward appearances, the house hadn't changed—beige with white shutters; window boxes out front. The lawn was well kept, bright green and glistening with dew from the sprinkler. Even the car in the driveway was the same, a sturdy blue Buick chosen for durability over style.

She climbed out of her car and wiped her sweaty palms on her pants. She wasn't ready for this—had tortured herself all the way, picturing worst-case scenarios—but she'd come this far. Might as well see it through.

She made her way to the door, noting with faint amusement that even the welcome mat was the same—DON'T STOP. BE LEAVING. Hilarious. She took a deep breath and rapped twice. Somewhere inside the house, she thought she heard a groan. Then she heard footsteps, Dad's heavy tread clomping down the hall. He opened the door, and Erin's face fell.

"Dad?"

She wasn't sure what she'd expected, but this wasn't it. Dad had shrunk like a sweater left too long in the wash. He looked tired, stoop-backed, as if he'd been carrying a heavy burden for a long time. His face had sunk in itself, revealing deep hollows at his temples and cheeks. He'd been larger than life once, but now he looked frail.

"Erin," he said. Then his fallen face lit up, and he said it again. "Erin! You came."

Erin forced a smile. "I'm in town on a case. I thought I'd stop by."

"Yeah, Eric mentioned." He unlocked the screen door to let Erin inside. "Saw you on TV. You're looking good."

Erin followed him to the living room, an odd sensation washing over her, like stepping into the past. Nothing had changed since she'd left home, not the pictures over the mantel, not the doilies on the end tables. Even the *firewood* was the same, the same five dried logs piled in their rack. A prickle of *déjà vu* walked down her back, and she itched to flee. Instead, she perched on the edge of the couch and studied her father. She hadn't seen him since her graduation from Quantico, hadn't updated the picture in her head.

Age hadn't been kind to him. New lines marked his face, and his hair was streaked with gray. His green eyes had faded, no longer the verdant emerald he'd passed on to her and Eric. Now, they reminded her of moss-covered rocks. Had the light gone out of them when she'd left, or after Eric's trial? Or had it been sooner, when Mom passed away? She couldn't remember, couldn't picture him back then.

She pushed her musings aside and asked, "How have you been?"

He shrugged. "Can't complain. Plenty of work, and the Lakers are kicking ass."

Erin's lips quirked up. The Lakers—trust Dad to bring *them* up. "But how are *you* doing? How's your health?"

Dad thumped his chest. "Can't complain of that either. I had my physical in March, got the all-clear. My knee still does its twinging thing when it's going to rain, but hey. I've got two of them." He rubbed the back of his neck, regarding her sidelong. "How about you? Doing okay, staying safe?"

Erin considered her answer. Dad was a lot of things, but stupid wasn't one of them. A blithe answer wouldn't satisfy him, but the whole truth would just upset him. "I'm doing well," she said. "It's tiring sometimes, a whole lot of travel. But we look out for each other, you know, my team. Brody's a hardass, but he's not a jackass. And Catherine's always there for me. I'd say she's a friend."

Dad bobbed his head. "Good, that's good."

A strained silence descended. Erin groped for something to say, but she took after Dad, the strong, silent type. Five minutes she'd been here, and already the well was dry. She scanned around for inspiration, and her eyes lit on the oven.

"What'd you do for Thanksgiving?"

"You really want to know?"

"I asked, didn't I?"

"Swanson turkey dinner in front of the TV." Dad pulled a wry face. "Your brother called, so there was that."

Erin looked away. She could picture it all too clearly, Dad hunched in his La-Z-Boy in front of the TV, his ersatz turkey dinner cooling in his lap. Heaving himself upright at the sound of the phone, maybe stopping a minute to massage his tender knee. The silence stretched out and grew stifling, and Erin got to her feet.

"I should go," she said. "I'm sorry I can't stay longer. I've got, you know..."

"You're busy." Dad stood as well, a trace of relief crossing his face. "Of course, work comes first. I'll walk you out."

She followed him, relieved, only to hesitate at the door. Dad had never been the hugging type, but maybe...but no. She nudged the screen open. "Take care, Dad."

"You too, Erin."

Erin turned and walked away, wondering why she'd thought anything would've changed. It had always been him and Eric, Erin on the outside. Maybe if she'd stuck with him after the trial—maybe then, they'd have bonded, but—

"I order pizza on Saturdays. For dinner." Dad called out to Erin as she bent to unlock her car. "You're welcome to come tomorrow, if you have time."

Erin turned to find him still standing on the porch. She'd thought he'd gone back inside. The fact that he hadn't got to her, somehow. Tears pricked her eyes, and she blinked them away. He looked horribly lonely, standing there by himself, an abandoned old man and his creaky old house.

"Okay," she called, hoarsely. "I'll make the time."

She climbed into her car, a lump rising in her throat. When she looked back at the porch, Dad was gone.

She went back to the prison the following day. A thick nostalgia had clung to her since her visit with Dad. She blamed his time-capsule house, his portal to the oughties. She'd stepped in and flashed back to all she'd lost—all she'd once dreamed of, all she'd once been. She didn't want to go back, but still her heart ached.

Eric met her with a wary look, a crease between his brows.

"If you're here to pick my brain again—"

"I'm not." She looked away, guilty. When had she got like this—calculating, manipulative? She'd come to Eric for answers, about herself, about her case. Had she even thought to ask how he'd been? "I thought we could talk," she said. "Or you could."

"About what?"

"About..." Erin bit her lip. "Does Dad come and see you?"

"He comes on my birthday," said Eric. "Sometimes around Christmas. Mostly, I call him. He, uh, misses you. When I told him I'd seen you, he got all choked up."

Erin's guilt rose, a black, sickly tide. "I saw him yesterday. Does he always look that tired?"

Eric reached for her hand. When she didn't pull away he squeezed it, stilling her fidgeting. "He *is* tired," he said. "He's like you, works too hard. But I don't think it's just that."

"What do you think it is?"

Eric was quiet a spell, maybe deciding what she needed to hear. What he could tell her without breaking her heart. "He has regrets," he said at last. "He told me once, years ago, he wishes he could go back. He wishes he could be different, you know, as a dad. I think..."

"What?"

"He thinks you might visit more if he'd been there for you."

Erin snorted without meaning to. "He's right about that."

"You can't hate him forever. He's trying to change."

Erin sighed. "I don't hate him. It's just, I've built a life for myself, and he's not part of it. Maybe he should be, but...I don't know. Being back here in Lancaster, I'm tripping over old memories I haven't thought of in years. Yeah, it was bad sometimes, but we had good times as well. I've tried not to think of them, but they happened. They did."

Eric sat forward, smiling. "What's your best memory?"

"My best?" Erin frowned, considering, though there wasn't much contest. The title of *best* could only go to one day. "Hurricane Harbor," she said.

"The water slides!"

"The water slides." She grinned. "The steps were so gross, slimy and spidery and smelling of feet. But then you'd get to the top, and that moment when you push off..."

"Remember Dad in the lazy river?"

Erin huffed laughter. "I swear, he set up camp in there, him and his inner tube and his Thermos of beer."

"And that sad spot of sunblock at the end of his nose?"

"And his sunburn after, between his fingers and toes?"

Erin slumped back, breathless with mirth. Eric laughed just as hard, muffling the sound in his sleeve.

"That was a great day," he said, when his giggles had passed. "Riding back in the car, singing along with the radio? What was that one song, *Baby, One More Time?* You kept smacking my head every time I sang 'hit me.'"

"Can't say you didn't ask for it."

Eric stuck out his tongue, and Erin saw him again as he'd been back then, a tall, rangy kid with just a hint of baby chub. He'd been happy back then, or he'd seemed that way.

"Eric?"

"Mm?" He wiped at his eyes.

"When did you—" She bit her tongue. Now wasn't the time to ask when he'd changed. When he'd dropped down the rabbit hole that ended in this room. "Remember our Go-Kart?"

"Oh, *that* was all you." Eric thumbed at the pale scar above his right elbow. "Pillows for airbags—what were you thinking?"

"Hey, at least there *were* airbags." She rubbed her own elbow. "And you're the one who climbed in. I didn't force you."

"No, you made chicken sounds until I got in beside you. Then you used me as a crash mat when we flew over the wheel. I smashed my shoulder. You got, what, road rash?"

"Epic road rash.*"* She chuckled, but this time her laughter came out flat. The Go-Kart had been eighth grade, their last year of junior high. The last summer they'd been *them,* the old Erin and Eric. After that, he'd got broody. His pranks had stopped being silly and taken on an edge of malice. Erin had still gone along, at least at first, but the fun had gone out of it, that pure, childish thrill.

"I'm glad you came," said Eric, as their time ran down. "It was good to catch up, just be us for a while."

"You're still in there, aren't you? The brother I miss?"

"Part of me, maybe." A shadow crossed his features. "You'll come back, won't you? Before you go?"

"I will if I can."

Erin left the prison half elated, half sick. Would she be naïve to believe he was in there, some version of Eric she might recognize? Would she be stupid to reach for him, or would she find peace in understanding? She'd missed him, missed Dad, even—missed having a family. Still, hope felt dangerous, a trap waiting to spring.

She headed back to her hotel with her insides all in knots.

———

Erin arrived back at Dad's right behind the pizza. She paid the driver and headed up to the house. Dad opened the door with his wallet out, and did a double take when he realized it was Erin.

She held up the box. "Pizza's here."

"Take it through to the living room." Dad held the door for her, then locked it behind her. He'd never done that when they were kids, locked the door when he was home. "I'll bring the plates," he said. "You still drink grape soda?"

Erin nodded. "Yes, thanks." She made her way to the living room and set the pizza on the coffee table. When she rose, she felt dizzy, like she'd turned a familiar corner and found herself somewhere strange. She'd thought the house hadn't changed, but she didn't remember the photo album spread out on Dad's chair. She perched on the footrest and pulled it into her lap. The first shots were familiar—her and Eric in Santa hats; the three of them at the beach. A couple with Mom, which made her eyes prickle. But a few pages in, the family snaps gave way to newspaper clippings. She brushed her finger over the first one, an inch-long blurb on her first case. She wasn't mentioned by name, but Dad had tracked it down anyway and filed it away. She flipped through the pages, flipped through her career. Dad had been following her, right from the—

Dad cleared his throat. Erin dropped the album like she'd been caught reading porn. Dad was standing in the doorway, plates and napkins in his hands. His expression was sad, but under that she saw...pride?

"You've done a good job," he said. "Got them answers, all those people."

Erin felt her chest swell. Had Eric been right about Dad's regrets? He *did* seem changed, and not just by age. He seemed gentler somehow, his rough edges filed off. Erin went to him and took the plates and napkins.

"Thanks, Dad," she said. "That's why I love my job, giving folks their closure. If you'll get the drinks, I'll set these out."

Dad grinned, and the stress lines smoothed out at the corners of his eyes. He headed back to the kitchen with a lightness in his step. Erin watched him, smiling, as she set the table.

Dinner went smoother than she expected—conversation was stilted, but still it went on. Dad fed her questions between bites of pizza, all about work, but it felt like a start. Erin told him about the time, as a rookie, she'd stumbled on a cache of stolen cheese so stinky she'd puked down Brody's back. Dad laughed at that, a genuine guffaw. Erin found herself relaxing, even having fun. When her phone rang, she scowled, resenting the intrusion.

"I gotta take this," she said. "Sorry. It's work."

"Don't worry about it." Dad stood, knees popping, and retreated to the kitchen. "I'll see what I've got in the way of dessert."

She waited until he'd left the room, then answered her phone. "Hey, Randy, what's up?"

Her supervisor heaved a sigh. "Nothing good, I'm afraid."

She tensed, her free hand curling into a fist. "What's going on?"

"I've been debating whether it's prudent to leave you on this case." Randy's chair creaked, far away. Erin pictured him leaning back, closing his eyes. Slipping his glasses off to let the world go foggy. "Brody's been fighting for you, but Erin, you assaulted a reporter. I had to call in a hell of a favor to keep her from pressing charges. And I hear you're not sleeping, hanging around that prison—"

"Visiting my brother!"

"I'm worried about you. Worried about your mental health, if you stay in Lancaster."

Erin couldn't speak, unnerved by the gentle but clear censure in his voice. She wanted to protest, but the words stuck in her throat.

"I've gone back on forth with this, but in the end it comes down to whether I can afford to lose a good agent from an active case. The fact is I can't, so you get a reprieve. But one more outburst—"

"That was a one-time deal. And it's been a week since then, and I've been playing ball."

"You have," said Randy. His chair creaked again. "But, Erin, I need your word it won't happen again—no outbursts, no screwups, no playing rogue agent."

"No Hasty Hastings," she said. "I promised Brody already."

"That's what he said as well," said Randy. "And he claims he needs you...which brings me to the other reason I'm calling. The police found Vernon Hayes's vehicle in a ditch outside Coyote Springs. Your team's headed up there already, and I told Brody I'd send you along. But, Erin—"

"I know."

"No more Hasty Hastings. I need you at your best."

Erin swallowed hard. She didn't want to imagine how close she'd come to heading home in disgrace. "Thank you," she said. "I appreciate you not benching me. I won't let you down."

"I know you won't." Randy's voice warmed, and she knew he was smiling. "Go get him, kid."

Erin hung up, composing herself as her father walked in. "There's been a break in the case," she said. "I need to head out."

The skin around Dad's eyes tightened, but he managed a smile. "Do what you've got to do. And take care out there."

Once again, Erin debated whether to hug him, but then her phone buzzed, an update from Sasha. She fired off a quick reply, already heading for the door.

12

Erin arrived in Coyote Springs to a frantic buzz of activity. Brody was barking orders like they were going out of style, fielding calls with one hand, directing agents with the other. A line of sweat ran down his back, darkening his shirt between his shoulder blades. Catherine emerged from the hustle and pulled Erin aside.

"Finally! Where've you been?"

"I came as soon as I could. What's going on?"

Catherine raked a hand through her hair, exhaustion clear on her face. "Gathering evidence. Can't afford to let Hayes walk on a technicality."

Erin scowled at the thought. So far, they had nothing tying Hayes to the crime scenes, not a hair, not a fiber, not even a witness. "What are you looking for?"

"Seed pods from those trees on Sandy's street. We've been scraping the tires, taking dirt samples, vacuuming all the seats. Here's hoping he drove there and didn't take a bus."

"Fingers crossed." Erin glanced at Brody, who was pacing up and down. His hair had come ungelled, and hung limply in his eyes. "Is it just me, or is he looking extra-stressed?"

"Hannady's been on his back." Catherine lowered her voice. "I don't know what's up with her, but it's like she's not so much interested in catching the killer as closing the case. She's been calling all day, demanding results."

"She called last week too, when Hayes got away. Gave Brody quite the earful, from what I could—"

"Hey! Erin, Catherine." Brody waved them over, phone still glued to his ear. He hung up at their approach, and raked his hair off his face. "We've got a receipt here, some Dunkin' Donuts outside Vegas. I need you to run down there and see if anyone remembers Hayes."

Erin suppressed a groan. She'd been on the road what felt like all night, mainlining caffeine to keep from dozing off. "We can't have the locals do it?"

"I'm not leaving anything to chance." Brody looked her up and down, lip curling into a scowl. "Do I have to go myself?"

"No, of course not." Erin couldn't quite muster a smile, but she shot him the thumbs-up as she piled into Catherine's SUV.

"You can sleep on the way," said Catherine. "And, hey, it's Dunkin' Donuts. We can eat while we're there."

———

Erin and Catherine didn't get their donuts.

They arrived at the restaurant just before opening, only to learn the manager had been working alone the night Hayes swung by, thanks to a flu bug that'd gone through the whole staff. He lived in Coyote Springs, so they'd turned around and sped back the way they'd come.

They pulled up at the Lewis house right around breakfast. Harvey, the manager, answered the door, dripping pancake batter from a bright red spatula.

"The FBI, seriously? I don't mean to be rude, but what do you want with me?"

"We just need to ask you a few questions about one of your customers." Catherine peered past him. "Do you mind if we come in?"

Harvey led them to the kitchen, dripping batter all the way. A fat dog chased after him, licking up the mess. "Go ahead and sit down," he said. "Just watch out for toys."

Catherine stayed standing, but Erin sat down. Her foot hit a soccer ball and it rolled across the kitchen.

"So, I'm just going to need you to take a look at this mugshot." Catherine held up her phone, displaying a mugshot of Hayes. "Do you remember serving him two nights ago?"

Harvey glanced at the photo and his mouth turned down. "Oh, yeah. I remember him. He gave me the creeps. I thought it might be a stickup, the way he kept looking back at the door. Scanning for cops, you know? They always do that."

Erin raised a brow. "Do you get many stickups?"

"Not as many as 7-11, but a couple a year."

"That's tough," said Catherine, jotting something in her notepad. "Is there anything else you can remember about him?"

Harvey frowned. "He wanted to know about car rental places in Vegas. I told him I couldn't help him. I live in Coyote Springs. He said any place would do, so long as they have cars. So I told him about Blake's here in the Springs."

"Blake's?"

"Sorry, Blake's Car Services. Locals just call it Blake's. Good place, reliable vehicles. It's closed now, though. He opens at noon on weekends." Harvey stuck his spatula in his batter and leaned on the counter. "Did he do something, your guy?"

"He's a person of interest," said Catherine. "Anything else you can tell us?"

Harvey shook his head. "No. Soon as I told him about Blake's, he rushed out the door. I was glad to see him go. I got that weird vibe, you know?"

"Well, thanks for your time," said Erin. She nodded to Harvey and headed back down the hall. His dog followed her as far as the door, then watched from the welcome mat as she climbed into the car. Catherine piled in beside her, covering a yawn.

"We should find a motel," she said. "I don't know about you, but I've been up all night and I'm dead on my feet."

Erin groaned and agreed. "Let me call Brody. I'll brief him on the plan."

Catherine just grunted, already pulling out. She looked as tired as Erin felt, her eyes dark and glassy, her hair hanging limp. For all her badgering, maybe Hannady had a point—this case couldn't wrap up soon enough.

———

Catherine found a small motel just outside town. They booked into a double and immediately crashed, the past twenty-four hours catching up to them all at once. Erin passed out the second her head hit the pillow, not even bothering to kick off her shoes. She dropped into a dead sleep—so deep when the shot came, she'd stumbled into the wall before she realized she was up.

"Waffuck?" She dropped to the floor, fumbling for her gun. It wasn't there and she grunted, crawling back toward the nightstand.

"Was that a shot?" Catherine was on the floor, crouched behind her bed.

"Don't know. I can't—" Erin's breath caught in her throat. A perfect, round hole hung dead center in the curtains, still smoldering at the edges. Bright sunlight slashed through it, blinding in the gloom. Catherine had spotted it as well, and was moving toward it, back to the wall. She pulled back the curtain to reveal a spiderweb of cracks radiating from the bullet hole punched through the pane.

"A warning?" Catherine peered out the window at an angle. "I don't see anyone. Do you?"

Erin squinted out from the other side. "A drive-by, maybe. I thought I heard a car peel out, but it might've been a dream."

Catherine made a disgusted sound. "Call the police," she said. "Our shooter's not here, but we can't risk him swinging back and trying again."

They sat out by the pool while the police cleared the scene, waiting for noon and the chance to chase their lead. The motel had offered a new room, but Erin's blood was up, and Catherine was the same—too wired to sleep; too tired for much else.

"These sandwiches are okay," said Erin. "For a motel vending machine."

"You're braver than I am," said Catherine. "Egg salad from a vending machine—better you than me."

Erin took another bite. "Is Brody coming up?"

Catherine shook her head. "Not much he can do here. But he thinks this is a sign we're on the right trail."

"Too close for comfort." Erin yawned hugely, so wide her jaw popped.

Catherine dug in her bag and found a bottle of nail polish. She leaned forward in her deckchair and started painting her toenails. Erin leaned over, laughing.

"What color is that?"

Catherine checked the bottle. "Ectoplasm green," she said. "Noah got it in his loot from Halloween. He doesn't wear nail polish so...what do you think?"

"Ghostbusterrific." Erin flashed her a grin. "How *are* the munchkins? Holding up okay?"

Catherine smiled at that, her shoulders relaxing. "Izzy's whining about her next piano recital and how her teacher is too strict. Noah's shot up another inch, grown out of all his pants. John says he's eating like a lumberjack, can't get enough."

Erin let out a chuckle. Catherine's kids never failed to amuse her with their antics. "What's got Izzy so bothered? She adored her teacher, last I heard."

"Oh, she does. But she insisted on learning 'Clair de Lune' for her recital. Now she says it's too hard, but Lisa won't let her quit. And she won't let her fudge the more difficult sections."

Erin leaned back, laughing. "I remember that phase. I went through it myself. I boasted to Eric I could learn Russian, of all things. He didn't think I could, so...*yaitso na yevo litse?*" She chuckled. "Tell Izzy I'll come to her recital if she sticks with it."

Catherine laughed. "I'll pass that along."

Erin finished her sandwich and went back for sodas, grape for herself, Dr. Pepper for Catherine. It felt good to sit a while and let Catherine's stories wash over her, especially the ones having to do with her kids. It brought back a feeling she'd almost forgotten how to feel—the comfort of home, the shelter of family. Maybe she'd find that again someday. Maybe even soon.

13

By a surprising stroke of luck, Blake himself greeted them when they arrived at the rental agency. He ushered them into his office, his salesman smile fading as the door swung shut behind him. "What can I do for you agents?"

Catherine held up Hayes's mugshot. "Has this gentleman come in to rent a vehicle?"

Blake studied it for several moments. "As a matter of fact, he has. Quinton Hicks, right?"

Catherine made a *tch* sound. "That's Vernon Hayes, currently a person of interest in an active murder investigation. You didn't request ID when you leased him a vehicle?"

Blake's face paled a shade. "He paid in cash and tipped on top of that. He said he'd lost his ID in Vegas, in his hotel. Besides, I don't like to argue with—"

"Yes?"

He let out a pent-up breath. "A man with a gun. Plus, he had crazy eyes, like—" He made a bug face to demonstrate, eyes bulging from his head. "If you give me a second, I can tell you exactly what he's driving right now."

Erin nodded tightly. "I think you'd better."

Blake hurried to a filing cabinet and rifled through its contents. He pulled out a paper smudged with carbon print. "Yep, here we go. He rented a 2019 black Honda Accord. I even have the license plate— 952-X28. I'll just make a copy and you can take it with you."

"And next time someone shows up with a gun on his hip and no ID?"

"I'll still rent to him," said Blake. "I've got a family who'd miss me. But I'll call the cops, cross my heart."

"You'd better," said Catherine. "Unless you want an accessory charge on your record."

Blake turned white at that, and dropped down at his desk. Catherine left him there, Erin trailing at her heels.

Erin waited until they were safely in their vehicle to laugh. "I thought he might pass out when you gave him that look."

"I hate guys like that," said Catherine. "If he'd done his job, Hayes would still be looking for wheels. We might even have him, but no. Stupid Blake."

"Still, don't most rental cars come with a tracker? Sasha can trace him, and it'll work out okay."

"Maybe. Maybe not." Catherine dug out her phone and called Brody, putting him on speaker. "Agents Hannon and Hastings reporting. Your lead was good: Hayes did rent a car. Erin's sending the details to Sasha. What should we do next?"

124

Brody let out a sigh of relief. "Get in touch with both the California and Nevada state police and have them issue a BOLO. I'll pull together a press brief and get the word out to the public. This might be the break we were looking for. Good work."

Erin opened her mouth to thank him, but Brody had hung up.

Catherine shrugged. "You want California or Nevada?"

Brody was true to his word. In less than an hour, he'd gathered the press. Erin and Catherine were listening to the breaking news report when Erin's phone buzzed in her pocket.

"Hey, Sasha. What's up?"

"Do you know how many junk tips we're getting from that stupid tip line?" She huffed down the line, so loud Erin winced. "You want to trade places? 'Cause I'm ready to tear my hair out. Some crackpot from New Jersey just called to inform us Hayes is driving a blue Cadillac, not a black Honda Accord, because he saw it in a dream three years ago."

"At least it's not UFO freaks."

"Oh, we've got those. There's *always* UFO freaks." Sasha blew a raspberry. "Anyway, I have a message from Brody. He says not to come home. You're to stay in the area in case any new leads come in."

"We'd figured as much." Erin went to hang up, then broke out in a grin. "Good luck with the tip line. Or as they say on Mars...beeble-beeble-beeble."

Sasha squawked and hung up. Erin turned to Catherine. "What do you say we follow up with the police, see if they've got anything on our shooter?"

Catherine nodded. "Sounds like a plan." She swung the car around, headed back toward town. They'd just pulled into the station when Sasha called back. This time, her voice was animated, bright with excitement.

"Hayes's rental car was just left with the valet at McCarran International Airport. The locals are on it, but Brody wants you to—"

It was Erin's turn to hang up on Sasha. "McCarran International Airport. Hayes is there *right now*."

Catherine reversed and peeled out, flipping on her cherry light though the road was deserted. Erin fired off a text to the team.

Hannon and Hastings en route. ETA 1 hr 15.

She settled her phone on her lap and leaned forward in her seat. That familiar anticipation rose in her gut, every instinct she had telling her this was it. Hayes was waiting, unsuspecting, just an hour down the road. By tonight, she'd have her answers—was he guilty of murder, or only of being a colossal pain in her ass? Her pulse picked up, and she found herself hoping he'd evade the local cops long enough she could nab him herself. Hoping he'd *resist* her, so she could show him how she felt.

"Almost there," said Catherine.

Erin grinned, wide and wolfish. "Almost there," she agreed.

14

They made it to the airport in forty minutes flat, thanks to light traffic and Catherine's foot sitting heavy on the gas pedal. Airport security met them at departures—along, to Erin's surprise, with Las Vegas SWAT. She'd expected regular uniforms, Hayes in custody already.

"What's going on?" Erin jogged up to join them, securing her vest as she went.

A gray-haired man stepped forward, quick on his feet. Erin put him in his sixties, grizzled and leathery, but still fit and trim. "Carter Smith, head of airport security. Vernon Hayes walked into the terminal fifty minutes ago. He made his way to the ticket desk and requested a seat on the next flight to Mexico. The agent assisting him recognized him from the news."

He gestured to where a young woman was giving a statement. "Veronica's smart, and she thinks on her feet. She asked for his valet info, and when the license number he gave her matched the one on your BOLO, she hit her silent alarm."

"Smart girl." Catherine gave an approving nod. "So, I'm assuming something went wrong?"

Smith pulled a face. "He saw us closing in and whipped out a gun. He tried to take Veronica hostage, but she kicked him and ran. He fired on security and ran the other way, straight into the employee locker room. We'd have gone in already, but that chief of yours, Hannady? She insisted we hold back until you two arrived."

Erin frowned. "Any hostages?"

Smith's scowl deepened. "We've got two ticket agents unaccounted-for. Hayes might be holding them, or he might not. But SWAT's cleared the area, and we're working on an extraction plan."

"Okay," said Catherine. "This guy's wanted in connection with a string of murders in California and Nevada. I know he's not making it easy, but we want him alive."

"That's our aim, too." The SWAT captain, Markov, beckoned them over to a wide table spread with maps of the airport. He tapped on a long room circled in red. "This is the locker room. It has two exits, here and here. Hayes is in the middle, between the lockers and the stalls, but we're not sure he's aware of the rear exit. It's partially hidden, see, behind this wall." He pointed at a wide door nestled in the back corner. Erin narrowed her eyes.

"So, what's the plan?"

"We want to send a negotiator to talk to Hayes through the front. While he's distracted with that, our team will enter from the rear. We'll appraise the situation and go from there."

"I'd like to be on that team," said Erin.

Markov gave her a long look, and Erin thought he might argue. Instead, he blew out a long breath. "All right. You're in. I'll handle negotiations."

Erin shifted from foot to foot as the captain helped her wire up. The first wisps of adrenaline thrummed through her veins, sharpening her senses until her palms began to itch. Hayes was so close she fancied she could smell him, that faint mildew tang from his moldering couch. She couldn't wait to lay hands on him, to sweat the truth from his—

"Wait at the back till I establish a rapport," said Markov. "Then you head into the bathroom, quiet as you can. I'll talk loud, give you cover, but still, take it slow."

"Got it." Erin moved into position behind three burly SWAT guys. She practiced moving silently as they circled through the lounge. Security had cleared the area, and the high ceilings amplified their every breath, every creak of their boots.

They crept up on the rear door, slowing as they went. Someone whispered *in position,* and for a moment, all was still. Then came Markov's greeting, booming through the door.

"Vernon Hayes? You okay in there?"

Hayes didn't answer. Erin thought she heard a whimper, somewhere up ahead. She glanced at the man beside her to see if he'd heard it too, but he stood impassive, breathing slow through his nose. Markov called out again, more gently this time.

"I'm not going to burst in on you," he said. "You're totally safe. I just need to know, you got hostages in there?"

"Five! I've got five of 'em!" Hayes's voice was a squeak, high and trembling with panic. "You come in here, I'll start shooting. I'll—"

"No need for that." Markov's tone was soothing, warm and calm. "I just need to ask you, is anyone hurt?"

"Not yet," said Hayes.

"That's good, then. You're good. You haven't done anything you can't walk away from. Now, listen, we're—"

Erin eased forward, hardly daring to breathe. She slid ahead of the others, soles soft on the tile. She pushed the door open, one inch at a time, and slithered inside with her back to the wall. She could hear dripping water, and the whirr of a fan. Hayes was tapping his foot, a nervous staccato. And someone was sniffling, so close, for a moment, Erin thought it was one of her guys.

She took a deep, cleansing breath and held it in her lungs. Markov was still talking, all meaning lost in a torrent of sensory input—the sharp smell of drain cleaner, the breeze from the fan. Erin timed her steps to match Hayes's tapping, working her way down the wall. The sniffling was coming from just around the bend, the dank little alcove between the wall and the lockers.

"I need a minute," said Hayes. "I need to *think*. Can't you shut up while I—"

Erin darted around the corner. There in the alcove, a young man crouched, cowering, one ankle cuffed to a hanging padlock. His eyes went round at the sight of her, and Erin pressed her finger to her lips. She dug in her pocket, pulled out her notepad, and scribbled.

OTHER HOSTAGES BESIDES YOU?

The man shook his head.

Erin knelt down beside him and unhooked his cuffs. He surged up, tensed to run, but she caught him by the shoulder. "*Slowly,*" she mouthed, and he crept past her, past her backup. He made it out quiet, then he let out a sob. Hayes gasped, and the game was up.

"What was that?"

"Just someone outside," said Markov, but Hayes was moving, darting into a stall. The door slammed, then the lock clacked home, and Erin heard him breathing hard.

"Don't come in. I'll start shooting."

"I'm afraid that's off the table," said Markov. "Your hostage is out, and we know it's just you. But we can still do this easy. If you lay down your weapon and put your hands on the wall—"

Erin inched forward. She could see Hayes in the mirror, his dusty gray shoes peeking under the door.

There you are. Got you. She held her breath.

"I'm coming in now," said Markov. "Me and my team." The front door thumped open. Hayes yelped aloud.

"Stay back! I'll shoot." He shuffled back, clumsy, heels bumping the toilet. "I'll blow your brains out, so—"

"You shoot, so do we. Drop your weapon and step out, and no one gets hurt." Markov's voice echoed in the tight space. Erin slunk forward, toward the line of stalls.

"We can all still walk out of here," said Markov. "You want to—"

Vernon fired twice. The long mirror crumpled in a dazzle of glass. Erin dropped down instinctively, and inspiration struck. Even in her riot gear, she could slide under the stalls, crawl up behind Hayes and surprise him from below. She signaled to her team leader and pointed at the gap. He cocked his head, uncomprehending, then frowned and shook his head.

"I'm giving you thirty seconds," said Markov. "Thirty seconds to surrender, or—"

Hayes fired again, into the ceiling. A shell clinked at his feet and rolled toward Erin. She jerked her head at the gap again, and this time, she got the nod.

She dropped to her belly, checked the space one more time. It would be tight, but she'd make it—if she didn't breathe too deep.

Please, let this work. She held her breath and pushed off. The floor was slick, newly waxed, and she squirted into the first stall like a watermelon seed. Her hand slapped the toilet bowl as she flailed to stop her slide. It hit with a loud *smack*, and she paused, breathing hard.

"Just go. Get out. I need time to think." Hayes squeezed off another round, straight through the door. Erin sagged with relief: he hadn't heard her. She took a moment to breathe, to slow her pounding heart, then she wriggled forward on her elbows, down the row of stalls. Every cell in her body urged her, *hurry, hurry,* but she went slow and steady, an inch at a time. She breathed through her nose, soft, shallow breaths.

"If you wanted to hurt us, you'd have done it by now," said Markov. "You're a good guy. I can tell. How about we keep talking?"

Erin stopped just short of Hayes's stall, close enough to reach out and tug on his shoelace. She was tempted to try it—a wild, goofy urge— but she held her position, biding her time. She'd get one shot at this, one chance to take him down.

"That's a PPK you're packing, right? Eight rounds in the clip, maybe one in the chamber. That means you've got—"

Hayes let out a howl. He flung himself at the door. Erin grabbed his foot and *yanked.* Hayes screamed and pitched forward. His gun hit the floor. He went down like a sack of concrete, headfirst through the door, letting out a loud *whoof* as his belly hit the floor. His gun skidded wide, past the stalls and out of sight.

Erin scrambled to her feet and sprinted from her stall. Hayes was up on his knees and she slammed him down, pinning him in place with a knee in his back. She grabbed his wrist, cuffed it, and reached for the other one. Hayes struggled weakly, to no avail. Erin's cuffs clicked home with a satisfying *snik*.

"All clear," she said.

The SWAT teams converged, moving more confidently when they saw Hayes subdued. Erin sat up and pushed her hair from her face. "His gun's over there. He should still have four rounds—five if he loaded one in the chamber."

"Got it," said Markov. He leaned down to offer her a hand up. "How about you? You good?"

"Not a scratch on me. Help me get him on his feet so I can arrest him."

He did as she asked, hauling a red-faced Hayes to an upright position. Erin smirked at him.

"Remember me?"

Hayes scowled and looked away. Erin marched him from the locker room. "Vernon Hayes, you are under arrest for false imprisonment, and, for reckless discharge of a firearm in a public place. You have the right to remain silent. Anything you say can and will be used against you in a court of law..."

Hayes didn't struggle. He kept his head down all the way to Erin's vehicle. She deposited him in the back seat, secured him, and locked the door. Markov peered in at him, thick brows drawn together. "Reckless discharge of a firearm? Didn't you say he was wanted for murder?"

She flashed him a half-smile. "Judges can be picky. We *want* him for murder, but we can *prove* he took that hostage and shot up that bathroom. And there's nothing to say we can't add additional charges while he's in custody." She held out her hand. "Thanks for the backup."

Markov shook it easily. "All in a day's work. This *is* Sin City."

Erin laughed. "Still, we appreciate it. We've been chasing this guy for days."

Catherine ambled up to join them, visibly relieved. "All right, Hayes is ours. Airport security will send their footage to Sasha. With that and your body cams, we'll be in good shape." She clapped Erin on the shoulder, a fraction too hard. "Ready to head back to Lancaster?"

"Never thought I'd say yes to that, but yes. Yes. *Yes.*"

Catherine chuckled, fishing for her keys. "What's this I hear about you crawling on the bathroom floor?"

"I wasn't—" Erin broke off sharply. At the time, she'd just done it, high on the hunt. Now, with the adrenaline ebbing in her veins, she couldn't hold back a shudder. "I don't want to think about it. Let's just get somewhere equipped with a shower."

"Yeah, well, that's what you get, worrying me like that." Catherine flicked her arm, and Erin flicked her back. They both laughed a little shakily, loose with relief.

Erin showered at the police station, in the gray locker room. She showered a long time, until her fingers went pruney and the ceiling dripped condensation. It felt good to scrub the day off her, scrub off the case. She tilted her head back and let the spray drum her face. She rinsed her mouth, spat, and rinsed it again, and stepped out as pink and fresh as though she'd shed her old skin.

She took her time toweling off and wriggling into her clothes. Brody would just be starting his interview with Hayes. He'd have let him sweat a while first, let him get good and anxious. Poured him full of Coke so he'd be buzzed on caffeine and needing to pee.

Erin fixed her hair in the mirror and headed for the observation room. She strode in with a cheerful greeting on her lips, only to choke it back at the unmistakable whiff of tension.

"Catherine? What's up?"

Catherine reached over and turned up the speaker. Erin went to the window and pressed her hands to the glass. Brody was standing over Hayes, who was handcuffed to the table, foot jiggling furiously as he yammered his innocence.

"You snatched my wallet," he yelped. "But go get it, go check, and you'll see for yourself. I couldn't have killed that bitch. I was at the Days Inn off Polaris, by the Burger King—fifty bucks for the room, ten on the minibar. I got the receipt. Go check. I'll wait."

"You could've fished that receipt out of the trash," said Brody. His Texas drawl was strong, betraying his frustration. "If you're so innocent, why'd you go on the run?"

Erin leaned forward, ears pricking up.

"I was scared," said Hayes. "You were going to find...I guess you found it. My wall of retribution."

"You mean this?" Brody pulled out a photo and slapped it on the table. "Your statue? Your pictures? What's that all about?"

Hayes stared at the photo, a greedy light in his eyes. He reached out to touch it, but Brody jerked it out of reach. Hayes pooched out his lower lip, a kid denied his candy.

"They're everyone I—everyone I was gonna punish."

"You want to punish these nuns? These women of faith?" Brody shook his head in a parody of confusion. "What'd they ever do to wind up on your wall?"

Hayes opened his mouth, then closed it again. His face twitched, then contorted into a terrifying mask. "Women of *faith?* Let me tell you about those women. Those bitches are the *devil*, sadists in veils!" He slapped his own palm, so loud Erin jumped. "You ever get that? You ever get the ruler? You can't close your hand after. You can't write, can't wipe your ass, but that's not the point. It's so you can't grab yourself, so you can't—" Hayes grabbed his crotch, staggered to his feet. The chain caught on his ankle and he thudded back into his seat.

"The flesh is corrupt," he screamed, his voice high and reedy. "Mortify thy flesh, that thy soul might be saved!" He smacked his palms on the table, again and again. "Repent! *Repent!*" His voice hitched and cracked, and he dissolved into laughter.

"That'll do," said Brody.

Hayes hiccupped and giggled, and stared at the table. His breath came in short bursts, almost like sobs. When he raised his head, a chill ran down Erin's spine.

"They deserved it," he croaked. A goblin grin split his face, all jagged teeth. "I saw the news and I knew this guy was just like me. He sniffs out evil and removes it from this world. You call them victims, but those women deserved it. They deserved it and then some. I knew they were evil, so I put them on my wall. You know, *inspiration.*" He groped for the photo again. "Take that one there, in the bottom corner. She's not one of mine, but she got what she asked for. And that one up top. You can tell just by looking at her, she put her husband through hell. I only wish I'd witnessed her penance."

"Fantastic. A wannabe." Erin stepped back from the window, acid rising in her throat. "I'll go check his wallet, see if he's got that receipt."

"It's late," said Catherine. "You should go get some rest."

Erin grunted assent, but she knew she wouldn't sleep. She went to the evidence lockup and signed out Hayes's wallet. She spread out its contents across the big desk in the briefing room, coupons and flyers, receipts going back years. A piece of fuzzy hard candy stuck to her finger, and she shook it off in disgust.

The door swung open behind her what felt like minutes later, but when Erin checked her watch, the dial read midnight. Brody stood in the doorway, rumpled and pale.

"Checking his alibi?"

Erin sank down in a hard plastic chair. "He's clear for Sandy," she said. "The clerk at the Days Inn remembers him. He's sending over their tapes." She shuffled through the receipts, didn't find what she wanted, and put her head down instead. "He didn't do Alice either. He was at Walmart at noon, checking out a list of groceries as long as my arm. I haven't reached out to them, but I will in the morning."

"You did well today," said Brody. He sat down beside her, rested his hand on the arm of her chair. "Have you had dinner?"

"Too grossed out to eat." Erin thought of Hayes, and her stomach burbled sickly. "The flesh is corrupt," she said, and Brody slapped his forehead.

"Let me drive you back," he said. "We can talk on the way."

Erin followed him out. His stride was heavy, his shoulders tense and stooped. She guessed hers were the same. Even climbing into his SUV felt like a monumental effort. The radio came on when Brody turned the key, but he slapped it off again with a grunt of disgust.

"I thought we had him," he said, as he pulled out. "You had your doubts, though. Catherine said."

"His thesis statement wasn't clear," she muttered, thinking of Eric.

"Excuse me?"

She sat up a little straighter, pinched herself alert. "I kept asking myself why he did it—why those victims, why now—and all I got was maybe. *Maybe* they were surrogates. *Maybe* he just snapped. *Maybe* he's Catholic, and they're all divorced. But none of it jelled. None of it made me go *that's it. There's our why.*"

"Agent Mirza said the same thing," said Brody. "Too convoluted, too...shaky. Still, we couldn't just leave him. Not after he ran."

Erin stared out the window, watching the dark buildings zip by. By night, they looked abandoned, forgotten. Condemned. A lump rose in her throat, too thick to choke down. This town swallowed light, swallowed hope, swallowed lives. It'd happened with Eric and it was happening again, one tragedy after another, young lives cut short. She hadn't stopped Eric, and she wouldn't stop—

"Erin." Brody touched her elbow and she nearly screamed.

"*What?*"

"I thought you were sleeping. You shouldn't sleep in the car. That's how you get arthritis, sleeping in cars."

Erin didn't know what to say to that, so she said nothing at all. Somewhere, the killer lurked, in that black, haunted night. Stalking his next mark, hunting her down. How would she find him, if she couldn't find his *why?*

Why'd you do it, Eric?

She leaned her head on the window, tired to the bone.

The killer hummed to himself, a bright, merry tune. All was right with the world: Sandy Morrison in a cooling drawer, where she belonged; the feds running in circles, chasing their tails. And the cherry on top, he'd just come from Whole Foods, laden with all he'd need to build the perfect sandwich.

He couldn't even feel bad about Vernon Hayes, run off his own land, hiding from the feds. Vernon would thank him, if he understood. Vernon was *twice* divorced, a victim in truth. He'd suffered, himself, at the hands of those strumpets. He hadn't had what it took to erase them from the world, but he'd sure as hell wanted to. The proof was in his record.

"I'd do it for you if I could," he said, and he reached for the onions. "Maybe I will—stop those whores in their tracks, before they ensnare their next marks."

He sliced into an onion and blinked back tears. Hayes had done well, drawing off the heat. Still, it was hard to watch him claim credit. This wasn't his crusade, or that blowhard VanRijn's. Crusades took *strength.* They took patience and wit and a deep sense of purpose— no. Not purpose. Conviction. Faith. A *calling,* that was key.

He piled his sandwich with onion and lettuce and tomato, reached for the roast beef and peeled off a slice. It'd been fun for a while, watching the feds scurry around. It had strengthened his faith, even, knowing they couldn't find him. He was blessed—he could feel it— but he was tired of being careful. Tired of them always peering over his shoulder.

He slapped mayonnaise on the top slice and spread it around. It was better for now, that he stayed out of the spotlight. At least until the word got out, and they all understood. That reporter did already, the one who'd dubbed him the Crusader. Soon enough, they all would—but, until then, the shadows were his cover.

The TV brayed and jingled, a breaking news alert. The killer looked up, wiped away onion tears. Helicopter footage was playing, a dizzy view of Las Vegas. The chyron blared, all-caps, *SHOOTOUT AT McCARRAN: HAYES IN CUSTODY.*

He turned up the volume, scarcely aware of his own avid grin. The picture switched to Hayes in cuffs, being led from the airport. A skinny fed muscled him into the back of her wagon. Her hair hung in her face, but he knew her silhouette—the same vicious vixen who'd swung at that reporter.

"Special Agent Erin Hastings." He took a bite of his sandwich and licked mayo off his lip. She'd been in the news almost as much as the murders—she and her brother, the Lancaster Slasher. Her evil twin...or was *she* the bad apple? She had that look to her, all smug and entitled. She probably felt pretty good right now, certain she'd caught the Crusader. How hard would she take it, he wondered, when she discovered Vernon Hayes was nothing more than a fool?

He took another bite of his sandwich, savored its rich taste. He could see it already, her snooty mask cracking, giving way to...surprise? Disbelief? She'd cling to her victory, try to pin the tail on Hayes. She'd hold on beyond reason, until that big agent stepped in, the one who'd marched her off when she'd thrown her punch. He'd cut her down to size, right in front of the cops. Would she run back to Atlanta with her tail between her legs? Or would she dig in deeper, resolved to root him out?

Vernon's clip played again, a longer version this time. Erin straightened up and said something to her partner. The killer studied her expression, her economy of movement. Maybe she *would* give up, but she didn't strike him as the type. She was like her brother, on her own quest to cull evil from the world. But she'd gone about it the wrong way, let the FBI warp her. She wouldn't know evil if it smacked her in the face.

He polished off his sandwich and grabbed an apple from the fruit bowl. People like Erin were how evil women prospered. They knew they'd be protected, knew they were safe. The world gave them permission to take and take. They took from good men, hardworking men—then they tossed them aside like they were garbage.

He took his apple to the living room and powered on his computer. He couldn't become complacent—that was how sin flourished. He couldn't stop, couldn't rest, until the world took up his crusade.

15

Erin slipped into the conference room and plopped down next to Catherine. The air hummed with nervous energy, and she felt her hackles rise.

Brody rose stiffly. "Good, we're all here. As I'm sure you all know, Hayes is not the killer. I've turned him over to Vegas Metro, and they'll be handling him from this point forward. On the bright side, we grabbed him by the book, and our evidence is solid. He's looking at a lengthy prison stint, even with good behavior." Brody paused briefly, but nobody made a sound. He glanced around the table, his expression grim.

"Hayes is ruled out, so we're back to square one. Hannady's not happy with our lack of progress. I'd like to say she's wrong, that we've done all we could. But my gut's telling me we should've caught him by now. What are we missing? What stone haven't we turned?"

Erin racked her brains, but nothing came to mind. Catherine sat just as silent, picking at her notebook. Brody exhaled sharply and drove his fist into his palm.

"Come on, people. Our team was called in for our high closure rate. Everyone's counting on us, not just the brass, but every divorced woman from Rebel Creek to San Diego. If we don't get results soon, Hannady's talking about calling in another team to take our place."

The table erupted in gasps and protests. Sasha scowled fiercely. "What does she want from us? There's only so much we can do with what we're given. Forensics still hasn't got back to me on the Morrison scene. I can't analyze data that's still in the lab."

"Noted," said Brody. "I'll speak with the lab and get a rush on the evidence. But that doesn't change the fact we're fresh out of leads. I need your theories, your ideas, however off the wall."

Erin raised her hand. "Why don't we all go back to the start? Review the case from the beginning—why each suspect was eliminated, who we might've overlooked. With all of us on it, one of us might hit paydirt."

Brody sat down heavily and reached for his laptop. "That's not a bad idea," he said. "Let's take today and go over what we've got. I expect your reports on my desk by end of day." He gave a vague wave, as though to shoo a swarm of flies. Erin grabbed her jacket and slung it over her shoulder.

"I'm going to work from my hotel room," she said. "I'll bring my report by when I'm done."

Brody just *humphed* at her, already absorbed in his work.

───────

Erin cruised by her hotel without meaning to, her thoughts on VanRijn and his paramour. What would their *why* be, if they were in it together? Two angry attorneys, sick of shepherding bickering couples through division of assets? Except VanRijn was strictly corporate, and while Green did divorce, she'd been through it herself.

She noticed her mistake two blocks past her hotel, but instead of pulling a U-turn, she kept heading north, a vague, poisonous anger unfurling in her chest. Eric's insights had been good—no, better than good. He'd been right on the money, so...had he known all along? Had he known and not warned her, Hayes wasn't her man? The manhunt had been all over the news. Eric must've had his suspicions, why they were chasing him down—so *why* hadn't he warned her? Some mean-spirited thrill? She drove on, stone-faced, all the way to the prison, and soon she was waiting in the now-familiar visiting room, counting the water stains on the pockmarked drop ceiling.

"You look serious today," said Eric, once the guard had made his exit. "What's on your mind?"

Erin squared her shoulders. "I have a question for you."

A brief, strange expression flitted across Eric's face—confusion, surprise—then he blinked and it was gone. "So ask it," he said.

"What do you want from this? From my visits, from...*this?*" She made a vague twiddling gesture, finger wagging to and fro.

Eric stiffened almost imperceptibly, tiny creases appearing at the corners of his eyes. "That doesn't feel like a question," he said. "It sounds like some kind of—some kind of accusation."

Erin's frustration rose, hot in her chest. "I feel like you're playing games with me. The first time I came by, all you wanted to do was be my Hannibal Lecter. Which, by the way, is creepy as hell." She scowled. "Then I asked for your help, and you acted all hurt. I actually felt *bad* for you, like I'd tricked you somehow. But that's what you wanted, so—"

"Are you serious?" Eric gaped at her, his expression caught somewhere between amusement and outrage. "Did it ever occur to you, maybe I was happy to see you? That I thought if I helped you, you might just come back? Fifteen *years,* Erin, without even a call. You never thought I might miss you?" His voice rose, gaining volume, his cheeks flushed bright red. "And the way I remember, you never asked for my help. You asked why I did it, tried to make me—I'm not stupid, Erin. You weren't asking about me. You meant why did *he* do it, your guy, your Crusader. You used me. You lied to me. You're—"

"Okay!" Erin half-stood, seized with sudden panic. Eric's outburst had shocked her, thrown her off her guard. She hunched over the table, catching her breath as his tirade sank in. "I'm—"

"Don't say you're sorry. Not unless you mean it."

Erin bit her cheek hard. *Did* she feel sorry? She wasn't sure she did. She felt exposed, mostly—guilty, embarrassed. Like she'd done something shameful and been caught in the act.

"I feel bad if I hurt you," she said. "*If,* because I'm still not sure I believe one word out of your mouth." She lowered herself down, stiff in her chair. "But I won't say I'm sorry, because...Eric, you were right."

Eric snorted. "You got your man, so that makes it all right."

"I didn't say that," she said. "But, yeah. Yeah, it does. If it comes down to your feelings versus nailing some creep, I'd do it again. I'd do it every time." Erin felt sick admitting it, but in some deep, hurt part of her, she knew it was true. She waited for Eric to yell at her or call for the guard, but he didn't say anything, just sat breathing hard. After a while, he closed his eyes.

"Do you know how fucked up that is? How utterly foul?"

Erin made a *hah* sound. "You want to talk fucked up? You, the Lancaster Slasher?"

"Don't call me that."

"Why not? You are." Erin glowered at him, poison welling inside her, toxic resentment built up over years. She wanted to hurt him, tear him down till he cried, but Eric just lowered his head and stared at the table. He was grinding his teeth, a dry, irksome sound. Erin pushed back her chair.

"So, I guess I should—"

"That's it, then?" Eric laughed, a harsh bark. "You've got your man, so it's 'goodbye, Eric.' I knew you were cold, but I never thought—"

"We don't have him." Erin sagged where she sat. "We picked up Hayes in Vegas, but he's not the Crusader. I thought you—I thought..." She realized she was stammering and sucked in a deep breath. "Look, I can't discuss the case with you, but you can talk to me. If I asked you, no tricks, would you tell me what you think?"

"Of your case?" Eric stared, disbelieving. "You're asking a favor? After what you just said?"

Erin met his eyes steadily. "I am. Will you help?"

"That depends. *Am* I your Hannibal, or am I still your brother?"

"You'll always be my brother." That was true too, and her guilt surged like nausea, ringing in her ears. "I had fun last time, just talking. You know that, right?"

"I thought you did," said Eric. "I thought I knew a lot of things, but you're...Erin, you've changed."

"And you haven't?"

They both laughed at that, both shaky, both raw. Eric leaned forward, elbows on the table.

"I'll help you," he said. "As long as you promise this won't be the end. You'll still call, still write, maybe visit when you can."

"I can do that," said Erin, unsure if she meant it. This lie, too, was worth it—and, oh, the things she was learning about herself, back here in hell.

"All right," said Eric. "Maybe your problem is, your guy's like me."

Erin's brow furrowed. *Like me?* "What do you mean?"

Eric's mouth worked, but at first, no sound came out. Then his eyes brightened and he straightened in his seat. "Let me ask you this: before I was the Slasher, what would you have said if someone had asked you my obsession?"

Erin thought about that, turned it over in her head. "I'm not sure," she said. "I wouldn't have thought you had one. You *liked* to do pranks, and you *wanted* to start a band. But I wouldn't have pegged you for the obsessive type."

"Exactly." Eric looked pleased. "I was normal, right? I never set fires. I never tortured small animals. I never even wet the bed, except that time *you* snuck in with a bowl of warm water." He grimaced at that, wiped his hand on his pants. "My point is, you wouldn't have said *there's a killer in the making.* I was normal, then I snapped, and I...did what I did."

"I hate that you won't say it. Won't say what you did."

"I murdered four women," he said. "But that's what you need to look for, someone who was normal, just living their lives. Someone who *was* normal, but now they're not. They're falling apart, and if you look, you'll see the cracks. You saw them with me. You'll find them here too."

Erin sank into her chair, mulling over Eric's words. What he said made sense. Eric had been a normal kid, at least to outward appearances. Then he'd been a killer, and she'd felt him go bad even before she'd found his jacket.

"That's how he got close," she said, almost to herself. "They just saw Joe Normal, some guy on the street." It fit, when she thought about it. Alice Newman had been killed in broad daylight, on her way back to work. She'd died within shouting distance of a busy street. The killer must've got close enough to seize her by the throat, to silence her forever before she made a peep.

"Thank you," she said. "I think that helped."

Eric flashed her a grin, but it never reached his eyes. "You always used to come to me when something was bothering you. I'd like to think maybe it could be like that again."

Erin laughed without meaning to. "Like, I'd get dumped and call you? Cry on your shoulder?"

"Why not?" Eric frowned. "I hoped, I don't know, we could find some new normal."

Erin stared at him, seized with sudden disgust. He really thought normal lay in their future? That one day they'd be *them* again, older and wiser but still Erin and Eric? That he thought he deserved that, after all he'd done—

"Erin?"

"Look where we are," she said. "Look how we got here. I've been to those crime scenes. I've seen what you do, the bodies, the blood, the sheer waste of life. I've given all that I am to hunting people like you, and you want—you want *normal?* Between you and me?" She leaned back and roared laughter. Eric made a choked sound.

"I should go," she said. "Thanks again for your help."

She turned and pounded on the door, and never looked back.

———

Erin sprawled on the floor, nose buried in her laptop. She'd been through the evidence half a dozen times, and nothing had popped. All the suspects' alibis checked out, their whereabouts documented and pinned down without question. She dug into the victims next, their friends and their calendars, their spending habits. Nothing overlapped, nothing worthy of note. Her heart leaped for a moment when she discovered both Alice and Sandy had tried a free yoga class, but that had been months ago, and none of the others had gone.

She tabbed back to the Cook case. Those fingerprints still bugged her, those mysterious prints that didn't match up to anyone. She stared at them again—four bloody prints on a shattered rear window. The blood wasn't Rayna's or Valerie's, and it wasn't Allen Cook's. *Blood type O-, male, DNA now on file.* The same prints had cropped up on Valerie's bedside table and headboard, and again on her light switch. Only in Valerie's room, and that broken window.

Erin chewed her lip. Why Valerie's room, and nowhere else? Rayna was the target, the one strangled and posed. Unless *Valerie* was the target, and the rest were, what? Cover? Erin shook her head. That didn't make sense. But someone had tucked her in, pulled the covers to her chin. He'd taken the risk of turning on the light, maybe to look at her, maybe for...what?

She slammed her laptop shut. She'd done all she could from the confines of her hotel room. She needed to get back to the Cook residence and see for herself. To see what the killer had, the way he'd seen it. Last time, she'd focused on the victims, on what they'd gone through. She needed a fresh perspective, and that's what she'd get.

16

Erin pulled up to the Cook residence and parked her SUV. Yellow crime scene tape still fluttered from the fenceposts, and the lawn was sick and threadbare where police boots had trod.

She sat and observed the house. It stood dark and abandoned, the shell of what had been. The light from the streetlamp gleamed dully on the eaves. Brody'd laughed when she'd said as much, but houses had memories. Life left its mark on them, for good or for ill. Dad's place was lonely—you felt that walking in. Catherine's was joyous, filled with the echoes of laughter and life. This place felt *bereft,* robbed of all it should've been.

A tap at her window snapped Erin from her reverie. She looked up to find Brody hovering outside.

"Didn't hear you come up," she said.

"Sorry to keep you waiting." He glanced at his watch. "Ready to go?"

Erin stepped out of her vehicle and stood regarding the house. "Let's go in the back," she said. "That's where the killer went. I want to follow his route."

Brody led the way around back, the pale beam of his flashlight cutting a path through the gloom. Erin stopped at the back door to examine the broken pane above the lock. The killer's prints were gone, washed away by the rain.

"I'd have needed a minute," said Erin.

"What?"

She closed her eyes. "It's so quiet here. I'd have stopped and listened before I broke in. Made sure she was sleeping, so she wouldn't hear."

"The element of surprise." Brody eased the door open. It creaked in its frame. "Breaking glass doesn't sound like much. You mostly hear the tinkle when it falls down."

Erin nodded. Rayna *hadn't* woken up. She'd been killed in her bed.

"I'm the killer," she said. "I've just broken in, so—no. Don't turn on the light." She caught Brody's wrist. "I want to see what he saw."

"Can't have been much. It's *ass*-dark in here."

Erin stood and waited for her eyes to adjust. Vague shadows emerged, and the black sockets of doorways.

"It's the house next door," said Brody. He pointed back the way they'd come. "See, we're on the corner. The back of their garage is blocking our light. Plus, those trees can't be helping, down by the shed."

"It's nearly pitch black." Erin shuffled down the hall. Her hip struck a low table, and it banged against the wall. "Shit. Where'd that come from?"

"Ready for the lights?"

Erin laughed. "Go ahead."

Brody flipped the switch and warm light flooded the hall. Erin rubbed her hip absently as she surveyed the scene.

"Either a light was on or he knew the place. There's way too much crap in here to sneak around blind."

"They didn't find any lights on, besides Valerie's room."

"He could've turned the rest off, but why leave just one?" Erin made her way down the hall, to the master bedroom. The bed was still rumpled from Rayna's final struggle, the mattress cover holding the ghost of her shape. A mug lay by the night table, chipped from the fall. "He came in and found Rayna asleep in her bed. He jumped on her, pinned her before she could scream. Got a pillow over her face..."

"Couldn't look her in the eye."

Erin nodded slowly. "Jessica, he strangled—up close and personal. Inhaling her last breath." Erin breathed deep, herself. "But with Rayna, I need—he needed that barrier. I can't watch her die...or *she* can't see *me*."

Brody cleared his throat. "You're thinking he knew her."

"Cared for her, even. Cared what she thought." Erin chewed her lip. "Maybe someone who'd admired her from afar. Someone she'd crossed paths with, maybe known to say hello. Someone she'd smiled at when he held the door. But when he approached, she rebuffed him, and..."

"What?"

Erin shook her head. "That kind of killer, there should've been signs. He'd have sent flowers, gifts. Her friends would've known."

"Maybe just first-time jitters?" Brody rubbed his chin. "His kills have been steadily increasing in violence—smothering to strangulation, then a slashed throat. He needs more and more as he devolves."

"Maybe." Erin turned away, toward the stairs. "He dragged her out here to pose her, out to the stairs." She moved to the front door to take in the scene. "I thought it was strange at first, how she was posed with her face to the stairs—facing the banisters, not looking at anything. But maybe it was more about *us* finding *her,* first thing we'd see when we walked in the door."

"Or maybe he was disturbed," said Brody. "Maybe that was when Valerie came home. She screamed, made a racket. His time was cut short."

"Could be." Valerie had gone out that night, to see a concert. What had brought her home early, into the hands of a killer? Erin went to the living room, where Valerie had died. Her blood stained the carpet, black in the dim light.

"He chased her in here," said Erin. "He hit her just once, and she dropped to the floor. Cause of death was technically stroke, but what are the odds she'd have stroked out asleep in her bed?" She scanned the room, eyes narrowed. "Whatever he hit her with, he took it with him when he went. You see anything missing?"

"Forensics is still working on identifying the weapon."

"Valerie was the one he cared about." Erin went to the doorway and gazed across the hall. "He humiliated Rayna. Posed her degradingly where everyone would see. Valerie, he tucked in, like she was only sleeping. He even pulled her covers up right to her chin. And he left prints." She peered at Valerie's night table, the book she'd left half read. "Anything else he touched, he must've wiped clean. But here, he got sloppy. Upset, maybe. Because she was an innocent, and Rayna was...?"

"It's a strange scene," said Brody. "Almost like two killers, or a killer and his accomplice."

"Two killers." Erin blew out a long breath. The thought had crossed her mind, but none of the other scenes suggested a second unsub.

Brody came up beside her. "Did you get what you need?"

"I got all I'm going to get." She peeled off her gloves and stuffed them in her pocket. "Come on, let's get out of here. This place is done."

Erin dialed Catherine on her way back to the hotel. The line rang and rang, and Erin was about to hang up when Catherine answered.

"Hey, Erin. You get my text?"

"Text? What text?"

"I was headed back to the hotel. I thought we could get manicures, but..."

"Too late now, huh?" Erin sighed, frustrated. "I went back to the Cook scene, but nothing jumped out. What about you, any new leads your way?"

Weariness laced Catherine's voice. "No. Honestly, I'm starting to wonder if we're dealing with multiple killers."

"Brody said the same thing, but...does it feel right to you?"

"No, but this case—" Something crashed in the background, and Catherine cursed. "Normally I'd trust my gut, but this case is just weird. What if it's a cluster of copycat kills? A bunch of angry people piggybacking on our 'serial' to dispose of their enemies?"

"Please, don't let it be that." Erin huffed laughter. "One killer's bad. Four would be disastrous." She stopped at a red light, drummed her fingers on the wheel. "I hate how he's always one step ahead."

"Just one?" Catherine loosed a tired chuckle. "We're back at square one. He's left us in the dust. Hannady's all wound up, won't leave Brody alone. He said he almost pissed himself trying to get rid of her so he could go to the bathroom."

"Charming." Erin smiled faintly, but her stomach felt sour. The way this case was going, the killer really *would* ride off into the sunset— no justice for his victims, no answers for their families. No collar for Hannady, no peace for Brody. Erin swallowed bile. "I know we can't take work personally, but this case, I can't help it."

"Because of your brother?"

Erin's breath caught. "Fifteen years, Cat. Fifteen years is a really long time. But still, coming back here, it's like it's only been a day." She licked her dry lips. "I couldn't stop Eric. This felt like a second chance, but—"

A loud beep cut in, Catherine's call waiting.

"That's Brody," she said. "Drive safe, okay? I'll call back when I can."

Erin hung up. Her own phone rang not even two minutes later, a number she didn't recognize.

"Hastings. Who's this?"

Static crackled briefly, then a gruff voice spoke up. "Ma'am, I'm Officer Fargo. I'm calling you from California State Prison in Lancaster. I regret to inform you there's been an incident involving your brother."

Erin's fatigue drained away. Her hands went numb on the wheel. "Eric? Is he—"

"Ma'am, your brother's alive, but his condition is critical. He's been transported to Los Angeles Community Hospital. I can give you the number, or—"

Erin smacked her phone so hard it flew off the seat and bounced under the dash. She pulled a screaming U-turn and sped back the way she'd come.

Erin drove in a daze, blood throbbing in her temples. The city lights throbbed with it, a sick, fevered pulse. Her phone rang for a while, but Erin couldn't reach it, wouldn't have cared if she could. She blew through a red light in a storm of honking horns. Her last words to Eric —what had they been? She couldn't remember. She'd got what she needed and moseyed on out.

Her phone rang again. She kicked it: *shut up.*

She arrived at the hospital with little idea how she'd got there, weak in the knees and copper on her tongue. She stood a full minute in the cold night air, but the calm she was searching for hung just out of reach. Fragments of thoughts chased their tails around her head, leaving her dizzy, trembling in her boots.

"Can't go to pieces," she muttered. It came out high, unhinged, and she bit her tongue. The pain did what the night air had failed to do— shocked her to stillness, calmed her racing heart. She straightened her collar, raked her fingers through her hair. Struck out for the entrance, heels clicking on the tarmac.

She strode up to reception, eyes fixed straight ahead. She had an idea she'd have felt something if her twin had left this world—the twang of a broken string, something snapping inside her. Still, her pulse picked up as she flashed her ID.

"I'm Agent Erin Hastings," she said. "My brother, Eric Hastings, was admitted to this hospital."

The nurse on the counter looked her up and down. Her eyes were bright and appraising, full of gossipy interest. Erin clenched her fists. One comment, one sneer, and she'd—

"Let me check on his status." The nurse tapped on her keyboard. Erin waited, tapped her foot. "Your brother came in an hour ago and went straight into surgery. Looks like they're still operating, so if you'd just like to—"

"What happened? Do you know?"

The nurse glanced at her screen. "Multiple stab wounds, mostly to the arms and lower abdomen. The waiting room's down the hall. Just follow the signs. Someone will be out to speak with you once he's out of surgery."

Erin stood for a moment, expecting something more—reassurance, maybe, or further instructions. When none were forthcoming, she headed down the hall. The smell of disinfectant rose to greet her, burning her nose. Her footfalls echoed off the sterile walls, beating out a grim refrain: *too late. Too late.*

17

Dad sat slumped in the waiting room, hair mussed, leg jiggling. His jacket was inside-out, label fluttering in the draft from the air vent. He looked up and saw her and stumbled to his feet, and then he was holding her, stubble scratching her cheek.

"Baby girl. You came." He squeezed her tighter, so hard she couldn't breathe. "Your brother's a strong boy. He'll pull through this, you'll see."

Erin hugged him back, drawing strength from his embrace. When she pulled back, she saw his eyes were wet.

"I talked to the nurse," she said. "She couldn't tell me anything, except he got stabbed."

"By another inmate." Dad swayed on his feet, caught himself on the wall. "That Fargo guy, you talked to him? He wouldn't tell me anything, except there'd been an *altercation*. That's how he said it, not a fight, an altercation."

"Here, sit down," said Erin. She took Dad by the elbow and guided him to a chair. He tugged at her arm, trying to pull her down with him.

"You don't look good. You should sit. You should—"

"I left my phone in the car." She pulled free and scurried off, nearly breaking into a trot. The lights were too bright in here, the air too thin. She had to get out, had to get her head straight. Eric would live or he'd die. She couldn't change that. But she couldn't go down with him. Couldn't fall apart.

Her phone was ringing again when she arrived at her car. This time she answered it, her voice a thick rasp.

"Hastings, go ahead."

"Erin. It's Brody. I heard about your brother."

"How?"

"On the news." He coughed lightly. "I've been trying to call you. Are you okay?"

"I'm at the hospital," she said. "I left my phone in the car."

"That's not an answer."

Erin drew a strained breath. She couldn't fill her lungs. "I'm not sure how I am," she said. "In limbo, I guess. They're not telling us anything, just wait and see. I keep thinking—" Her throat closed up abruptly, and her eyes swam with tears. The parking lot doubled, then trebled before her.

"It's okay," said Brody. "You don't have to talk."

Erin sank into the driver's seat, legs hanging out. "I saw him today, just this afternoon. I was such an asshole. I said..." *It was worth hurting him, if it helped with the case.* "I said awful things, and I meant them. But now, looking back, what was going through my head?"

Brody made a sympathetic sound. Erin closed her eyes.

"I don't want him to die," she said. "I hate what he did, but I don't want him gone."

"You don't have to explain yourself. He's family. I know."

Erin wondered about Brody's family, a fleeting burst of curiosity. Then she thought of Dad, alone with his thoughts. "I left my dad in the waiting room," she said. "I should get inside."

"You can take time off if you need to. I'll approve it, no questions."

"No." Erin got to her feet, blood surging to her head. "Or, I don't know. Maybe. Can I call you in an hour? Or once we know more?"

"Call whenever you need to. And take care of yourself."

Erin hung up feeling steadier. She headed back inside and stopped at the coffee machine. Dad would need caffeine. He lived on the stuff. She plugged in a dollar and punched for cream and sugar. A paper cup dropped down and wobbled on its shelf. Soon, the machine fired up, and the bitter smell of coffee filled the dim hall. Erin watched the cup fill up as though from a great distance. By the time it was done, she felt fit to face Dad.

"I brought you some coffee," she said.

Dad hadn't moved, but he perked up at the prospect of coffee. He reached for the paper cup and cradled it in his hands.

"You and Eric, you're... You've been visiting, right?"

Erin looked away, guilty. "We had a fight."

Dad snorted into his coffee. "Same old Erin and Eric."

"Same old—not exactly." Erin's breath hitched. "That's what we fought about. He wants to be us again, or at least some new us. I don't know what I want, so I've been jerking him around. One minute we're laughing, sharing old memories. The next I'm storming out, treating him like dirt. I should've picked, in or out, not sat on the fence."

"You feel guilty," said Dad. "I feel that way too. I look back and I think, what could I have done different? If I'd been around more, if I'd seen the signs... Or that old knife he used, if I'd thrown it out. I'd see it sometimes, cleaning up in the attic—your granddad's old Bowie, all worn and chipped. I *thought* about ditching it—Lord knows I'm no hunter—but throwing it out just never felt right." He took another swig of coffee and licked cream off his lip. "It's hard to be close to him, Eric, I mean. Hard to be his dad. He's my son and I love him, but what he did, I just...*why?*"

Erin had no answer, so she took his hand. Dad's palm was dry and rough from hard work.

"Pardon the interruption, but are you the family of Eric Hastings?" A surgeon stood framed in the doorway, scrub cap crooked on his head. Erin and Dad both stood, but it was Dad who spoke.

"Yessir, that's us."

The surgeon thrust out his chest, as though to deliver a speech. "Your son was stabbed nineteen times," he said. "Most of the wounds were superficial, and defensive in nature, but his bowel was badly perforated, and required extensive repairs." He pulled off his scrub cap and broke into a smile. "He's not out of the woods yet, but the good news is, he pulled through. With time and luck, he should heal good as new."

Erin clenched her fists, weak with relief. "When can we see him?"

"He's in recovery now. Once his anesthesia wears off, he'll be moved to the ICU, and you can see him then. He'll be pretty out of it, but if you talk to him, he should know you're there."

Erin turned to Dad. "Did you hear that? He'll live."

Dad caught her in his arms for the second time that night. His breath smelled of coffee, familiar as home. "You can tell him yourself, what you just told me. Tell him you're off the fence. You are, aren't you?"

Erin just nodded. She couldn't quite picture it, the new Erin and Eric. But she'd give him a chance—for him, for Dad, and even for herself.

Erin's relief was fleeting. Seeing her twin swathed in bandages, Erin felt sick. His face lax with sleep, he looked more like her than ever, same nose, same cheekbones, same thick brown hair. Even his hands, with their long, questing fingers—Erin glanced at her own, at her short, blunt nails. There, at least, they were different. Eric's were ragged, chewed to the quick.

Dad touched her elbow. "Can you go after him? The bastard who did this?"

Erin shook her head. "The California prison system's out of my jurisdiction. But I'll keep an eye on his case. If I can help, I will."

Dad grumbled at that, but he didn't argue. He took Eric's hand and held it in his own. Outside, the sky was gray, dawn kissing the horizon.

"I should check in with work," she said. "Be back in a minute."

She stepped out in the hall and dialed Brody. He picked up on the first ring, almost like he'd been waiting.

"How's your brother?"

"On the mend. How's the case?"

"Are you serious?" Brody let out a chuckle. "Well, now you mention it, I've got some good news."

Erin swayed slightly, caught between relief and exhaustion. She pinched herself hard. "Don't keep me in suspense."

"The autopsy report came back on Sandy Morrison. She had tissue under her fingernails, and traces of blood."

Erin's heart leaped. *Go, Sandy.*

Brody wasn't done. "We're still waiting on DNA," he said. "But once that comes back, we'll be able to compare with the blood from the Cook scene. This might be our proof we're looking at one killer."

Erin realized she was bouncing, jigging lightly on her heels. She forced herself to stand still. This was big, but not big enough. She needed her hallelujah moment—clouds parting, light streaming, angelic choirs overhead. "I can't wait," she said. "I need...I need—"

"What?"

"What you said at the Cook scene, how the killer cared for Valerie. How he couldn't bring himself to look Rayna in the eye. He had to have known them, maybe pretty well. I want to talk to Cook again, ask about their friends." She glanced back at Eric, pale and helpless in his bed. "If I leave now, I could be in Pahrump by ten."

She expected Brody to argue, but he hummed in approval. "I'll call Catherine," he said. "I want her to drive you, and you'll sleep on the way."

"I thought that's how you get arthritis, sleeping in cars."

"And *not* sleeping when you need to is how you get dead." Brody made a *pffft* sound. "I know you need to keep busy, but don't overdo it. Do I make myself clear?"

Erin flashed him the thumbs-up, though he couldn't see her. "Ten-four, boss," she said. "I'll let you know what we find."

Dad looked up as she made her way back to Eric's bedside. "Did I hear that right? You're going to work?"

"I don't have a choice," she said. "If we don't catch our killer, he'll do it again. But I'll be back as soon as I can." She reached out and laid a hand on Eric's forehead. "Be good, okay? I'll bring you some Jell-O, so...so you just be good."

It took six hours to reach Pahrump, thanks to an overturned semi slowing traffic to a crawl. Erin slept all the way, curled up in her seat. She arrived at Allen Cook's stiff-kneed, with a crick in her neck.

Catherine squinted up the drive. "You think he's awake?"

"He works nights, so my guess would be...probably not."

Cook didn't answer Catherine's first ring. She peered in the window and ding-donged again. This time, a door slammed somewhere upstairs. Cook answered the door in his bathrobe, his features twisted into a furious scowl.

"Don't you know it's rude to—" His brows shot up as he recognized Erin. "Excuse me, agents. I get a lot of solicitors, so..."

"That's okay," said Erin. "Do you mind if we come in?"

"Depends. Did you catch him?" Cook pulled a wry face. "Never mind. Come in." He stepped back, but not far enough, so Erin had to squeeze past him. She headed for the living room and settled on the couch. Cook stayed standing this time, hovering near the door.

"I'm sorry to say we haven't made an arrest. But we do have some new leads, and you might be able to help us."

Cook glanced behind him, toward the stairs. "Can we make this quick? I need to sleep before my shift."

"We realize that," said Catherine. "And we're sorry for the intrusion. But this is *our* job, following every lead. Would you mind sitting down?"

Cook's brows drew together, the hint of a scowl. His hands flexed and relaxed, and he plopped down on a hassock.

"It's just, I'm so tired," he said. "I'm afraid if I sit too long, I might nod off."

Erin laughed politely, but she wasn't sure Cook was joking. He was smiling, sort of, but his tone was sharp. He picked at his sleeve, plucked a loose thread. Erin pulled out her notepad.

"Last time we spoke, you mentioned you moved to Pahrump to be close to your family. How would you say that was going?"

Cook stiffened. "Excuse me?"

"What I'm asking you is, Pahrump's four hours from Lancaster when traffic is good. How often did you get down there?"

"Every weekend, without fail." Cook spat the words at her, then he looked away, shamefaced. "At least, that was the plan. I'm always so tired, and Val was busy with school. Last time I made it was...the end of September."

Catherine frowned. "If I might ask, why live in Pahrump when your family's in Lancaster?"

"I sued my last employer. Negligence resulting in injury." Cook held up his arms so his sleeves fell away, revealing a spatter of burn scars crawling up past his elbows. "*You* sue your boss and then try to find work."

Erin frowned. "How about phone calls? Did you still keep in touch?"

"As much as I could."

"And did Rayna or Valerie discuss their social lives? Any new friends they'd made? Any fallings-out?"

Cook shook down his sleeves so they covered his scars. "Rayna had her new job," he said. "They kept her so busy I'm not sure she had time for friends. As far as Val goes..." His eyes flicked to the empty space over the mantel. "Did you try her Facebook? She was always on that."

"We've done that," said Erin. "What we're here for today is anyone who stood out to *you*."

"Her boss was a piece of work," said Cook. "Rayna's, not Val's. He was like, from that show...Don Draper. *Mad Men*."

Catherine leaned forward. "How so?"

"Slimy. A creep. Looks at women like meat." His lip curled up. "I thought they might be involved at first, the way he'd touch Rayna. The way he'd walk by and pat her elbow or back. But he did that to everyone. She wasn't special, just...no."

"So, no affair. You're certain?"

Cook's gaze turned icy. "You think she'd throw her family away for a dirtbag like him?"

Erin twitched where she sat, surprised by his outburst. "Is that what she did? Threw her family away?"

"You're putting words in my mouth now. I'm tired, and you're— You're treating me like a suspect, and I won't—"

"No one's saying you're a suspect," said Erin. "We just have a—"

"A job to do, right. Why don't you go do it?" Cook got to his feet. "You *have* suspects, right? Go harass them. Rayna's *dead* and Val's *dead,* and they're not coming back. My family's just gone, my future,

166

my..." His voice cracked and he crumpled, sat down with a thud. "I'd like you to go now. Please go. Get out."

Erin rose slowly. "I'm sorry we disturbed you," she said. "But please be assured, we're doing everything we can to bring this killer to justice. If you'll just try to—"

"What do I care?" Cook hung his head. "Catch him, don't catch him, my family's still gone. I'll never wake up again and see...please just go."

Erin glanced at Catherine. "In that case—"

"We'll go, Mr. Cook. Next time we drop by, we'll try to give you some notice."

Cook shot Catherine a sour look, but he didn't say anything. He didn't get up to show them to the door.

"Angry man," said Erin, as the door swung shut behind them.

"Wouldn't you be?"

"I guess so. Yeah." She rubbed her stiff neck. "I saw this thing once, on some old detective show, how innocent people get mad when they think you suspect them. But so do the guilty ones, so what did we learn?"

"That Rayna's boss was a creep," said Catherine. "But he's also in Dubai, and he has been all month."

Erin got into the driver's seat, heading back to Lancaster. "Your turn to sleep," she said. "I need to think."

The accident had been cleared by the time Erin drove back through. She'd meant to spend the drive mulling over the case, but her thoughts wandered to Eric on a constant loop. Worst-case scenarios cluttered her thoughts—if he never woke up, if he woke up too damaged to know who she was. If the last thing she ever said to him amounted to a dismissal. He'd never again be that kid who loved waterslides, that kid with the big heart and the even bigger mouth. But Erin couldn't claim to know who he was now. He'd been the Slasher, no doubt about that. That would always be true, but maybe he could grow past it. Maybe she could help him. Maybe, maybe...

She stopped by the hospital to pick up her car. Dad's was still there, parked askew in its space. A twinge of guilt pricked her—she should go inside for a minute, at least—but she pushed it down and drove off, following Catherine from the lot.

Brody met them at the station. He looked as tired as she felt, and she wondered if he'd slept.

"Erin, you're back. Any word on your brother?"

"Not yet." She checked her phone anyway—nothing from Dad. "He'll probably pull through, though. Do you have a moment?"

He glanced around, frowned, then guided her to the conference room. "Yeah, what's up?"

"Allen Cook's kind of losing it. He's—"

The team chose that moment to pile in behind them, loaded down with Chinese food and stacks of paper plates. Erin's stomach growled loudly, and Brody gave a snort. "Eat something. Cook can wait. Unless the end of that sentence was about to be 'the killer'?"

Erin laughed. "I wish." She grabbed a plate and plopped down. "You guys get egg rolls?"

Midway through the meal, Sasha went quiet, eyes fixed on her phone. The chatter died off as the team took in the expression on her face, somewhere between surprise and triumph.

"You're not going to believe this," she said. She pushed her plate away and stood up. "That tip line of yours finally paid off."

Brody gave a whoop, so out of character Erin burst out laughing. He pumped his fist in the air. "Didn't I tell you?"

Sasha waited for the commotion to die down, lips pinched together like a small, angry frog. That got Erin giggling again, but she choked it back. Sasha shot her a stern look as she read from her phone. "The tip's from one Abigail Davidson. She called in half an hour ago to report a person of interest, which would be her tenant, a student, Benjamin Watt." She scrolled down, lips moving. "Blah, blah, suspicious; blah, blah, weirdo. He keeps strange hours, goes out at night. Ooh, maybe he's a vampire."

Brody stabbed at a wonton. "Get to the good part."

"Well, she figured he was just goth, y'know, until she went to do laundry and found bloodstains on the washer. That was the day after the Cook murders, but she didn't think much of it. Not until she realized his nightly excursions coincided with the murders."

Brody scowled. "That's it?"

"No, that's not it." Sasha stuck out her tongue. "That brings us to last night. She was down changing the furnace filter when she found his sketchbook left out, all filled with—drumroll, please—sketches of Valerie Cook. *Creepy*-ass sketches, like, how'd she put it? *Bondage and leather stuff, down on her knees.* She was so scared she couldn't call us until Watt left for his evening class."

Erin leaned forward. "So, you're saying—"

"*Shhhh!*" Sasha hissed at her, so loud she startled. "Here comes the best part: *she still has the rag she used to clean the blood off the washer.*"

A hush fell over the room. Erin and Brody exchanged glances. This could be it, the break they'd been waiting for.

"I'm going," said Erin. "Who's with me?"

"I am," said Brody. "Sasha, text us the address."

By the time their phones pinged, they were halfway down the hall.

18

Erin fidgeted on the drive, frustrated by the traffic, the constant stop-and-start.

"The recruiters don't tell you this job's so much *sitting*." She stretched out her legs and pulled them back in. "Sitting at desks, sitting in cars. Sitting in planes, forty thousand feet up."

"I once sat nineteen hours in a crawlspace in Palm Beach." Brody made a face. "Damp, full of spiders, and a rat the size of Lassie tried to hump my leg."

Erin snorted laughter. "Always got to one-up me."

"I like to win. What can I say?" Brody cruised through the intersection, smile fading. "I used to work with this guy back then, out of the Tampa office. Jenner, his name was. Couldn't stand that guy."

"Why? What'd he do?"

"Tchah—what *didn't* he do? We'd all bust our butts, our whole team flat-out, and our ASAC would come by to tell us good job. And you know what Jenner would say? He'd smile and say thanks, like he'd earned that headpat all to himself. Guy was a credit-grabber, a total glory chaser, and you know where he is now?"

Erin shrugged. "I don't know, where?"

"Still in Tampa, but now he's Special Agent in Charge. Groveling little creep leapfrogged over all of us." Brody's grip tightened on the wheel.

"I thought you were going to say he got everyone killed."

"I'm sitting here, aren't I?" Brody glowered at a blue Volvo hogging the lane. "I used to think you were like that—glory hound, you know? You'd do your Hasty Hastings thing, and I'd see a less subtle Jenner. But that's never been it. That drive you've got in you, that's all about—"

Erin reached over him and laid on the horn. The blue Volvo swerved sharply, out of the passing lane.

"Quit profiling me," she said. She didn't want to hear Brody's thoughts on her motives, especially if he was right. If he said *guilt* or *penance,* she might have to deck him. Or grab the wheel and swerve him straight into traffic. As long as she got results, her *why* was her business.

"This is us," said Brody. He pulled off down a side street and parked under a tree. "What I was *trying* to say was, I want this done too. I want this creep off the streets, and I want him off now." His voice had gone gruff, thick with emotion. "Sandy shouldn't have had to die. None of them should, but we—"

A loud *crack* punched through the evening calm. Erin flung herself out the door and crouched behind the wheel. She reached for her weapon, then hesitated, eyes narrowed.

"Erin?"

She straightened up slowly. Down the street, a man waved at her from a drift of spilled trash. Erin waved back stiffly, cheeks flushing hot.

"Not a gunshot," she said.

"A banging trash can." Brody set his hand on her shoulder. "Are you all right?"

"If I'd drawn my weapon, I'd say I had a problem." She let out a shuddering breath. "I think I'm just jumpy from Hayes taking that potshot in Coyote Springs. Assuming it *was* Hayes. Has ballistics come back?"

"Not yet," said Brody. "Come on. Let's get inside."

Erin slammed her door and locked it, and took a deep breath. She needed her head in the game, not jumping at shadows. She shifted her focus to Abigail Davidson's house, a once-tony Tudor fading into gentle ruin. An old Chevy Vega brooded in the driveway. Brody eyed the car as he thumbed the doorbell.

"Think that still runs?"

"Wouldn't bet on it." Erin pulled out her badge and held it up to the peephole. Moments later, a bolt snapped back, and the door opened a crack. A raspy voice demanded, "Let me see that close up."

Erin slipped her ID through and let Abigail inspect it. "We're here for your tip," she said.

Abigail slid the chain back and let the door swing open. "This was a nice neighborhood when I moved in. Now, it's all...well, you can't be too careful, let me put it that way."

Brody just smiled. "Ms. Davidson, I'm Agent Innis, and this is Agent Hastings. Let's all sit down, and we'll go over your tip."

Abigail led them to a sitting room straight out of 1950, complete with crochet pillow covers and a Bakelite radio. Erin took the opportunity to discreetly inspect her. She was in her mid-fifties, with brassy blonde hair. From the state of her voice and nails, she was a heavy smoker. From the smell of her breath, she liked her drink too.

"Why don't you start at the beginning?" Brody sat down across from her. "What can you tell us about Benjamin Watt?"

Abigail picked at the hem of her sweater. "I take in a renter to help cover expenses. Everything costs so much—almost six dollars for a gallon of milk, and saints preserve you if you like almond milk, or one of those..." She trailed off, frowning. "Sorry. I'm rambling. I take in college students, mostly young ladies, but Benny's so quiet I let him take the room. He's been a good tenant, no partying, no drugs. None of that funny smoke coming up the stairs. He's a student, you know, art, design, something."

Brody nodded along, hummed here and there to show he was listening. When Abigail stopped for breath, he leaned in with a smile. "What about personality? What kind of guy would you say Benny was?"

"Quiet. Oh, wait—I said that already." Abigail tittered, fingers to her lips." "He keeps to himself, doesn't say much. I feed him dinner sometimes, if he comes home and I'm cooking. We eat in the back room, in front of the TV. He says please and thanks, but he's not much for conversation. The only thing strange is the hours he keeps. I always thought it was an artist thing—those salons they have, Toulouse-Lautrec and so on—but then I saw that sketchbook, and then with the *blood*..." She did a theatrical shudder, wiggling side to side.

Brody's phone pinged and he glanced down. "We got the warrant," he murmured, just for Erin to hear. Then he turned to Abigail, expression carefully bland. "I'd like to see that sketchbook. But first, would you mind unlocking his unit so we can take a look?"

"So I'm right? Benny's *him?*" She rose, smoothing her sweater in broad, flustered strokes. "Just give me a moment. I'll go fetch the key."

Erin watched her bustle off. "She's enjoying this, isn't she?"

"Highlight of her year."

"How'd you get a warrant off a phone tip?"

Brody smirked. "Found me a judge with a niece who works at Highgate. He's inclined to be generous, as long as we don't make him look bad."

Abigail trotted in with a key on a lanyard. "Found it," she said. "If you'll follow me, please."

They followed her to the basement, down a narrow flight of stairs. A plain white door greeted them at the bottom. Abigail unlocked it and stood aside. "This door's usually open. It just leads to the laundry, but I didn't feel safe." She passed the key to Erin and pointed down the hall. "That's his door at the end. I'd rather not look, in case he has..." She made a vague gesture, hands flapping in the air.

Erin gloved up, heading down the hall. Abigail hovered a moment, then leaned out to call after her.

"Don't be too long. Benny's at school right now, but it's eight thirty and his class ends at nine."

Erin unlocked Benny's door and peered into his apartment. It was small, sort of stuffy, its high windows painted shut. Clothes hung over the furniture, mostly jackets and hoodies. Books littered the floor. The kitchen smelled faintly of pizza and decay. Erin scanned the mess, found nothing interesting, and headed for the bedroom. She flipped the light switch and hissed in surprise.

"Brody. Come see."

Brody came up behind her and let out a low whistle. Benjamin Watt's room was papered in posters, tattooed hulks, nearly naked, looming over his bed. Some had their fists raised, as though in victory. Others were roaring or baring their teeth. One had a leather mask over his face. His eyes burned through the eyeholes, narrow with menace.

"Who are those guys? Leather daddies?"

"UFC fighters." Brody nodded at the far corner, at a worn punching dummy. "When she said he was into art, I didn't realize she meant martial arts."

Erin frowned. "Hey, Ms. Davidson? Did you ever know Benny to get into fights?"

"Fights?" Abigail's voice had drifted closer. "Not that I know of, but like I said, he doesn't talk much. He's a skinny kid, though, one of those goths. Looks a bit funny, but..." Abigail stopped in her tracks, just behind Brody. "Are those—what *is* all that?"

Brody took her arm and steered her back toward the hall. Erin went to Watt's desk and leafed through his sketchbook. Art wasn't her forte, but she guessed he had talent. His sketches were crude, heavy-handed, but they had an urgency about them that might've drawn her in, had the subject matter not repelled her: women in bondage, women on their knees. Women gagged and handcuffed, their eyes wide and pleading. About halfway through the book, their faces became Valerie's.

"Brody. Check it out."

He came up and took the book from her. His Adam's apple jerked sharply, and Erin heard him swallow. "That's Valerie Cook."

"I thought so too."

Brody flipped to the next page and held it up to the light. A featureless woman knelt in a pool of either shadow or blood, hands outstretched, palms up. A male silhouette loomed over her, offering her an apple.

"Religious fixation?"

Erin frowned. "I'm not sure. Let's bag it up, and we'll worry about that later."

Brody slipped the sketchbook into an evidence bag while Erin went to find Abigail. "Ms. Davidson, we're going to call in a forensics team. Would you mind waiting upstairs while we secure the scene?"

Abigail's eyes lit up. Erin could practically sense the questions hovering behind her lips. "Will this be on the news? Will my name be—"

"Too early to say." Erin smiled broadly to hide her irritation. "Come on, let's go upstairs and wait for forensics."

Erin sat with Abigail as the forensics team worked, a glazed sense of disconnect washing over her in waves. Benjamin Watt didn't fit Mo Mirza's profile, or Eric's guess. But if she'd had to draw a killer—a Pictionary killer, a caricature of evil—she might've drawn him. The man was a walking red flag, drawn to violence and degradation. He was sneaky and secretive, asocial, sullen and resentful from a lifetime of rejection.

Brody paused at the head of the stairs, deep in conversation with the lead CSI. Erin strained to listen in.

"So, the rag from the laundry, how useful will that be?"

"Well, the good news is, it hasn't been touched. It's been buried in that trash can, out of harm's way." The investigator had a faint, musical accent, French maybe, or Dutch. "The bad news is, it's hot down there. It might be hard to get a sample, but we'll do what we can."

"Would doing what you can include making it a rush order?" Brody leaned in, almost flirtatious. "You'd be doing me a favor, not to mention the public."

"I'll handle it personally, see that your case goes to the top of the list."

"That's what I like to hear." Brody caught sight of Erin and frowned. "You're still here? I thought you'd have called it a day." He checked his watch and cursed under his breath. "Go on, it's one o'clock. Nothing left for you to do here."

"Only one problem with that: you were my ride."

Brody blinked stupidly, then slapped himself on the forehead. "Of course I was. I knew that. *Man,* I need sleep."

"You and me both." Erin stood, stiff-limbed. "Come on, let's head back."

Morning came too soon, and it came gray and gloomy, a curtain of rain blowing in from the west. Erin dressed in the half-dark and drove to the hospital. Eric had woken in the night, and she needed to see him.

She slowed as she approached his room, half expectant, half dreading. She'd never minded hospitals, not their smell, not their ambience, but today the flickering fluorescents had her on edge. The sharp tang of bleach made her eyes water. Dad had gone to work, leaving her to face Eric by herself.

About what I said... Would he believe her if she said sorry, after insisting she wasn't? Would he even want to see her, after—

"Erin? Is that..." His voice was hoarse and weak, and petered out into a groan. Erin froze where she stood. His room was still two doors down. How had he—

"Erin?"

She broke out in a sick sweat, down her neck, under her arms. Someone moaned, thick with pain, and she nearly turned and ran. Instead, she cleared her throat.

"Yeah, Eric. I'm here." She forced herself to get going. Marched into his room. Eric rolled his head to look at her, and her knees went weak. He looked sick, vaguely greenish, his hair matted to his cheek. He was cuffed to the bed, though he didn't look like he could sit up, much less make a break for it. A bowl of ice chips sat melting on the table. Eric looked like he'd been reaching for it, one arm outstretched.

Erin coughed. "Did you want that?"

"Please."

She moved the bowl to the bed and set it by his elbow. Eric groped for it, clumsy, cuff clinking on the rim. He got hold of an ice chip and raised it to his lips. It slid down his cheek and vanished in the sheets.

"Are you really that weak? I should call a doctor."

Eric shook his head. "Tired. Stomach hurts." He closed his eyes for a moment, breathing in and out. "Besides, if you...call the doc, he'll just try to make me fart."

Erin croaked laughter, a loud, startled *awk.* "Excuse me?"

"To make sure they didn't, like...sew my guts together." He took another ice chip and dropped it in his mouth. "Dad said you were coming, but I didn't think you would."

"Because of what I said." She sat down. Her chest hurt, a dull, wretched ache. "I was a dick."

"Yeah, you were." Eric showed his teeth, not quite a grin.

"I know it might not mean much, but I hate what I said." Erin closed her eyes. "I don't trust you, not yet. Maybe I never will. I don't *understand* you, but I want to. I do. I want to keep talking, if that's still what you want."

"I—" Eric turned toward her, then his face contorted in pain. He bared his teeth, groaning, a deep, ragged sound. "Think I...might be sick."

Erin found a kidney bowl and held it under his chin. Eric heaved weakly, but nothing came up. He fell back, teeth chattering, clutching the sheets.

"I should leave you," said Erin. "You need to rest."

"No. No, don't go." Eric's tongue flicked out. "Just sit down. Let's talk."

Erin sat. She took Eric's hand without thinking, twined her fingers with his. His palm was cool and clammy, but his grip was tight. Erin wanted to cry.

"What happened? Who stabbed you?

"It got around the prison I was meeting with a fed." He laughed, almost soundlessly. "They made me for a rat, so..."

Erin's stomach turned over. So this was on her. "I guess 'sorry' doesn't cover it."

"Sorry...no." Eric made a pained sound. "But you know what might? Your Netflix password."

Erin blinked. "What?"

"I can get Netflix here. If you stream it from your phone. We could watch *BoJack Horseman*. Always wanted to see that."

Erin logged into her Netflix and paired it to the TV. She fired up *BoJack Horseman* and Eric grinned like a kid. For a while, they watched in silence, Eric struggling not to laugh. Then he closed his eyes, and Erin thought he went to sleep. But when she went to pull her hand away, Eric held on tighter.

"This isn't on you," he said, without opening his eyes. "I'm in prison for murder. For murders I committed. If I'd only thought back then, what that would do to you..."

"Don't say that." Erin looked away. "I think it's been good for me, coming back here. Like opening an old wound, letting the poison drain out. All this time, I've been out there trying to change the past. But I can't. You can't. So don't say that. Move on."

Eric watched some more *BoJack,* but his eyes had gone dull. "Can I ask you, do you believe me? About—remember I told you I only killed four?"

Erin scowled. She'd hoped he'd dropped that. "I don't," she said. "All the evidence said six. For me to believe otherwise, I'd have to see better evidence showing it was four."

"Thanks for being honest." Eric sank into the pillows. He let go of her hand. "I think I can sleep now. You can stay if you want, but..."

"I'll come back soon." She got to her feet. Her left leg had gone to sleep, and she shook out the pins and needles. Somewhere out there, another killer was stalking *his* sixth victim. Benjamin Watt, maybe. He'd never come home last night, still hadn't by morning. If that didn't scream *guilty,* she didn't know what did.

She called Brody from the parking lot. He picked up right away.

"Watt's still in the wind," he said, not bothering with hello. "Could be he saw us, or someone tipped him off. Good news, though: the prints from his room will be in by noon, the blood from the rag by tomorrow morning."

The tension in Erin's chest loosened an inch. "That's fast," she said. "I was thinking, since I'm not busy, why don't I check out the community college? Valerie went there too. Maybe someone saw something that'll put them together."

"Way ahead of you," said Brody. "Catherine's down there already, but you're welcome to join."

"I'll let you know if I find anything." Erin hung up without saying goodbye. She got into her car, and moments later, she was peeling out.

19

E rin sat on a bench under an oak tree, waiting for Catherine. The rain had cleared up, and the day was warm and sunny. She surveyed the students headed up the main stroll, trying to guess from their looks how they'd ended up here. That kid with the scooter and the pot leaf on his backpack—his parents had made him come, or they'd quit paying his rent. That middle-aged woman had young kids at home. Erin could tell from her limp hair and the spit-up on her shirt. She was here for a leg up, a better life for her family. The giggling girls behind her were here just for fun, to hang out and party and maybe pair off. To have kids of their own, and spit-up on their sleeves.

Catherine plumped down beside her and handed her a coffee. "Having fun?"

Erin took a long sip, savored the rush of caffeine. "I miss this sometimes, the whole college thing. Getting up at eleven, grabbing breakfast on the run. All that possibility, all that, uh..." She broke off, self-conscious, and took another gulp. Catherine glanced at her, brow raised.

"How's your brother? Hanging on?"

"He's awake." Erin stood up. "How's it coming over here?"

Catherine fell in beside her, heading up the path. "Brody had me call Watt's parents. Talk about a dead end. They're just in Santa Clara, but they haven't seen him since he left for college. To be perfectly honest, I'm not sure they've tried. They never even asked me why I was calling."

Erin grimaced, the parallels with her own family hitting too close for comfort. "Did you find out what caused the split?"

"Drugs in his room senior year. Mom was disappointed. Dad hit the roof. He threatened to call the cops, and Watt moved out the next day. He said he never wanted to see them again."

"Guess he was serious." Erin bit her lip. "So, rough home life, possible drug use, no support network. That could contribute, but it's not the whole picture." She gulped the last of her coffee and tossed the cup in the trash. "Let's go find someone who actually knows him."

"What is this kid, a ghost?" Erin threw herself down on a bench by a fountain. "Even his teachers barely remember him. He's like the Invisible Man."

"Or the man who wasn't there."

"What?"

"He wasn't there again today. Oh, how I wish he'd go away." Catherine winked. "The poem, you know?"

"If you say so." She flipped through her notepad with a scowl. "I've got ten pages on Valerie, just from those girls from her statistics class, but on Watt—check it out." She held up her pad for Catherine to see.

Across a mostly-blank page, she'd scrawled QUIET. BLACK CLOTHES.

"Excuse me?"

Erin turned around. A girl in pink had crept up from behind. Erin offered a smile. "Can we help you?"

"Are you the FBI?"

"We are. And you would be...?"

"Alison Cardiff. I heard you were asking about Val." She shifted from foot to foot. "I knew her pretty well, so if you wanted to ask me anything..."

Catherine shifted to make room on the bench. "Why don't you sit down? Every little bit helps."

Alison perched on the edge of the bench, her pink see-through back-pack poised between her feet. She looked about eighteen, maybe even younger, a slight, nervous girl with prominent buck teeth. She glanced at Erin, as though seeking approval. "Is this okay?"

"That's perfect." Erin relaxed visibly, hoping Alison would do the same. "So, what can you tell us about Val's social circle?"

"It was big," said Alison. She fidgeted with her zipper. "She'd talk to pretty much anyone. Like, we passed by this bum one time, and she didn't have any money, so she gave him this ring she had so he could go pawn it. Then she played with his dog a while, and I thought they were friends—like, she knew him from before. But when I asked her later, she said she didn't know him at all."

"Do you know if she spent time with Benjamin Watt?"

Alison's brow creased. "Benjamin Watt? I don't think I know any— oh, you mean Benny?" Her expression turned eager. "I wouldn't say they were friends, but, yeah, she knew him."

"Would you say they were close?"

"Close? I don't think so, but he did ask her out."

Erin's chest tightened. She sensed paydirt. "And how did that go?"

"Well, Val wasn't...she was stressed about her dad. Her folks just got divorced, and I guess they were trying to work it out?" Alison glanced at Catherine, seeking confirmation. "Anyway, she wasn't dating. She wanted to do the college thing, hang out with her friends. She didn't want a boyfriend, and that's what she told Ben."

"How'd he take it?"

Alison shrugged, now playing with the hem of her oversized shirt. "He was cool, I guess. He didn't get mad, just kinda slunk off. And he didn't, like, stalk her or anything. Not like that one guy, who changed all his classes to Amy Wheelwright's when they broke up. *That* guy was creepy, but Ben just went away. I don't remember even seeing him after that. Did he drop out, or something?"

"No—no, he didn't." Erin frowned. Watt really *had* been the man who wasn't there.

"Can I, um, go now?" Alison shifted where she sat. "I have class in twenty minutes, and I don't want to be late."

"Of course, that's fine." Erin handed her a card. "Call me any time, if anything else comes to mind."

"Just one more thing," said Catherine. "You said she was stressed about her dad. Stressed in what way?"

Alison paused, backpack clutched to her chest. "She didn't say much about him. But they'd meet for coffee sometimes, and she'd be tense the next day."

"Thanks, Alison," said Catherine. "You've been a big help."

186

Alison scurried off, beaming. Erin watched her go, bemused. "Well, this doesn't line up with his whole chamber of horrors." She kicked at a loose stone. "Did you hear from Brody yet? Weren't those prints supposed to come in by noon?"

Catherine checked her phone. "Nothing for me."

Erin exhaled harshly. "This doesn't make sense to me. Does it to you? I mean, okay, I get why he'd target Valerie. But what about Rayna? What about the rest? Why would a college kid hunt divorcées? And cross state lines to do it? Does he even have a car?"

"He doesn't," said Catherine. "As for the why, your guess is as good as mine. Thrill kills, maybe? One step up from ultimate fighting?"

"This case just gets weirder every time I turn my back."

Catherine only chuckled. "Come on, let's get out of here, grab something to eat. You always get grumpy when your blood sugar drops."

"Do not."

"Do too." Catherine nudged her, and they both broke out laughing. They headed back across campus in search of food.

———

Erin was munching her way through an order of onion rings when Brody called. She put him on speaker so Catherine could hear.

"You've got Hastings and Hannon. Go ahead."

"We've got him," said Brody, his tone downright gleeful. "Those prints from the Cook scene are a match to Watt. All we have to do is find him, and—let's not jinx it, hm?" He chuckled. "I'll be holding a press conference in just a few minutes. In the meantime, I've got every officer in the city on alert. Once we get eyes on him, Erin, I'll want you on the scene. We'll head up the collar, you and me—no room for screwups."

Erin tried and failed to hide her surprise. No room for screwups, and he'd picked *her*? Her heart swelled with pride. She wouldn't let him down. No Hasty Hastings fumbling the ball.

"Erin? Still there?"

She blinked hard. "Yep, got you. Should we head back to the station?"

"I'd hold off on that. This place'll be a feeding frenzy once I call the press. Keep doing what you're doing, and wait for my call."

"Sir, yes sir!"

Brody let out a snort. "I like your enthusiasm. Okay, got to go." He hung up, and Erin sat staring at her phone. "Does this mean I'm forgiven for the Anderson mess?"

Catherine took a bite of her sandwich. "He's giving you a chance," she said. "You're a valuable asset, and he wants to see you grow. What do you want to do while we wait?"

Erin licked mustard off her thumb. "Let's canvass the campus again. We should have a whole new crowd now, for afternoon classes. And let's send some uniforms to swing by Watt's house. Did I miss anything?"

"Not that I can think of." Catherine finished her sandwich and crumpled the wrapper in her fist. "Okay, let's go. Time's not our friend."

Erin dropped her last onion ring back onto her plate. She felt cold all of a sudden, that creeping chill Dad would call a goose crossing her grave. Time was her enemy, right enough. Every second Watt was out there was a second he could panic. A second he could decide to squeeze in one last kill.

She tossed her plate in the trash and got to her feet. "All right, I'm done. Let's catch this bastard."

The killer watched the press conference with mounting discontent. It was the prissy one again, that big square-jawed tightass with his fussy cheap suits. Innis, his name was, Agent Brody Innis. Even his name smacked of a sphincter in need of relaxation.

"Thanks to your tips," he droned, "we've identified a new person of interest, a student at—"

He hit MUTE on Agent Tightass and watched him yap on. His face barely moved, apart from his lips. His hair perched on his head like the world's dullest helmet. Soon a headshot popped up, a kid around twenty with scruffy black hair—BENJAMIN WATT, according to the caption. So this was the dream team's latest wild goose.

"How'd they get *you*, Watt? You look at some girl wrong? Tell her she was sweet?"

Agent Innis filled the screen again, still blabbing on. The wind blew up, but he'd buttoned down so tight his tie didn't flap. The killer unmuted him, curiosity getting the better of him.

"—prefer not to call him that," said Innis. "The Crusaders believed their mission was holy. We don't know that's the case here. And, on a personal note, I find it distasteful. Let's not mythologize him, paint him larger than life. He might be a sick man. He might be evil. But he's not a celebrity, or anything but a—"

The killer flung the remote at the TV. It bounced off harmlessly and landed on the carpet. Meanwhile, another reporter called out a question.

"This Benjamin Watt, is he wanted for murder?"

"Once again, no." A tiny line appeared between Innis's brows, and then it was gone. "We want to ask him some questions about what he might have witnessed."

The killer laughed out loud. "Tell you what, Watt: if you believe *that*, you deserve to get collared." He scooped up the remote and turned off the TV. He'd had it with Innis and his Captain America chin. They should've put Hastings on. Now, *there* was an agent. A jittery sensation ran through him, not quite a shiver, not quite a thrill. Hastings was *creepy*, not to put too fine a point on it—the mirror of her twin. She had his cold green eyes, his penetrating stare. She had a smell to her, too, a sort of thunderstorm tang—sharp and metallic, lightning poised to strike. Hastings could be a problem, if Innis let her off her leash.

He clapped his hands smartly to dispel his nerves. Hastings was bright, but she hadn't seen through his mask. He was still a free man, for all her prying. His mission *was* holy, not in the Catholic sense, but something far broader. He was cleansing the world of a deep, rotten stain.

He went to his computer and powered it on. As he stared at the loading screen, he thought of Agent Hastings. It was a shame, really, her sins weren't mortal. His cock stirred at the thought of her down on her knees, her icy green eyes milky with death. She'd need somewhere special for her final pedestal—not some hidden corner, not behind closed doors. Somewhere high up, lit from below. The top of a water tower, or...the cop shop, on the roof. A bright jolt shot through him, like lightning to his groin, and he let his hand drop to his lap. The picture was too sweet, too sweet to pass up.

Maybe he could make an exception, just this once…

20

Sasha's call came in at five on the dot, just as Erin and Catherine were wrapping up at the college. Erin picked up left-handed, opening her car door with her right.

"Tell me it's good news."

"If you like catching killers." Sasha didn't wait for her response. "Watt's just been spotted entering a residence in LA. The task force is headed over. You're to meet them there—I'll text the address."

Erin reached for her seat belt. "Let Brody know we're on our way now."

"I'm on the line," said Brody. "The locals are watching the house, but they won't go in without you. It's all riding on you, so don't drop the ball."

Catherine put on her cherry light but left off her siren. Her color was up, her grip tight on the wheel. "Fifty bucks says I have us there in forty minutes."

"A hundred says we make it before our warrants come through."

Catherine laughed, high and wild. Erin reached for her phone and set about chasing their warrants. The road flashed by and she sat on hold, and Catherine laughed at her, but Erin barely noticed. In her head, she was already planning their approach—how they'd surround the house, how she'd soothe Watt into a quiet surrender. How she'd corral him if he failed to comply. Their warrants came through by the time they hit the suburbs. Catherine flashed her a smirk.

"So, who won the bet?"

Erin glanced at her watch. "I make it thirty-eight minutes, warrants in hand. Guess that means we both did."

They pulled over a block from Watt's hidey-hole. The team was waiting already, geared up to go.

"I want three of you around back," said Erin, "and two on the side door. Me and Catherine'll take the front. We'll try first the nice way, then storm on my go."

Erin hung back while the team circled the house. At their signal, she moved, striding up the walk with Catherine on her heels. She freed her gun from its holster, ready to draw.

"All set?"

Catherine nodded. Erin raised her fist. She pounded on the door, so hard it shook.

"FBI!" she thundered. "We've got you surrounded, so come out with your hands up."

Nothing happened. Erin waited for the commotion of someone fleeing out the back, but the house remained quiet, crickets chirping in the yard.

"Okay. He had his chance." Erin held up three fingers, counted down three-two-one. She booted the old door just under the knob. It broke loose from its frame with a sharp gunshot *crack*, crashing down in the foyer in a shower of splinters and glass.

"Hey! What the—" A big man jumped up from the living room table, headphone cord jerking loose as his laptop tumbled to the ground. He spotted Erin's gun and jumped back with a shriek, tripped over his own feet, and went down on his ass. Catherine rushed to secure him and the team charged in. The team fanned out on Erin's command, and soon shouts of "Clear" echoed down the dusty halls.

"Crap. Where'd he go?" Erin stalked back to the living room, holstering her weapon. "We're clear—it's just him. You can let him up."

Catherine got to her feet. Her captive pushed himself upright, drawing up his knees to cover a dark spot at his crotch. Erin crouched before him, her expression stern. "What's your name?"

"My, uh...it's Xavier Whedon. Xavier Whedon, ma'am."

"Where's Benjamin Watt?"

"I don't know. He left." Whedon shook his head furiously. "Whatever he's into, we're just friends from school. I don't *know* him, know him. We're not, like—"

Erin resisted the urge to slap him. "Where did he go?"

"I don't know, I swear! He took off ten minutes ago, looked out the window and I guess something spooked him, because he ran out the back. I had my headphones on, so—"

"Did he leave on foot, or was he driving?"

"I didn't see, but on foot. He doesn't know how to drive."

"What was he wearing?"

"I don't—uh, black. He only ever wears black." Whedon's eyes widened. "What did he do?"

Erin flicked on her radio to address her team. "He slipped by the locals. Subject on the move." She rounded on Whedon. "You sure it's been ten minutes? Not fifteen? Not half an hour?"

Whedon nodded miserably. "Three songs, ten minutes. Prob'ly twelve since you got here. Hey, are you guys gonna pay for my—"

Erin turned her back on him. "Cat—you, White, and Wells are with me. Santos and Hughes, you stay and search the residence. See if Watt left anything behind—and interrogate Whedon. He might know more than he thinks."

Santos nodded. "Leave it to us."

Erin turned and jogged from the house, the others hot on her heels. They jumped in their vehicles and fanned out, Erin and Catherine speeding in the direction Whedon had indicated, the rest covering the neighborhood in case he'd led them astray.

Luck was on Erin's side. She spotted Watt running down the sidewalk just a couple of miles away. She hit her siren and closed in. "Suspect in sight. Hastings in pursuit."

Her radio crackled to life. "Ten-four. Right behind you."

Watt glanced back, eyes round. He abandoned the sidewalk and tore across a narrow strip of lawn. He reached a hedge and vaulted over it, sprinting for the black maw of a five-story parking garage.

Catherine surged forward and pounded on the dash. "Don't let him get in there!"

Erin screeched after him, but Watt lunged for the darkness and was swallowed by it. Erin screamed to a halt just short of the speed bump.

She was out of her vehicle in the same instant, darting for cover as her eyes adjusted to the gloom.

"Where the hell is he?"

"I don't see him."

Erin crouched in the shelter of the ticket machine, senses on high alert. The chill of the garage settled on her skin, raising the fine hairs down the back of her neck. The reek of warm rubber and gasoline hung heavy in the air. She scanned the shadows for movement, but saw none; pricked her ears for footfalls, but heard only her own breathing.

"He's hiding," she whispered.

Catherine made a low sound. "Let's wait for backup. We can't clear this whole place and cover the exit."

Erin didn't respond. She held her breath, strained her ears, but the only sounds she could hear were the sigh of the wind and the tick of cooling engines. Somewhere, a bird twittered, scolding some unseen foe. Erin ground her teeth so hard her jaw creaked. Outside, brakes squealed, and then a door slammed.

"That's our backup," said Catherine. Erin reached for her radio.

"White, stay out front and secure the main gate, and get someone on the rear exit. Wells, search the north end. Me and Catherine will split the south. Check in cars, under cars, and get some uniforms in here. We need everyone on this, everyone we've got."

Her radio blipped "Affirmative." Erin eased along the east wall, weapon raised. She cleared each row efficiently, but the work was slow, rattling every handle, thumping every trunk. Watt had vanished like morning mist, without a trace.

The uniforms arrived and spread out across the floor. Erin circled back toward the up-ramp. Her nose itched from the dust, and she stifled a sneeze.

"Boots! I've got boots." Catherine popped up twenty feet to her left, clutching a pair of well-worn Doc Martens.

Erin reeled like she'd been slapped. "Socks," she hissed. "Everyone shut up! Everyone stand still."

A pregnant hush settled over the garage. Erin eased forward, Catherine on her heels. They flanked the ramp and inched upward, noiseless in the gloom. Erin could hear birds again, nesting overhead. Water dripped. Rats scurried. Cloth caught on concrete, a tiny Velcro sound. Erin's heart leaped.

"Second floor, I got him! Heading for three!" She plunged ahead, Catherine hot on her heels. A shadow danced on the wall as she rounded the corner—not her own, but Watt's, lurching up the ramp. Erin hurtled after him, breath hot in her lungs. Her footfalls echoed strangely in the cavernous space, seeming to bounce back from every direction at once. She caught sight of Watt sprinting for four, the bright white of his socks flashing up ahead.

"Stop! FBI!"

Watt hooked around the corner. Erin pushed herself harder, blood thundering in her head. Watt panted, loud and frenzied, almost close enough to grab. Erin was gaining, she could feel it, and she put on a burst of speed. She whipped around the bend and a black wall rose and struck her, cold metal to her face.

Erin didn't cry out. She had a moment to register a steel door clanging shut—the same one that had opened and slammed her off her feet—and then she was on her back, vision pricked with stars. She gripped her weapon reflexively, and then Watt was on her, grasping the barrel.

She jerked it away. He lunged after it. She seized him by the collar, twisted it in her fist.

"Let go."

Erin twisted harder. Watt let go of her sidearm and grabbed her by the hair. He slammed her head into the concrete and her vision went black. She jerked her knee blindly, aiming for his crotch. Watt hit her again, drove his fist into her temple. A bolt of pain shot through her, and all her muscles seized at once. She tried to roll away and only twitched. A stray thought ran through her head—*guy hits like a train*—and then Watt was gone, socks shushing up the ramp.

Erin fumbled for her radio. She couldn't feel her hands. Her ears buzzed with nausea, and she thought she might puke.

"Erin! Hey, look at me."

Erin forced her eyes open. Catherine was crouched over her, her face a pale blur. Erin squinted, tried to focus, and the world slitched to one side, cars and tarmac dancing a disorienting ballet.

"Help me up," she said, only it came out more like "*hfughh.*" She needed to get up. Watt was getting away. She rolled to her hands and knees, and the garage flew apart in a woozy drift of stars.

"He's on five," snapped Catherine, from somewhere far away. Boots pounded by her head—Wells, Erin thought.

"Get him," she muttered. *Ge'um. Go 'head.*

"Don't try to talk." Catherine eased Erin into a sitting position. "Breathe for me, okay? Can you focus on my finger?"

Erin crossed her eyes. Catherine's finger danced and jittered. It looked funny and she laughed, except instead of laughter, she coughed up her lunch. It missed her vest somehow and splashed Catherine's instead.

"Sorry," she managed.

"That's okay," said Catherine. She grabbed her face gently and tilted it to one side. "Did you hit your head?"

"My weapon..."

"You're holding it. Now, *did you hit your head?*"

With her nausea fading, Erin's head felt more clear. She holstered her weapon and felt a little better. "I ran into the door," she said. "And he hit me, twice I think. Guy packs a punch."

Catherine poked up her finger. "Let's try this again. Follow me side to side—okay, up and down."

Erin focused as best she could, but the movement made her sick. She closed her eyes and waited for the spinning to pass.

"Looks like a concussion," said Catherine. "Are you hurt anywhere else?"

"Don't know. I..." Erin patted at her body. Her hands felt big and clumsy, trembling with shock. "My back's kind of aching, but that's from sleeping in the car. And I fell on my ass, so you could say I'm butthurt. But mostly, it's just my pride. Can't believe he got the jump on me."

"He wouldn't have if you'd waited." Catherine slapped her lightly, backhand across the shoulder. "What were you thinking, charging off by yourself?"

"By myself?" Erin's brow furrowed. She'd heard Catherine, she was sure of it, mere paces behind her. "I could hear you," she said. "Your boots—you were—"

Catherine swatted again. "You know better than that. The acoustics, a place like this, you need visual confirmation."

Erin blinked, slow and owlish. "Wouldn't have mattered. The door just swung out, the...it happened so fast. So fast, like a freight train. The door just swung out."

Catherine sighed. "Excessive repetition, obsessive fixation. You're definitely concussed. We're going to talk about this when your brain isn't scrambled."

Wells jogged up to join them. "How is she?"

"She hit her head in the scuffle," said Catherine. "She'll need to be checked out. You didn't find him?"

Wells shook his head. "Just a fire extinguisher on five. Looks like he used it to bust through a security door. I've got the team sweeping the area. You need anything else?"

Erin's head throbbed. "We have to find him," she said. "He'll go to ground, and then...d'you know how many people are in the state of California? I'll tell you: too many. It'll be a needle in a haystack, like..."

Catherine cut her off with a hand on her arm. "Sorry, Erin, but you're babbling." She turned to Wells. "Okay, I'm in charge. Get the locals on the search, as many as they can spare. Watt can't have gone far, so let's run him down now. Officer Wells, call for medical. And arrange a ride for Agent Hastings back to Lancaster. She's not driving anywhere in her current condition."

Erin wanted to protest, but whenever she blinked, galaxies danced in her vision. If she stayed here, she'd only puke all over the scene.

"I'll keep you updated," said Catherine. She squeezed Erin's shoulder. "Don't worry. We've got this."

Erin nodded, nearly gagged. She leaned back against the wall, letting the cool concrete soothe her throbbing head. "Be careful, okay? He's more dangerous than we thought."

She watched, dull-eyed, as Catherine walked away. Brody was going to kill her, to say nothing of Randy. She'd done it again, lost situational awareness and put her whole team in danger. Watt had nearly snatched her sidearm—would've got away with it if Catherine hadn't caught up.

She drew her knees to her chest, her face hot with shame. Stupid Hasty Hastings—how had she done this *again?*

21

Erin slunk into the conference room covered in shame, still smarting from the indignity of being poked and prodded by medical. She was a bad patient, always had been, twitchy, impatient. She didn't like being pawed at, especially by strangers. Especially when she *hurt,* miserable aches and pains settling into every inch of her body. She pulled out a chair, but didn't sit down. She wanted to be standing when Brody let her have it.

"You're back," he said. "Why?"

She squinted at him through a sick whirl of vertigo. His question didn't make sense to her. "Why?" she echoed. "Why what?"

"Why are you here, and not resting at the hotel?"

She mulled that over, eyes fixed on a spider-crack jagging down the wall. "I can't sleep," she said at last. "I have a concussion. I need to stay awake."

Brody stared, disbelieving. "And you expect me to, what? Keep you awake?"

"Give me some work to do, anything. I'm fine." Her head throbbed and she staggered, and Brody gestured at her chair.

"Sit down, why don't you? I've got some new evidence. We'll go over it together."

"You don't want to yell first?"

Brody slumped forward, buried his face in his hands. He shook his head side to side, shoulders hitching with laughter. When he raised his head again, he was wiping his eyes. "You know what you did, and you'll be hearing from Randy. I'll yell if you want, but have you looked in a mirror? I'd call that instant karma."

Erin touched her face where Watt had punched her. Her cheekbone was tender, her eye swollen half shut. "Touché," she said, and slid into her seat. Brody pulled a folder toward him and flipped it open.

"This is from the lab," he said. "The blood from the laundry came back a match for Valerie Cook. Not only that, but they were able to match skin cells from Watt's home with the blood from the Cook scene."

Erin closed her eyes to keep the room from spinning. "He was there the night she died."

"Beyond a doubt. It's not enough to prove he killed her, but it ties him to the scene."

"And I let him get away. First Hayes, now this clown. I can't—" Her head throbbed sickly, and Erin gulped to keep the bile down.

"Drink this," said Brody. He slid a Sprite across the table. Erin sipped and felt better, the fizz settling her stomach. She tipped her chair back and stared at the ceiling.

"You're going to break that chair," said Brody. Erin ignored him.

"I'm Watt," she said. "I'm twenty years old."

"He's nineteen," said Brody. Erin ignored him again.

"I'm in college, pulling Bs, but I don't fit in. It's like I'm invisible. Nobody talks to me, and if they do, they don't remember. Even my teachers, it's like I'm just *there*. Part of the scenery, not a whole person." She rocked in her chair, the slow motion soothing. "I've got to fit in somewhere, but...where would I go? Who'd be my tribe?" Erin jerked upright. "What about all that fighting stuff? Anyone run that down?"

"Sasha's checking out boxing gyms, but no luck so far."

"He could've paid cash. Used a false name. Or what about those fight clubs? Do those exist in real life?"

"They exist," said Brody. "But no way he'd find one without joining a gym."

Erin leaned forward, drummed her fingers on the table. Sitting still didn't agree with her. She needed to move, needed to *hunt*. She needed to redeem herself, cancel out her mistake. "How about his socials? Anything there?"

"Not a lot," said Brody. "He doesn't have many contacts, no recent activity. Mo's building a profile, though. We might get something there."

Erin stood up. "I'm going back to the college," she said. "We hadn't finished our interviews."

"Over my dead body." Brody moved to bar her way. "Come on, you know the rules. No field work for at least twenty-four hours." He scratched his chin, considering. "You can do phone interviews, if you'd feel up to that."

"I can't read their body language over the phone." She bounced on the balls of her feet. "See, I'm not dizzy at all. Why don't I go down there and—"

"Hasty Hastings." Brody jabbed a finger at her. All trace of humor had vanished from his expression. "You know the protocol for injuries in the field. Squawk all you want, but you're riding a desk. If you need to see body language, do a video call. Tomorrow'll be soon enough to get back in the field."

Erin wilted, defeated. Brody was right. He'd gone out on a limb not sending her home. Pushing for more would just be ungrateful.

"I'll take the media room," she said. "And, Brody? Thanks."

He flapped his hand at her. "Go on, and stay hydrated. It'll help your headache."

Erin slammed her laptop shut. The sound hurt her head, but it felt good to abuse something, even an inanimate object. Watt's professors had all sung one song, like a record on repeat—*depressingly average. Quiet kid, not much spark.* Two of them had needed a photo to recall who he was, and one of those had just stared at it with blank, puzzled eyes.

"You're *sure* he's in my class? He doesn't ring a bell."

"Look again. Zoom in. How big is your class?"

"It's a lecture class, about eighty, but I don't know him at all."

Even Watt's drawings had failed to arouse much recognition. One woman had even chuckled, waved them aside. "Those are a dime a dozen," she'd said. "You've got to understand, these are kids. They're out on their own, mostly for the first time. They're pushing the boundaries, testing what fits. We see a lot of that stuff—sexual exploration."

"So a sketchbook like that wouldn't raise a red flag?"

"Not on its own, no. Like I said, dime a dozen."

Erin rubbed at her forehead, trying to ease the blooming ache behind her eyes. What had she learned? Watt was a quiet kid, but not overtly creepy. He didn't speak up much, didn't excel. His attendance was good, but he pulled Bs and Cs. Average in every way—maybe Eric had been right. Watt had been normal, so normal he'd gone unnoticed. Then he'd latched onto Valerie. She'd become his obsession, the prize he had to have.

"But then, why keep going? Why Rayna? Why Alice?" And why hadn't he posed Valerie to fit his fantasy?

Erin glanced at her notes, frowning. They'd got sloppier with each interview, sentences becoming fragments, short and disjointed. The last page was just a scribble, a jagged mark of frustration.

A sharp pain shot through her eye, and she pressed her fist into it. How long had she been at this? *And why bother at all?* She'd turned up nothing, not the shadow of a clue. The pain finally passed, and she let her hand drop. When the ache didn't return, she reached for her phone. She dialed Dad's number and listened to it ring.

"Erin? That you?"

She licked her lips, tasted sickness. "Yeah, Dad. It's me. Thought I'd check in, see how you're holding up."

"I'm with Eric," said Dad. "He keeps falling asleep."

"That's good. Sleep's good for him." Erin closed her eyes, groped for something to say. "I'll try to come by soon. Tell him I'm thinking of him."

Dad was quiet a moment, then he breathed a harsh sigh. "You're a good girl," he said. Erin was saved from having to respond to that by Dad hanging up. She eyed her laptop, but couldn't summon the will to reach for it. A deep exhaustion lay over her like a blanket made of lead.

She glanced at the clock—nearly seven. Catherine hadn't called, which meant Watt was still in the wind. She laid her head on the table, savoring its coolness. Her Advil was wearing off, and she felt scraped raw inside. Brody had been right. She should've left hours ago.

She scooped up her laptop and headed out through the bullpen. Brody looked up as she passed, and she gave him a nod.

"I'm headed back to the hotel," she said. "Let me know if you nab Watt, or if anything comes up."

"I'll do better than that. I'll drive you." Brody pulled out his keys and flipped them in the air. He slung a brotherly arm around her as he led her out of the station. "Cheer up, kid," he said. "It'll look better in the morning."

22

Day dawned bright and blinding, a rare, hot December day. Erin woke to her phone buzzing, rattling off the nightstand. She snatched it as it fell, answered hoarse and muzzy.

"Hastings. Whaddaya want?"

"Good morning to you too," said Brody. "And also, good news. Catherine's got Watt. She's transporting him to Lancaster as we speak."

Erin sat up so fast she saw stars. "I want to be in on this. Let me run the interrogation."

Brody made a clucking sound. "How's your head?"

"Tender. Clear."

"I don't like the tender part," said Brody. "Catherine will take the lead, but you can sit in." His breath whooshed down the line, and Erin wondered what he was doing. Working out, maybe, or running upstairs. "You'll want to head in through the side," he said, interrupting her speculation. "We've got press swarming already. Let's not add fuel to the fire."

"I'll be there in ten," said Erin. She looked down at herself, saw she wasn't dressed. "Make that fifteen."

"Don't break any speed limits. They're still forty minutes out." Brody hung up and Erin sprang into action. She felt better after resting, sharper, more focused. Her eye still throbbed where Watt's knuckles had connected, and her cheekbone felt like a warm, soupy pillow. But her brain fog was gone, her head free of static.

"Swiggity swooty," she said. "I'm coming for that booty." She laughed, disbelieving—had she said that out loud?—then groaned in pain as the outside light hit her eyes.

Watt stumbled into the station in a flurry of camera flashes. He ducked his head to evade them, squinched his eyes shut. His stringy black hair fell in his face. Erin swallowed thickly, seized with sudden nausea. In the bright morning light, he reminded her of Eric—not Eric now, but Eric back then, shuffling down the driveway, hands cuffed behind his back. Eric hadn't let his fear show, except when he'd caught her eye. She'd seen his dismay then, a kid's naked shock. Then he'd looked away, and his face had gone blank.

Watt glanced at her too, as the doors slammed behind him. He took in her bruised face, the sunset down her cheek. His jaw dropped just slightly, and he looked away.

"Get moving," said Catherine. She marched him down the hall, past the vending machines. Erin followed more slowly, and waited outside while Catherine secured him to the table.

"Brody says you'll be joining me," said Catherine, once Watt was settled. She stood watching him through the one-way glass, eyes cool and narrow. "How long d'you want to give him before we head in?"

Erin snorted. Watt was craning around already, sizing up the room. "I figure five minutes," she said. "He's been stewing an hour already, in the back of your car."

"I left the AC off. He's not just stewed. He's *tender*."

They shared a faint laugh at that. Erin went to the vending machine and got herself a Coke.

"I'm going to drink this in front of him," she said. "Remind him who's in charge."

Catherine smirked. "You can if you want. But all the tough guy went out of him once we got him in cuffs. I'm not sure, but I think he cried some on the way into town."

Erin's insides knotted up again, thinking of Watt shedding a tear. She hadn't seen Eric cry since they were nine or ten. But his eyes had been red-rimmed the day they'd read his verdict. Dad had blamed her for that, for refusing to see him.

"Let's go in," she said. "Think he's stewed long enough."

Catherine went ahead of her and took a seat across from Watt. Erin stayed standing, leaning by the door. She cracked her Coke open and took a long swig. Watt eyed her thirstily, just as she'd hoped. Catherine ignored him. She started her recorder and set it on the table.

"Agent Catherine Hannon and Agent Erin Hastings interviewing Benjamin Watt. Please state your name, age, and occupation for the record."

Watt slumped in his seat, a skinny kid dressed in black but for his white socks. "Benjamin Joseph Watt," he mumbled. "Um, nineteen. College student."

"Mr. Watt, have you been read your Miranda rights, and do you understand these rights as they have been read to you?"

He nodded slowly. "I understand."

"Okay, Mr. Watt. You've been brought in for questioning regarding the deaths of Rayna and Valerie Cook, Jessica VanRijn, Alice Newman, and Sandy Morrison. Are you willing to answer our questions at this time?"

Watt glanced at Erin. She regarded him blandly until he looked away.

"I guess so," he said.

"Where were you on the night of November third?"

Watt chewed his lower lip, nipping off dead skin. "The third, I, uh...studying." He licked at his lip, where he'd chewed it smooth and pink. "Studying in the library. I had a test the next day."

Catherine made a note. "And what class was that for?"

"Visual culture. Or, no, intro to psych. It was about group dynamics, how outcasts differ from preferential loners."

Erin raised an eyebrow. "What's a preferential loner?"

Watt didn't look at her. He sat with his head down, eyes fixed on the table. "It's someone who chooses to be alone, usually an introvert or an innovator. An outcast is someone who's ostracized by his peers."

"I see," said Catherine. "And can anyone confirm you were there that night, studying for your test?"

Watt shrugged. "Probably. The place was packed. I was tucked in the back, but I left a couple of times to get food. They'd have seen me go by, unless..."

Erin narrowed her eyes. "Unless what?"

Watt still didn't look up. Red spots had appeared high on his cheeks. "I don't know if you've noticed, but I kind of blend. They might've seen me, but seeing's different from noticing. And then remembering's a step up from that. You could ask if they saw me, but..." He shook his head.

Erin pursed her lips. Refusal to make eye contact could mean an inexperienced liar. Or it could indicate shame, something to hide. Watt was nervous for sure, squirming and fidgeting, pinching the skin on the backs of his hands. He was jumping at shadows, twitchy as a mouse.

"How about November seventh?" said Catherine. "Where were you that night?"

"I don't know," said Watt. "Wait, what day was that?"

"That was a Sunday."

"At the gym. No, the park. I don't know. I forget."

Erin moved around the table, to stand just behind him. "How'd you do on that test? The one you were studying for?"

"What?" Watt flinched, just barely, as though surprised by the question. "Okay, I guess. I don't...I'd have to check."

Catherine leaned forward, noticing his discomfort. "And why did you run from the FBI?"

"You were chasing me with guns."

"You ran before that," said Erin. "You ran to Mr. Whedon's house. Why'd you do that?"

"Because—because..." He shrank deeper into his chair. "I came home to grab a textbook. Ms. Davidson was on the phone. I heard my name, so I listened, and she was on the phone with you. She said I killed Valerie, and she had the blood to prove it. I didn't do it, but I knew you wouldn't believe me." He raised his head at last, his eyes big and wounded. "No one ever believes me. No one takes my side, not my parents, not my teachers, not—okay, let me tell you. I was thirteen, at summer camp, and this kid killed a swan. I said I'd tell, he told them *I* did it, and guess who got kicked out? My folks made me see a shrink, and he put me on loxapine. I was a zombie all year, and I *never killed that swan.*" He stamped his foot hard, chains rattling between his legs.

"We're not interested in the swan," said Catherine. "Valerie, on the other hand—"

"I *never* killed Valerie, or her mom, or anyone. I'd never do that, never!" The words burst from him in a rush, and his eyes glistened with tears.

"I see." Catherine tapped her pencil on her notepad. "Back to November seventh, where did you say you were?"

Watt stared at the table, tight-lipped and sullen.

"I'm going to need you to answer me."

Watt hunched his shoulders and didn't say a word. Erin studied Catherine instead. She was fiddling with her pencil, scratching her nail along the raised print on its side. She always did that when she sensed disappointment in the air—when the truth she saw emerging wasn't the truth she wanted to find. Erin sipped her Coke, but the sugar turned her stomach. She was starting to sense something amiss, herself. Their man was methodical, cold and detached. He killed and posed his victims and got out without a trace. Watt was emotional, out of control. He might've killed Valerie, but as for the rest—

Erin drained her Coke and tossed the can in the trash. Watt flinched at the sound, and she shot him a smile.

"How about we start over?" She sat down next to Catherine and leaned in, still smiling. "Tell us about Valerie. You went to school with her, right?"

Watt's eyes narrowed with suspicion, but as Erin had hoped, he couldn't resist the opportunity to talk about Valerie. He gazed into nothing, a smile tugging at his lips. "She was in my psych class," he said. "She sat two rows ahead of me, had the prettiest dark hair I'd ever seen. It looked so soft I wanted to touch it, but of course I never did. I didn't even talk to her until *she* talked to *me*." He glanced at Catherine, defiant. "She was nice to everyone, not just her friends. She'd ask how your day was and actually listen, not just pretend to listen and then blow you off. That's why I asked her out, but she said no."

Erin nodded, feigning sympathy. "What'd you do then?"

Watt licked his lips. His tongue was rough and dry-looking. "I really liked her, y'know? And she didn't say no, exactly. She said she wasn't dating right *then*. I thought I might ask again when she was ready. I figured I'd make friends with her, so when she got lonely, I'd be right there." He looked down at his hands again, the color high in his cheeks. "This is gonna sound creepy, but I followed her a few times. I wanted to catch her alone, so it could be just us. That's how I knew where she lived."

"And you followed her on the third?"

"No. Yes. I mean, I *was* in the library, but I swung by her place on my way home. I didn't follow her, though. I went on my own." Watt frowned. "It was late when I got there. The whole place was dark. I thought I'd peek in the window, you know, just to see. That was when..." He sucked in a shaky breath. Erin saw he was sweating, his brow slick and shiny. "I didn't mean to stalk her. I just wanted to talk. I had this bracelet she'd dropped, and I was going to give it back. But when I peeked in, I saw—" His Adam's apple bobbed up and down in his throat. He swallowed convulsively, the color draining from his face.

Erin lowered her voice to a soothing pitch. "What did you see?"

"I saw her mom. She was... Dead." He gulped hard, ducked his head. "She was in her pajamas, kneeling by the stairs. I could tell from how her head was...I knew she was dead." He tilted his own head back to demonstrate, at a broken-doll angle. "I thought someone might see me if I broke in through the front, so I went around back and busted in there. I checked on her mom, but she—"

"Wait." Erin held up her hand. "You broke in yourself? The back door wasn't open?"

"No. It was locked." Watt held up his hands to show a fading scar on his wrist. "See, there, I cut myself."

"Okay," said Catherine. "What happened next?"

Watt hugged himself. He was shaking all over, teeth rattling in his head. The words came pouring out of him like he'd held them in too long. Tears came along with them, great salty drops streaming down his cheeks. "I checked on her mom, but she had no pulse. And then I saw Valerie laid out on the floor—in the living room, in the moonlight, like an angel, or..." He coughed. "I was stroking her hair, like 'wake up, wake up,' but she was cold and all bloody, and she looked angry like—like it was my fault. Like I could've saved her." A rasping sound burst from him, a great, braying sob. "I couldn't just leave her there, so I put her to bed. I lay with her a while to warm her up, but she just got colder and colder, so I...I tucked her in and I ran." He hunched over miserably, wiped his nose on his sleeve. "I'm sorry. I tried to help her, but she was already dead."

Catherine waited until Watt had his sobs under control. "If that's what happened, why didn't you call the police?"

"Because, I told you, no one ever believes me." He laughed, half-scream. "I knew this would happen. I knew you'd arrest me while the real killer walked free. Losers like me, you always—"

"Can you prove what you're saying?" Erin cut in, heading off his hysteria. "This doesn't look good for you, but if you can back up your story—"

Watt wiped his nose again and clenched his fists tight. "I get a lawyer, right? I want my lawyer now."

"Fair enough, Mr. Watt. You're entitled to a lawyer." Catherine got to her feet. "Did you want to review your statement while we wait for—"

"No. I want my lawyer *now*."

Erin tried to catch Watt's eye, but this time he wouldn't look at her. She shoved her chair back and followed Catherine from the room.

Watt's lawyer arrived promptly, inside half an hour. Erin disliked her on sight, her boxy black heels, her stiffly starched suit. Her hair was smooth as LEGO, scraped into a bun so tight it tugged her brows into a permanent expression of surprise. She had tiny eyes like a shark's, and a predatory smile. She introduced herself as *Irene Daniels, attorney*, as though there were any doubt.

"He's all yours," said Catherine. Irene pursed her lips.

"I hope that's true," she said. "Because if I find you've questioned him after he invoked his right to counsel—"

"You're welcome to our recordings," said Erin. She ushered Irene to the interrogation room, following a little too close. If Irene felt uncomfortable, she gave no sign. She smirked over her shoulder as she shut the door in Erin's face.

"I hate her," said Erin.

"I'm not crazy about her, myself." Catherine peered through the one-way glass. "I don't think he did it, but that shark in lawyer's clothing is gonna make us work for every inch."

Erin got herself a coffee while she waited for Irene to work her witch-craft. Brody caught her drinking it and insisted she add a bear claw. She ate it in small bites, and by the time she was done, Benjamin was ready to make his statement. He made it nearly in one breath, never taking his eyes off Irene.

"The third of November, I was studying for my psych test, just like I said. I had to sign for a reference book, the kind you can't take home. I signed it back in around eleven thirty. I went to see Valerie on my way home, and that's when I found them, her and her mom. I was home by three thirty, in bed by four."

Catherine scratched at her pencil. "Why didn't you provide this information the first time we asked?"

Watt opened his mouth, but Irene waved him to silence. "My client was concerned he'd be blamed for the Cooks' deaths—as, indeed, he has been. Nor is he required by law to volunteer information that might implicate him in a crime."

Catherine tried again. "When you discovered the Cooks, why didn't you call for help?"

Irene placed her hand on Watt's shoulder. "The victims were beyond help at the time of discovery. My client was in a state of extreme distress. He acted emotionally, not rationally. That's not a crime."

Catherine pinched the bridge of her nose, but plowed on. "Mr. Watt, how often did you visit the Cook residence on your way home?"

Irene cut in again. "How is that relevant?"

Erin squared her shoulders. "If Mr. Watt visited regularly, maybe he noticed something out of place that night. Something that didn't make sense at the time, but now it does, given the circumstances. Is that the case, Mr. Watt?"

Irene's lips turned down. "Mr. Watt declines to comment at this time."

Mr. Watt went right on declining to comment, and soon Erin and Catherine ran out of questions. Erin rubbed at her temples, her headache flaring anew. "Ms. Daniels, your client has refused to provide alibis for the time of the murders. By his own admission, he was at the first crime scene, and we have evidence to prove it."

Irene's eyes narrowed. "Agent, I—"

"I do have an alibi. Alibis for the others." Watt glanced at Irene, then barreled on. "I don't know where I was for the last one, on the twenty-fourth. But on the seventh, I went out drinking. The receipts are in my wallet. On the thirteenth, I went to...I was LARPing, okay? There's pictures on Instagram. I should be in some."

Erin cocked a brow. "LARPing?"

"Live-action roleplaying. I'm a vampire lord. You can check it on Insta, hashtag Lancaster masquerade."

Erin rose from the table. "Excuse me a minute. I'm going to go verify your, uh...all that." She shot him an evil look, but she had to admit Watt was looking less and less like the killer, and more like a dorky kid out of his depth. At least she could grab some Advil while she was out of the room.

Watt's alibi checked out, in all its bloodsucking glory. Erin gazed in disbelief at his black-cloaked form streaking across the park, a dull plastic scythe raised over his head. His mouth gaped open to reveal a set of Halloween fangs. The picture was timestamped one thirty AM.

"You've *got* to be kidding me."

She dug through his wallet and found the receipts for the seventh, and just like that, another suspect bit the dust. Her head throbbed and swam as she trudged back through the station. Irene greeted her in the interrogation room with a satisfied smirk.

"Well? Will you be charging my client or not?"

"He'll be charged with assaulting an officer and contaminating a crime scene. He'll be held pending his bail hearing, but for now at least, our interest in him is done. An officer will be along shortly to get him processed." Erin turned to go. "Coming, Agent Hannon?"

Catherine followed her out, her mouth a tight line.

"Show me the pictures," she said.

Erin blinked. "Pictures?"

"Watt's vampire weekend. Come on, let me see. I need a good laugh."

Erin fished out her phone and punched in the hashtag. "See, there, that's him, waving the scythe."

Catherine's face twitched. She pressed her hand to her mouth and doubled over laughing. "Those fangs—God, those *fangs!* I chased that creep half the night, and...damn, he's just a kid."

"A kid who packs a mean punch." Erin touched her cheek and winced. Catherine straightened up.

"I shouldn't laugh," she said. "But it's all so ridiculous. We keep thinking we've got him, and..." She waggled her fingers in a flying-away gesture. "*Poof.* Just like that." She looked Erin up and down, as though seeing her for the first time. "Jesus, that's bad. Shouldn't you be in bed?"

"It looks worse than it is." Erin stifled a groan. "Though, speaking of vampires that lawyer resurrected my headache."

"Hey, Hannon, Hastings." Brody called out as they passed the conference room. He held up a hand for them to wait and turned back to his phone call. "No, that was just...yeah, exactly. I appreciate it." He hung up the phone.

"So, Watt's off the hook."

"For murder, at least. We turned him over to the locals."

Brody nodded. "I'll make sure they throw the book at him. He doesn't get to walk away from an assault on my team. Speaking of which, that was the Nevada state police. They have the ballistics on the bullet from Coyote Springs." He turned to Catherine. "Can you follow up on that while I deal with the press?"

Erin gathered her determination. "Uh, could I go instead? I have a hunch I want to follow up on."

Brody frowned, but he motioned for her to continue. "What hunch might that be?"

She took a deep breath. "It's about Allen Cook. First of all, we've been relying on Gary Hubert for his alibi. But have we ever investigated Gary himself? We know he's not protecting Cook out of loyalty, but what about blackmail? Second, we haven't checked the security footage from the museum for signs of tampering. *Third,* Watt just told us *he* broke that back window. That means either the killer picked the lock, or he had a key."

"Or he got in some other way," said Brody. "For all we know, that door was never locked. But I see your point. We're short on leads at the moment, so go ahead. Chase your hunch. But you're still on light duty, so no heroics, understood?"

Erin nodded. "Just a fact-finding mission. Hasty Hastings is done."

"If that's true, I'm glad to hear it." Brody turned to Catherine. "Hannon, get some sleep. Good job catching Watt. You did us all proud."

When Erin slipped out the side door, the press was still swarming. She resisted the temptation to flip them the bird.

Erin ran out of gas twenty miles outside Pahrump. She was relieved to pull over, relieved to take a break. The drive had been miserable, the germ of a headache blossoming behind her eyes. The heat-hazed road was hard to look at, the blast of the AC unpleasant in her face. It hurt to listen to music, but silence made her head buzz. In the end, she found an ambient noise station, and she drove through the desert to the song of the seashore.

She pulled into a Shell station, her fuel light blinking red. It felt good to get out of the car, good to stretch her legs. The kiss of the sun eased the tension from her back. The red cleared from her vision, and she could breathe again. She closed her eyes, tipped her head back, and drank in the breeze.

A car pulled in behind her, jolting her back to reality. Erin got the pump going and watched the numbers run up. That, too, was soothing, the dizzy whiff of gasoline, the spinning white tally, fifteen bucks, twenty, thirty. Good thing Uncle Sam was footing the bill.

The whirr of a car window caught her attention and she looked up. She blinked. There, at the pump across from her, sat a cherry red Ferrari. And there, behind the wheel, sat Allen Cook. He didn't seem to have seen her. He had his radio cranked, and was nodding to the beat.

Erin's pump disengaged with a click. She reached for it, fumbled it, and it clunked on her fender. Allen looked up and their eyes locked. Neither averted their gaze, and the moment stretched and grew awkward. Then Allen grinned and sketched a salute. Before Erin could respond, he pulled out and was gone.

Erin stared after him, head spinning in circles. Allen drove a Honda. She'd seen it herself, a boxy old beige thing with dice on the mirror. He'd never mentioned a second car—but his alibi hung on his Honda parked in front of the museum.

She slid back into her car and pulled out her phone. She found the museum's address and plugged it into her GPS. She'd swing by on his shift tonight, give his cage a rattle. Eric had once told her: if you wanted to know a man, his deep-down dark self, you had to mess with him good. Tug at the strings of the world he took for granted.

She shot a quick text to Brody: *need to hit the museum, see what's going on there. Spending the night in Pahrump; will head back tomorrow. Any news on your end?*

His response came back quickly. *Understood. No news here.* A few seconds passed, then her phone binged again: *fact-finding ONLY!!! Don't forget.*

She found the exclamation points excessive, but sent back a thumbs-up. She tucked her phone away and set off in search of a motel. Her head was pounding, and she needed to lie down. She'd rest up an hour or two, and then she'd get to work, first the ballistics report, then Allen Cook.

23

Erin slept until noon and woke with the Anvil Chorus banging in her head. She gulped two cups of coffee and a handful of Advil, and the red fog rolled back enough she thought she could drive. But when she called to set up an appointment to go over the ballistics, the state cops blew her off. They'd just had a break in a case of their own, and couldn't spare anyone to meet with her.

Erin cursed, fully caffeinated and nowhere to go. The day stretched empty before her, until Allen clocked in at eight. She flopped down on her bed and dialed Catherine, wincing at the line ringing on the other end.

Catherine picked up on the third ring. "Erin. How's Pahrump?"

"Pah...rump." Erin drew out the word, her headache making her silly. "What kind of name is that? Pah-rump. Rump. *Rump.*" She reached for a pillow and tugged it over her face. "Uh, anyway, I'm good here apart from this headache. Any updates on the case?"

"Sifting through the same evidence we've been through ten times. What about that bullet? Did you get the report?"

"NSP blew me off. I'll have to try again tomorrow."

"Tomorrow?" Catherine's voice sharpened. "What are you not telling me?"

"I'm staying the night," she said. "Guess who I spied on the drive, gassing up his Ferrari?"

"Warren VanRijn."

"Good guess, but no." It hurt to grin, but Erin did it anyway. She took a deep breath to let the tension build. "Allen Cook."

"In a Ferrari?" Catherine snorted. "You sure it was him?"

"He was maybe ten feet from me. I saw him clear as day. And get this —he *saluted* me, this cheery little snap. How creepy is that?" She stretched out until her back cracked, curled her toes. "What did you make of him, when we did his interview?"

"I guess if I had to sum him up, I'd go with...frustrated." Something clunked in the background—a can, Erin thought, dropping from a vending machine. Catherine let out a strained breath. "I mean, what's he got going for him? He's got that dead end job, and not much hope of a new one. He's stuck in Pahrump, four hours' drive from his family and no friends to speak of. And even before she died, it doesn't sound like Rayna was in any hurry to reconcile. Valerie either, so—"

"So he's disgruntled, disappointed, just like our profile." Erin sat up, eyes sharpening. "I keep going back to that moment when he lost his temper. When he said, what was it? She threw their marriage away."

"Threw their *family* away." A soda can hissed, and Catherine took a slurp. "Resentment, I caught that. But did he resent Rayna, or does he resent *us?*"

"I'm thinking both," said Erin. "To be honest, I'm liking him more and more for the killer. I came out here to clear him, but his whole alibi hinges on his Honda parked at the museum. If he has that Ferrari, if he's keeping it a secret—"

"Don't get ahead of yourself," said Catherine. "Could be it's a loaner, or he gassed it up for a friend. Or his Honda's in the shop, and he thought why not treat himself?"

"Could be." Erin frowned. "Or *could* be he drove that Ferrari to Lancaster and walked in Rayna's front door. Could be he found her sleeping and smothered her in her bed."

"And drove back to Pahrump before the end of his shift? He'd be cutting it pretty fine."

"His shift's seven to seven—twelve hours, not eight."

Catherine made a *humph* sound. "Check out his story," she said. "But remember what Brody said. This is a fact-finding mission, not your excuse to play Spy vs. Spy. You see what you can see, then you come back safe."

"Sure, Mom." Erin's lips quirked up. "I'll check in when I'm done, okay?"

"Mind you don't forget." Catherine hung up the phone and Erin slid off the bed. Her headache had eased off, and her limbs buzzed with energy. She paced the room briskly, socks catching on the carpet. She pulled up the crime scenes in her mind's eye, first Rayna and Valerie's, then Jessica's, Alice's, and Sandy's. Allen Cook fit right in, she thought—standing over Rayna's body, sketching a cheeky salute. Bending over Alice to tuck her hair behind her ear. Struggling with Sandy as she fought for her life.

"Ten days," she muttered. "Ten days since Sandy." And her scene had been violent, out of control. A devolving killer was an addict like any other, needing stronger doses more often to achieve the same high.

Cook would be jonesing, itching for his next fix. He'd strike any night now. Maybe even tonight.

Erin reined herself in with an effort. If this wasn't getting ahead of herself, she didn't know what was. Cook was weird. Cook was creepy. Cook had a secret Ferrari...or maybe he didn't. Could he have left the museum without showing up on camera? And what about Gary Hubert? If Cook had snuck out, Gary had covered for him. Why had he done it? Loyalty? Fear? *Involvement?*

Her headache pulsed weakly, asserting its presence from beneath its blanket of Advil. Tendrils of pain unfurled down her neck, up the back of her skull and out across her shoulders. Erin poured some more coffee and took a long gulp. It was cold and she gagged on it, but she drained her cup anyway. A fresh pulse of energy coursed through her veins.

She needed to see the museum, that was the thing. To drop by unannounced, midway through Allen's shift. Maybe she'd even catch him sneaking out. A spark ignited in her chest, maybe excitement, maybe heartburn. She swallowed it down. Tonight was about fact-finding, and about sending a message: *we've got our eyes on you. Best mind your step.* Any plans Cook had brewing, he'd have to at least consider putting them off.

Erin slipped on her shoes and scooped up her room key. She needed a walk, a chance to think, to blow off steam. She'd need a clear head for her trip to the museum.

Erin stepped from her vehicle just shy of three AM. She'd been parked since six thirty, staking out the museum. Cook had driven up at six forty, in his boxy beige Honda. Hubert had come close behind, in a green Ford. Cook had walked the perimeter shortly after seven, and she hadn't seen either man since. She hadn't seen much of anyone, besides a stray cat.

She headed straight up the driveway, making no effort to hide her presence. Caffeine buzzed in her veins, setting her teeth on edge. Cook would be tired by now, his wits and his instincts worn down by boredom. His mental defenses would be at their nadir.

Erin counted six cameras around the perimeter of the building, two pointed at the parking lot, two at the main entrance. The one at the fire exit seemed to be broken. The one at the side exit gazed pointlessly at a Dumpster. Erin circled back to the entrance and stood under the floodlights. She stood there six minutes before anyone came.

"You there! What are you doing?"

"Gary Hubert?" Erin swallowed back acid and pulled out her badge. "Agent Erin Hastings, FBI. I talked with Director Whipley this afternoon. He gave me permission to stop by and look around."

Hubert leaned in, bug-eyed, to inspect her badge. He frowned at it for a long time, like he suspected some trickery. "I'm sorry, Agent Hastings, ma'am. It's just, our boss didn't say anything about the FBI coming by."

Because I told him not to. She plastered on a sweet smile. "It was rather last-minute. But if you'd like to call and check with him...?"

"And get him out of bed?" Hubert's bushy brows shot up in a show of comic horror. "Better not, I don't think, if I want to keep my job."

"Then, do you mind if I come in? I'll need to look around, and then I'll have some questions for you and Mr. Cook."

Hubert shifted uneasily, but he stood aside to let her in. "You can look around," he said. "But please, please don't touch anything. The alarms go off, and they take forever to reset. The noise is incredible, leaves your ears ringing for hours. One time, I was opening, and I forgot to cut the system. And *then* this first grade class showed up to see the LEGO show. They all ran for the blocks, and just—*ee-eee-eeee!*" He made a loud squealing sound. "Half of them peed their pants. A few number-two'd. The smell was unbelievable, so—"

"Got it. Watch my step."

Hubert regarded her, dull-eyed. "Should I go get Allen?"

Erin nodded. "If you would."

Hubert trotted off. Erin did a lap of the room, taking in the exhibits. They'd set up the main hall for local history month, and the displays were charming in a small-town sort of way. But the security was shoddy and easily circumvented. Only a few exhibits were locked under glass, and none of the cameras covered the walkways. The lighting was so dim she wasn't sure an intruder would show up as anything more than a shadow.

Two sets of footsteps echoed down the hall, Hubert's quick and skittering, Cook's crisp and heavy. He was marching, almost, each tap of his heel as sharp as a gunshot.

Erin turned to greet them with a cordial nod. "Evening, gentlemen. Thanks for seeing me."

"Did we have any choice?" Cook's voice was steady, but his stance was so tight it was a wonder he didn't creak. Erin ignored him. She drifted between the exhibits, too close for comfort. Hubert bleated in dismay.

"The alarm! Watch the—"

"Is this camera on?" Erin pointed overhead. "Its power light is out."

"The *bulb's* out," said Cook. "The camera works fine." His voice was unsteady. "This is harassment," he said. "First you show up at my home, no call, no warning. Then I catch you following me, lurking around the gas station. Now you're here at my workplace. What do you want?"

Hubert took a step back, but Erin stood her ground. "Mr. Cook, this is an active murder investigation. You should expect to see a lot of me until that investigation is closed. You do want justice, don't you? For your wife and daughter?"

Cook's face contorted in anger, but only for a moment. He brushed at his jacket, as though ridding it of lint. "Of course I want justice," he said. "Which is why I'm so puzzled. I'm the bereaved spouse. Shouldn't you be chasing the killer?"

"I'd love to," said Erin. "Any idea who that is?"

She thought Cook might explode. His face went brick red, an unhealthy shade.

"Agent Hastings," he said. The words came out staccato, sharp as glass. "You've interviewed me multiple times. You've verified my alibi for each...incident. You need to leave now. If I see you again, I'll file a restraining order against you. I'll sue the FBI for harassment and stalking. Is that clear, Agent Hastings?"

Erin didn't bother to conceal her amusement. "I'll make a note of that," she said. "By the way, whose car was that you were driving today?"

"If I said 'mine,' would you be jealous?"

"On my salary? Absolutely." Erin tipped him a wink and pretended to flounce off. She paused in the doorway, as though struck with a sudden thought. "Oh, while I've got you here, you didn't happen to have a key to your ex-wife's house?"

"A key? No, of course not. Why would I—"

"I just thought, if you were reconciling..." Erin gave a shrug. "Well, never mind. It doesn't matter. Rest assured, though, I *will* discover who killed your wife and daughter—and they *will* pay for their crimes. Enjoy the rest of your night."

Erin stepped out into the warm, dry night and let the door bang shut behind her. She was shaking, she realized, unsteady on her feet. The tarmac seemed to lurch and heave under her feet. Her Advil was wearing off, her headache back with a vengeance. She crumpled into her car and sat for several minutes, letting her breathing return to normal. She'd yanked Cook out of his comfort zone, but he'd unnerved her as well. He hadn't struck her as frustrated so much as *enraged,* a molten lake of fury bubbling just beneath the surface. She wouldn't have been surprised if he'd lunged at her, or even pulled a gun.

She exhaled and inhaled, held her breath for a five-count. Her heart pounded then slowed, and she pulled out into the street. Cook *could've* sneaked out, she thought, any time he wanted. The camera at the side door was pointed the wrong way. He could've cut across the parking lot brazen as he pleased, picked up his Ferrari and sailed into the night. The only problem was Hubert. Where did he fit in?

She stopped at a red light, drummed her fingers on the wheel. She couldn't prove anything, and there was the rub. She had a hell of a hunch and a handful of possibilities. Her whole case, as it stood, hung on *if* and *maybe. If* he snuck out, *if* he had that Ferrari. *If* he hated his ex-wife enough to end her life. *Maybe* he'd done it, but—

The light switched to green, and she laid on the gas. Horns blared, tires screeched, and her world exploded around her. She jerked side-ways, then back, through a fall of shattered glass. The shriek of metal filled her ears, then her vision went white. *The airbag,* she thought, and her next breath was heavy with the stench of gunpowder. Her car spun out and skidded to a stop.

Erin choked on a curse, coughed out a puff of talc. She fumbled her belt off and nearly fell out the door. Something dripped on her hand, something warm and dark. She sniffed, tasted blood, and prodded at her nose. It felt tender, not broken, and she leaned over and spat. She couldn't see the other car, but she could hear its engine ticking, the sound of rhythmic thumping as someone fought to open the door.

"Hello?" She straightened up, wincing, and stumbled around her car. Her head was a nest of bees, full of noise and chaos and bursts of clashing colors. A red Camaro had T-boned her, buried its grill in the side of her vehicle. She took a step toward it. Two of its doors burst open and three men spilled out, flushed with drink or anger. Erin stepped out of reach.

"Are you all right?" she called.

The driver turned toward her, eyes dull and bleary. "You smashed my Camaro."

Erin could smell him now, the sour reek of whiskey. She eased back another step, in case the situation took a turn.

"Hey, lady! Hey—"

Erin cut him off smoothly. "Is anybody hurt?"

"Just my baby. I think you killed her."

Erin's stomach did a nosedive, then the driver leaned over to stroke his crumpled hood. Erin squinted at him through the spots in her vision. He wasn't a young man, as she'd first assumed. He was middle-aged, graying, belly bulging over his belt. Old enough to know better than to drink and drive. His friends were milling around yelling, at her and each other. One had wandered off and sat down on the curb. Erin backed off herself, putting her car between herself and the drunks. She fumbled in her pocket and found her phone unscathed.

"What are you doing?" The driver was peering at her, thumping on her roof. She rolled her eyes, out of patience.

"What do you think?" She pried her door open, ready to slam it in his face. The driver just glowered at her as she dialed 911.

"Hi, this is Agent Erin Hastings with the FBI." She said that part loudly, a warning for anyone of a mind to start trouble. "My vehicle was struck by a speeding Camaro at the corner of West and Main. I'm counting three passengers and the driver, no obvious injuries. But we'll need you to send both police and EMS."

"Acknowledged, Agent Hastings. Help's on the way." The operator's voice was soothing, calm in a crisis. "We should have someone out to you in under ten minutes. In the meantime, are you safe?"

Erin eyed the drunks, frowning. "For the moment," she said. "But the occupants of the other vehicle are intoxicated and aggressive. I'm alone, so the faster you get here, the happier I'll be."

The police descended in five minutes flat, followed closely by an ambulance. Erin shrank from their sirens, their bright panic-lights. Her headache was gonging, every throb, every twinge ricocheting through her body. She needed an Advil, or maybe a whole bottle.

A medic bent over her, the reflective strip on his jacket glaring in her eyes. Erin offered him a tired smile.

"I'm sure this isn't what you were expecting tonight."

He shrugged. "Better than a pack of vultures robbing a convenience store."

Erin coughed laugher. "Is that something that happens?"

"It was last week." He set down his bag on the roof of her car. "I'll just look you over, then an officer'll take your statement. Sound good?"

"As good as it gets." Erin sat back and endured her second round of poking and prodding in just seventy-two hours. It didn't help that the medic looked a lot like Brody, same solid shoulders, same slicked-back hair. She hadn't screwed up this time, but when she closed her eyes, she still saw his thin lips tight with disapproval, his eyes black with reproach.

"Looks like the airbag did its job," he said. "You're going to have a nice pair of shiners, and you'll want to watch for a concussion, get yourself to a doctor if you feel dizzy or sick. But apart from that, I'd say you're in good shape."

Erin touched her face experimentally and hissed in pain. "Tell me you've got ice with you, maybe some Advil. I don't want to spend the next few weeks looking like I lost a fight."

He laughed. "Let's finish checking you over, then I'll see what I've got." A drunken shout went up from across the intersection. "*They* seem pretty lively."

"They're drunk," said Erin. "Totally wasted. They wouldn't feel a thing, even if they'd lost a limb. They'll be feeling it tomorrow though, I guarantee it."

"I'm sure you will as well." He walked her through a thorough examination, his quips and wry comments keeping her unrest at bay. Erin bore it without complaint, and as a reward, he presented her with a freshly-chilled ice pack and a handful of Advil. Her head was still spinning, but her nerves had stilled, and the ice eased her headache enough for her to power through her statement. At last, she was done, and she stood staring at her car.

"This is going to be a hassle," she said. "I was only in town for a case." She didn't address her complaint to anyone in particular, but a nearby officer looked over, concerned.

"Stranded, huh? I can give you a ride if you want, help you find a hotel."

"I've got a room already, the Sunrise Motel." She offered him a tired half-smile. "Let me grab my purse and phone, and then I'd love a ride."

She gathered her belongings and half-collapsed into the police car. Her head throbbed like a ripe abscess, hot and full of poison. She buried her face in her ice pack, crushed it to her eyes. *Cook would love this,* she thought, a little disjointedly. *Spiteful little dick.*

24

Erin scowled at her own bleary-eyed reflection. *A pair of nice shiners*—that medic hadn't been kidding. She looked like she'd dipped her face in a bucket of shoe polish. She poked at a sore spot along the bridge of her nose and frowned at the coppery trickle of blood down her throat. Last time she'd been this beat up, she'd been eight years old, fresh off a fall from the Sumners' oak tree. Eric had taken one look at her and offered to beat the tar out of whoever'd smashed her face. When Erin admitted *she* had, he'd kicked her in the shin. She'd laughed until her eyes streamed and he begged her not to cry.

A knock at the door drew her from her nostalgia. A young man stood waiting in a red AVIS shirt, a clipboard clutched to his chest. He yelped at the sight of her, and she might've been amused if her head hadn't been pounding.

"Car crash," she said. "Airbags save lives, but gentle they ain't."

"Right, I knew that. Sorry, ma'am." He nodded over his shoulder. "We have the car in the parking lot, if I can just see some ID."

Erin traded her badge for his clipboard and signed for the car. The guy gawped, eyes wide, and Erin managed a smile. "Your car's safe with me, don't worry. A drunk smashed the last one, not FBI business."

The guy's eyes just went wider. Erin filled out her paperwork and handed it back.

"Here's your keys, ma'am, and you have a great day."

"You too," she said, and retreated to the bathroom. She daubed concealer around her eyes—an exercise in futility—and slipped on her shades. That didn't help much, so she let her hair down. It hung limp, lank and greasy, and she tied it back up.

"Good as it gets," she muttered, and reached for her jacket. If she didn't get going soon, she wouldn't make it back by dark.

———

Erin nearly cried, driving up on the Lancaster town marker. Her vision had doubled somewhere around Barstow, and the sign read more like LANCASTERANCASTER. The sunset blazed behind it like a blood-drenched halo. Erin nearly plowed into it, swerving like a drunk. She zagged back just in time, a bright jolt of pain blazing down her neck. She'd puked twice in the last ten miles, once on the shoulder, once between her shoes. The AVIS guy wouldn't like that, no, not at all. She laughed, weak and watery, and clung to the wheel.

Her phone started ringing a mile from her hotel. It rang again in the parking lot, and again in the elevator. She ignored it—she had to. If she tried to speak, her whole stomach would escape. It was jumping already, twitching at the gates.

She bumbled into her room and kicked off her shoes, peeled off her pantyhose and left them by the door. Her phone buzzed again as she made for the can, and this time she squinted at it and saw it was Brody. She waited until he hung up, then fired off a text.

Just arrived @ hotel. need a shower & a nap, but will bomb toucan letter.

* be in touch later. damn it..

She dropped her phone on the bed, but it buzzed again right away. Brody's text swam and doubled, and she had to screw her face up to read it.

Calling back NOW. Pick up or else.

Her phone rang again, and Erin nearly sobbed. She hit accept mostly to shut off the ringer, but Brody was louder, his voice harsh with panic.

"What the hell, Hastings? I hear you're in an accident and you don't pick up for hours? I was about to put out a BOLO, and—Jesus. Are you okay?"

Erin crouched down, curled into a ball. "I was driving. Didn't hear you. Listen, I need a shower. I threw up on my shoes."

"You did *what?*" Brody was nearly shouting. "Don't get in the shower. Don't move an inch. I'm coming up right now. I'll be there in two minutes."

Brody hung up. Erin let her phone slip through her fingers. It felt good to be off the road, to let her eyes drift shut. Her head was rotten inside, pulsing with sickness, but here it was dark. Here, she could rest. An hour, maybe two, and she'd get it together. She'd clean herself up and feel good as new. Just first, she would sit a while, let her pain ebb away.

A thump at the door made her moan. Then Brody was yelling, demanding to be let in. Erin didn't move. He came bursting in anyway

—maybe he had a key. She opened her eyes, closed them again, and his palm was on her forehead. She burrowed into it like a kitten, eager for its coolness.

"Okay, I'm calling an ambulance." He pushed her hair off her face. "Hey, Erin? Talk to me. What's going on?"

Erin just groaned. She turned her head to the side, searching for his hand. Brody was barking orders somewhere far away, down a long tunnel on the other side of the world.

"Erin. I need you to talk to me."

She forced her eyes open. "What?"

"The ambulance is on its way. Can you tell me what year it is?"

"Twenty twenty-one." She looked down unhappily. "I barfed on my feet."

"I know. I can smell it. Who's our current President?"

"Joe Biden," she said. "Sasha thinks it's funny when she calls him 'Bidet.'"

"I laughed the first time," said Brody. "After the fiftieth, it wore kind of thin." He held up his hands. "How many fingers?"

"Six and a thumb."

"Okay. Not bad." Brody sank down beside her, seeming to deflate. "Doesn't look like you're dying, but Erin, what the hell? You drove two hundred miles like that—two hundred and fifty. What were you thinking?"

Erin sagged against him without meaning to. Her spine had gone wobbly, like a column of jelly. "Didn't mean to," she said. "Wasn't bad when I started, just a headache, sore neck. Then I was in the middle of nowhere, and it just... I was driving, and it hit me all at once." A sob rose in her throat and she choked it down hard.

"It's okay," said Brody. "Keep talking, okay? How was your trip before you got rammed?"

"I checked out the museum," she said. Her thoughts seemed to come clearer when she focused on the case. "Cook was...he gave me this look like he wanted to kill me. Creepy as hell, but the good part—" She broke off, surprised, as Brody reached for her hand. She thought he was going to hold it, but he slid his fingers up her wrist to check her pulse. Erin cleared her throat and went on. "The place wasn't secure. There's a camera at the side exit pointed straight at a Dumpster, a huge dead space he could walk through and not show up at all. Inside's just as bad, old hardware, crappy coverage. If he wanted to sneak out, he could do it no sweat."

"Good work," said Brody. "I think you're right about Cook. I think something's not—"

A siren blatted outside and cut off just as suddenly. Brody stood and peered out. "That'd be your ride."

"I've got to go like this? With my feet covered in puke?"

"You can soak 'em at the hospital. I'm sure they've got one of those...you know, like old folks have, those bubbling foot baths."

"That'd be nice," agreed Erin. "Maybe some Jell-O as well."

Brody knelt down to help her zip up her jacket. "Do you need me to ride with you? Or I can call Catherine, and she'll meet you there."

"Actually, I think I'm good. Dad should be there already, so I ought to be covered." Erin let out a weak laugh. "He's gonna love this, me and Eric both laid out, and he's all we've got."

"You know that's not true," said Brody, his voice hard and gruff. "We're here, your whole team, and we're not going anywhere."

Erin groped for a response, some appropriate expression of gratitude, but before she could find one, the paramedics had arrived. Next thing she knew, she was being wheeled out on a gurney, and all she could think was what a relief it was to stretch out—what a relief to lie back and not worry about a thing.

Erin felt better by morning, more clearheaded, more steady. She could move her head without wanting to do the technicolor yawn, and the throb behind her eyes had eased to a murmur. She ate some toast and struck out in search of coffee, but a nurse in Pokémon scrubs shooed her back to her room. She went to Eric's room instead, and perched at the end of his bed.

"Erin?" He sat up halfway, blinking in the half-dark. "Dad said you were in here, but holy shit. Your face."

Erin gave him the finger. "Yeah, love you too."

"You always could take a beating and bounce right back up." Eric propped himself on his elbow to get a better look. "All that's from a drunk driver?"

"Drunk as a skunk." Erin saw no reason to tell Eric about Watt. "Came tearing through the intersection like a bat out of hell. My airbag did its job, but no one ever tells you those things pack a *punch*."

"Everyone tells you that," said Eric. "You just don't listen."

Erin had to laugh. The motion made her ribs hurt, and she hugged her arms across her belly. Outside, the sun was rising, all shades of pink and gold. Cook was out there somewhere, maybe wrapping up his shift, maybe driving into the sunrise in a new red Ferrari. Maybe gloating over a fresh kill, leaning in to whisper secrets to carry to the grave.

"Erin? What's wrong?"

"Just watching the sun come up." Her lips twitched, not quite a smile. "Gonna be a nice day."

"Then why are you crying?"

Erin touched her cheek. Her fingers came away wet. "I'm not crying," she said. "It's the airbag, the chemicals—I keep sneezing, too. Doesn't mean I have a cold."

Eric snorted. "Defensive much?"

"I'm not crying." She dried her eyes on her sleeve and turned away from the sun. "I swear, though, this place is cursed. I come back here and suddenly—" Erin's throat closed up, and she couldn't go on. She stared at the floor, at its frustrating pattern of beige and green tiles. Her eyes swam and prickled, and she wiped them again. "It's me. I'm off my game. I keep chasing these leads, but over and over, I'm just chasing—"

"Me?"

"What? No!" She slapped him hard across his ankle, but no sooner had she done it than her anger subsided. She felt hollow instead, all cored out inside. "I don't know. Maybe a little. Maybe a lot. I keep getting this *déjà vu*—the bodies keep dropping, but what can I do? Every lead that comes in, every viable suspect, I'm off like a shot, but it's just like back then." She went to the window and pressed her forehead to the glass. "I wanted so badly for it not to be you. I wanted that so much I'd halfway convinced myself the killer was Dad. I'm doing the same thing again, pinning that killer hat on everyone I see. Can't trust myself, can't—"

"Erin."

"My instincts are all off, my judgment, my—"

"*Erin.*"

She closed her eyes. "What?"

"You didn't want it to be me. But you knew it was."

Erin's head hurt again, not the throb of her concussion, but the itchy, hot fullness of unshed tears.

"You'll know when you find him," said Eric. "You'll get that feeling again, but this time you won't want to push it away. You'll know in your guts, and you'll—"

"I think I already do." Cook was it. She could feel it, like an ache in her gut. His *why* made sense without squinting: his life had come undone and he needed someone to blame. He'd had his injury, then his long recovery—deep burns, slow to heal. Rayna would've tried at first, changed his dressings, cleaned his wounds. But Cook had a temper. She could picture it clear as day, Rayna slopping soup on his bedspread; Cook surging up, flinging the bowl at the wall. Maybe Rayna bumped his burned wrist, and maybe he couldn't help himself. Maybe he grabbed her, or even took a swing. She drifted away, maybe found someone new. Cook woke up one morning and the life he knew was gone. The more he clawed after it, the farther it drifted—his job, his friends, his dreams. His future. Rayna had been the last of it, all he had of who he'd been. Of course he blamed her. Who else could he blame, besides himself?

"You can't give up," said Eric. "Not when you've come so far, not just with this case, but...so far from where you started." He shifted, shackles rattling. "You know Dad stopped living when I went away. He hit pause in that instant before the gavel came down, before he had to admit I did what I did. We never talk about anything that happened after high school. I'll try sometimes, but it's like he doesn't hear me. But you, you kept going. You built this whole life. Erin, are you listening?"

She nodded. "I'm listening, but you're wrong. I haven't moved on." Her voice dropped to a whisper. "I'm still trying to save Althea Morris."

Eric made a soft sound, a sad flat-tire hiss. Erin opened her eyes. The sun hung over the horizon, bathing the parking lot in orange. The sky overhead was a flat brushed-steel gray. Cook would be home by now, maybe making dinner. He'd eat it in his living room, in front of the TV. He'd follow his own story like a favorite soap. She wondered how he liked being cast as the Crusader. She guessed he liked it just fine.

"I should get back to my room," she said. "Doc says I can go today, if I can walk a straight line."

"Okay," said Eric. "Uh, do you want a hug before you go?"

Erin's breath caught in her throat. Eric looked like he could use a hug, still pale from his surgery, his hair tangled on the pillow. She wanted to go to him, but she was still thinking of Althea. Of all six of his victims, bleeding out in the dark. No one had held them through their final, awful moments. She touched her shoulder and grimaced.

"My seat belt—I don't think—"

"It's okay. Next time, right?"

"Sure. Next time." She managed a sick smile. She wasn't sure she'd ever hug her brother again.

Erin made it back to her hotel room just before noon. She drew a hot bath and sank in to her chin, moaning as a million knots loosened and unspooled. Her eyelids went heavy and she let herself drift, half dreaming in the steam. In her dreams, Cook was running, but she outpaced him in a flash. He wept as she cuffed him, and she laughed with delight.

She woke to her phone buzzing on the edge of the tub. Her finger squished when she pushed ACCEPT, all pruney and fat.

"Hastings," she croaked.

Randy's voice came through crackly and laced with concern. "Erin, are you all right? You sound, I don't know..."

"Like death warmed over?" She coughed. "I took a nasty hit, but my headache's mostly gone. Doc said take it easy, but I'm good to go." She rubbed at her face. "Where are you calling from? You're all full of static."

Randy cleared his throat. "Brody called me last night. He told me you were assaulted in the field. And then you had an accident, on top of that?" He clucked his tongue. "I want you back in Atlanta for a full medical workup. Assault's a serious thing, not just for your body, but your mental health. You need time to process, to—"

Erin jerked upright, water sloshing over the tub. "What are you saying? You're kicking me off the case?"

"I'm not kicking you anywhere. I'm looking out for your health."

"You can't." Erin shivered all over, sick to her bones. "I can't leave like this. We're close—I can feel it. I can't walk away."

"You can and you will." Randy's response was calm, but his tone brooked no argument. "I'm flying in right now to take over the case. From what I've seen, you've done a great job. You've dug up all the pieces, and all that's left for me is to put them together. And *you* need to get healthy, to fight another day."

Erin's throat had closed up again. She made a strained sound, but no words came out.

"I've got to go," said Randy. "I'm at the airport, about to head through security. You rest up now, and we'll talk when I get there."

Erin just grunted. Her bath had gone cold and she wanted to cry.

"Okay, Erin. Be good. See you in a few hours."

Randy hung up and she dragged herself from the tub. Gooseflesh pricked down her arms and she reached for a towel. She had time still, she thought, before she was officially off the case. Randy's flight would be five hours, then an hour's drive from LAX. She could use that time—but how?

She dressed quickly in sweats and a pair of fuzzy slippers. "I'm Cook," she said to no one in particular. "I get up in the morning, and I...no, I get up at night. I get up and it's twilight going on dark. I nuke a burrito and head off to work." She paced up and down, not seeing her own room but the children's museum, its bleak little exhibits, its dingy green halls. "I'm bored," she said. "This job is beneath me. Feels like a trap. Night after night, it's always the same, dark and depressing, nothing to do. Nothing but shoot the breeze with a guy who, uh..."

Erin stopped, scratched her head. What *would* Cook make of someone like Gary Hubert? Gary seemed pleasant enough, not the sharpest knife in the box. Cook might find him annoying, or hardly notice him at all. Or he might see him as a patsy, someone he could use. Cook had it in him, that manipulative streak. He'd cried convincingly for Erin, at their first interview.

"I'm bored," she said slowly. "I'm bored and I'm angry, and I'm going nowhere. I want...I want what I had, but I want more than that. I want what I'm *owed*. A reward for all I've been through." She thought of the Ferrari, gleaming bright red. It didn't belong to Cook, that much was clear. It didn't belong to Hubert, or anyone else he'd know. A rental, then, but...

"An escape?" Erin scuffed at the carpet, at a small heart-shaped stain. "I want to feel powerful. I want to feel like someone else. I want to be *seen*—" She made an *oh* sound. That was it. Cook had wanted respect. He'd wanted to be treated like someone who drove a Ferrari, so he'd rented one, and that's when he'd realized he could slip behind the wheel and be someone else—be in two places at once, even, Cook with his Honda, the Crusader in his chariot.

"I'm taking my power back," she whispered. "Rayna took it from me, so I took it back. And it felt so good I took it back again. Only question is, where does Gary fit in? What did I tell him, what'd I do to him, to make him go along?"

No answer presented itself, so Erin moved on. "Rayna, poor Rayna. She threw it all away. Threw *me* away like a dirty old shoe." Erin's movements grew jerky. She paced back and forth, quick stomping strides. She let her rage build, *Cook's* rage, and where had it led him? "Bitch didn't need me, so I'm out on my ass. But I showed her. I showed her. She deserved what she got. That's it, isn't it? Punishment? But who deserves it? How to choose?"

Alice had worked with Rayna, and Sandy as well. Not Jessica, though. Jessica didn't work. Erin flopped down on her bed and reached for her laptop. Finding divorced women was easy: those records were public. There had to be something else, some trigger, some trait he couldn't resist.

Erin's phone buzzed again, and she reached for it without thinking.

"Hastings, go ahead."

"Hey, Erin. It's Brody. You're sounding better."

"I'm feeling better. Had a bath." She rolled onto her back. Did Brody know yet, she'd been kicked off the case? "We should check into those cars," she said. "The ones Cook's been driving."

"Already on it," said Brody. "At least, Sasha is. And I've got a couple of state cops canvassing the rental agencies. Showing his face around in case he used a fake name."

"Good." She stretched out, wiggled her toes. "I was about to dive back into the victims. I want to know how he's picking them, see if I can work out who's next."

"Should you really be reading?" Brody's tone was sharp. "You had a concussion. You need to rest your brain."

"What'd you do, Google it?"

"What if I did?" He made an exasperated sound. "You need to take care of yourself. Catherine says the same. She says to tell you, drink water, don't load up on Coke."

"Yeah, well, tell her *pthbbt* from me." Erin turned back to her screen. "Seriously, though, don't worry. I'll lie down right away if my headache comes back." Her headache was already back, but so far, it was bearable, just a faint hint of pressure at the backs of her eyes. She went to the window and lowered the shades all the way.

"Hey, Brody?"

"Yeah?"

"Did you talk to Randy?"

"He called a couple of hours ago. He's headed our way." Brody let out a groan. "Listen, I had to tell him about your accident and your assault. He's going to want to bench you, so don't give him a reason. Sit tight, rest up, and remember I'm on your side."

Erin smiled. Randy hadn't told Brody she was off the case. That meant it wasn't a done deal, or at least, she hoped it did. If she could present him with new intel, he might reconsider. He might see he needed her right where she was.

"I should get back to work," she said. "Let me know if you find anything."

"Same goes for you." Brody hung up. Erin stretched out on her belly and pulled her laptop toward her, and that was when it hit her: *Cook had already picked his next victim.* He'd been driving his cover car when she'd encountered him at the gas station. He'd have made his move that night, if not for Erin's presence.

She grabbed for her phone, a feverish energy coursing through her veins. She had to nail Cook, and she had to nail him *now.*

25

Erin dove down the rabbit hole, into Cook's victims' lives and into his head.

She started with Jessica VanRijn, with her social media. Jessica had been active, but never outspoken. Her posts had been sweet and cute, cupcakes and baking memes and fundraising links for her local cat rescue. She'd never mentioned her divorce, at least not directly. She'd described moving back home with her parents, the bittersweet pleasure of reconnecting with old friends. Where Warren was concerned, she'd taken the high road, keeping her dirty laundry firmly under wraps.

Alice was brassy, unrepentantly political, but her divorce was well behind her, and she and her husband had made peace. They'd even become friends, it seemed, in the past year. They tagged each other on Facebook, shared pictures of their kids—Christmas with Dad, hiking with Mom. He'd retweeted a video she'd posted just a day before she died, a man leaf blowing a crocodile off his front lawn. He'd added a comment—*LOL, that blows.* Erin wondered if that was the last thing he'd ever said to her.

Alice's last Facebook post was sad in its own way, a photo of Venice tagged *ha, someday.* Her friends had filled the comments with heartfelt tributes. Erin had read them before, but this time, at the bottom, she spotted something new. Her neighbor had added two lines and a link: *miss u so much sweetheart. BwT posted ur interview and Ive watched it 50 times.*

Erin clicked the link. *BwT* proved to be *Breakfast with Tiffany,* a local morning show. They'd posted an in memoriam for Alice, complete with an interview she'd done a week before she died. Erin watched without much interest as Alice showed off her winning entry in the Victorville Birding Society's annual photo contest. Tiffany seemed bored as well, rattling through the standard questions.

"And how long have you been a shutterbug? Going by this masterpiece, I'd guess all your life?"

The studio audience tittered. Alice shook her head.

"Actually, I took my first photo last Christmas. I mean, I'd done selfies, shots of the kids, but my first *photo*-photo, it's a whole story to itself. I'd just come out of a relationship—a fifteen-year marriage—and okay, I'll admit it. Honestly, I was lost. It had come to a point, we were holding each other back, but once I was free I was like...what now? I got stuck on 'what now,' just spinning my wheels all that first year apart, then my daughters presented me with this fantastic used Nikon. I marched straight to the window and snapped a cardinal at the feeder, and the rest—"

Erin scrolled back and hit PLAY again. Alice's smiling face filled the screen. "We were holding each other back," she said. "But once I was free—"

Free. Erin frowned. Cook wouldn't have liked that, but would he have seen it? Was he the type to watch breakfast TV? She checked the show's air time—weekdays at eight, right around the time Cook might be sitting down to dinner.

"Is that where you saw her? Celebrating her win?" Erin's brow furrowed. Sandy had been on TV right before she'd died. Erin searched for her interview and found it on YouTube. Her chest hurt at the sight of Sandy's obvious fear, the way she gaped into the camera with her hands clasped to her chest.

"First, they were saying he's stalking divorcées. Now it's Highgate employees, and look at me. I'm both!" She exhaled nervous laughter and Erin tasted bile. Had Cook heard that laughter and taken it for mocking? Had Sandy sealed her fate with a thirty-second spot?

She clicked Sandy's spot away and flipped back to Jessica. Jessica hadn't been on TV—or had she? Erin picked up her phone and dialed Sasha.

"Lancaster morgue," said Sasha. "You stab 'em, we slab 'em."

Erin rolled her eyes. "One day you'll do that and it'll be Randy. Or Hannady."

"Calling from your phone?"

"You never know." Erin straightened up. "Anyway, do you know if Jessica VanRijn was on TV at all, just before she died?"

"No, but give me an hour and I can find out."

"Thanks, Sasha. Appreciate it." Erin hung up and fell back on her bed. Her headache was back in force, a warm, diseased pressure inside her skull. Like an overripe watermelon, ready to split. She closed her eyes for a moment, woke to her phone burring in her ear.

"Sasha?"

"Guess again."

"Brody. What's happening?"

"Not much. Stuck in traffic." A horn honked and he cursed. "I'm headed up to Pahrump to coordinate surveillance on Cook. Sasha's tracked down his rentals, and you're right. He's picked up a luxury car one to two days before each of our murders. Not only that, but he's just signed out a Lambo. We're thinking he'll strike tonight, tomorrow at the latest."

Erin's scalp crawled, an unpleasant sensation like fingers in her hair. "What's the plan?"

"Give him some rope and hope he hangs himself." Brody's tone was grim. "It's not enough just to catch him stepping out on the job. That busts his alibi, but it doesn't nail him for murder. We need to nab him red-handed, or as close as we can without letting him near a victim."

"So you'll follow him when he slips out, see where he goes?"

"It's not perfect, I know. But we catch him mid-break-in, that'll give us enough to hold him. Buy us time to build our case." Brody made a frustrated sound. "It'd be easier if we knew how he was picking his victims. If we knew where he'd strike next, we could get there first."

"I'm working on that," said Erin. "Alice and Sandy were both on TV. I've got Sasha checking if Jessica fits the pattern."

"Let me know if she does," said Brody. "And don't push yourself. Get Catherine to help you. You scared the pants off me last night."

Erin snorted at the notion of a frightened, pantsless Brody. "Keep your pants on," she said. "I'm all good here."

The air hung hot and still in the cramped little kitchen. Outside, the sky was bright, the sun high overhead. Hours lay between him and the ecstasy of the kill, sluggish, slow-moving hours. Time drowned in honey. His fingers twitched and he drummed them on the counter. He'd choke this one out with her book, he thought. Make her eat her words, page after page until her eyes bugged out of her head. *Untying the Knot: Life After Divorce*—he'd show her there was none, not for her. Not for anyone.

He sank down at the table. He couldn't breathe, himself. He'd let it build up too long, the anticipation, the tension. That awful, pent-up feeling squeezing the air from his chest.

The Crusader closed his eyes. It'd been too long since his last one. Too long since he'd *breathed.* He inhaled through his nose and fancied he could smell her, the tang of her fear. The hot, meaty rust stink of her arterial spray. Sandy'd been good for him, a fresh breeze in summer. He'd felt his lungs open as he opened her throat. It was like he drew life from them, sucked up their last breaths and made them his own. If he stopped now, he'd die. Suffocate and die.

He flipped on the TV. Channel 5 was running a profile on Agent Erin Hastings, but most of the commentary was really about her brother. He muted the sound and watched a young Erin emerge from the Lancaster courthouse, her weird, cold green eyes revealing nothing at all. Then she was older, hair cropped to her chin, marching some perp down a wide flight of stairs. She paused at the bottom and locked eyes with the camera. The Crusader reached out, trailed his fingers down the screen. Sooner or later, he'd have to deal with her as well. But not tonight. Tonight, he'd be safe.

He grabbed his trash from under the sink and walked it out to the garage. The van he'd spotted an hour ago was still parked down the street—*phone company, my ass.* Who still kept a landline in this day and age?

"Think you're so clever," he muttered. "I got you right where I want you." After tonight, they'd have to move on. *Slink away*, even, covered in shame. Sleight of hand, it was called. Make the suckers look one way, slip off in another. If he played his cards right, they'd be chasing shadows for weeks.

He dumped his trash in the big can and trudged back inside. Erin was gone from the TV, and that was a relief. He needed to focus on tonight's festivities. Tonight, his crusade would kick into high gear. Tonight was his mission statement, the night he'd show the world what lay in store. He'd write his manifesto in blood: *take what's not yours to take, get what you deserve.*

Women took and took. That was their nature. They took a man's love, his protection, his money. They took these things as their due, and that was fine. Giving was men's nature, the other side of the coin. Men gave, women took—only some women, the wicked ones, didn't know when to stop. They lapped up a man's love, then they went for his dreams. They took his home and his future, his family, his pride, and just when he thought they were done, they snatched his dignity and ran.

"I'm taking it back," he said. "After tonight, they'll see. They'll understand."

The brave ones would join him—men of integrity, with the courage of their convictions. They'd take back what was stolen, take back their lives. They'd know what he knew, how it felt to reclaim what was rightfully theirs. How it felt to be downtrodden, and to rise again.

"Watch me, Erin," said the Crusader. "Watch and learn."

26

Erin's headache was a living thing, snorting and stomping in the dark behind her eyes. She ignored it until she couldn't, then she marched down the hall and filled a Ziploc bag with ice. She perched it on her head like a fat, sloppy beanie, and she could only imagine what Brody'd say to that. *I told you, don't push yourself. Lie down. Close your eyes.*

"Time's running out," she said. Already, the sun was setting. Cook would be up by now, moving about his lair. Showering, maybe, or rustling up some breakfast.

Erin's phone was ringing when she got back to her room. She dove for it, anticipating an update from Sasha, but the sight of Randy's name took the wind from her sails.

"Hastings, go ahead."

"Where were you?" Randy's voice was sharp. "I've been calling and calling and getting your voicemail."

Erin sat down heavily, holding her icepack to her head. "Believe it or not, I'm human. I have human needs. Like, when I drink water all day—"

"Okay."

"I can go into detail if you're curious."

"*Okay*, Agent Hastings. I get the idea." Randy hissed through his teeth. He was still in the airport. Erin could tell by the hum of background chatter, the gentle robot voice announcing upcoming flights. "Listen, I'm at McCarran. I'd hoped to see you in person, but for obvious reasons, I'm headed straight for Pahrump. Your flight back leaves—"

"Wait." Erin cut in, panic rising in her chest. "I know what we talked about, but I did a deep dive on our victims. I think I've found how he's picking them, and I have a couple of names—"

"See, this is what I'm talking about." A door slammed in the background, and Erin heard a car start. Randy made a huffing sound. "I told you, you're off the case, and what do you do? You jump straight back in, classic Hasty Hastings."

"But—"

"Sasha told me all about it, and you know what I thought? I thought, *why'd she do all that legwork when Sasha could've done it in half the time?* And you know why I think? Because you're not thinking straight. Because I told you to rest and you didn't listen, and you're making yourself sick all over again. Stand down, Agent Hastings. I'm giving you an order."

"But I've got—"

"You've got a seat on the redeye back to Atlanta," snapped Randy. "Catherine'll drive you when it's time to go. Until then, I want you resting, in bed, no screens. Do you think you can do that, or do I need to send an officer to babysit your ass?"

Erin sagged where she sat. She'd never heard Randy yell before—and he wasn't *quite* yelling now—but he'd said *ass*, and since when did Randy use words like *ass*? She swallowed, tasted acid. "Don't send anyone," she said. "I'm going to bed."

"Right now. No detours."

"No detours," agreed Erin. She hung up, pulled the covers over her, and immediately dialed Sasha. Sasha picked up on the first ring, popped her gum in Erin's ear.

"I'm not supposed to talk to you," she said. "What do you want?"

"To talk to you, obviously. You going to rat me out?"

"I haven't decided yet," said Sasha. "Depends what you've got."

Erin sat up, scowling. "What's that supposed to mean?"

"It means you were right. Check your tablet. I'll wait."

Erin set her phone down and reached for her tablet. Sasha had sent her a video clip, just thirty seconds long. Erin pushed PLAY and a little girl filled her screen, maybe five years old and cute as a button. The girl stretched tall, took a deep breath, and launched into a series of cartwheels and flips, coming to a neat stop at the end of the mat. She flashed a bright smile, charmingly gap-toothed, and the camera cut to a backstage shot—the same girl in her locker room, a shiny gold medal hung around her neck. A reporter crouched next to her, her microphone stamped with the Channel 5 logo.

"That was quite a performance! Your mom must be proud."

The little girl glanced over her shoulder. "That's not my mom," she said. "That's my aunt Jessie. She's getting a divorce."

The reporter's brows shot up. The camera cut to a thunderstruck Jessica VanRijn, who covered her embarrassment with a gracious smile.

"I guess the cat's out of the bag," she said. "But, hey, silver lining: now I have all this time to spend with Katie."

The little girl beamed, delighted. The video cut out. Erin grabbed her phone.

"Sasha? Still there?"

"Yeah. What do you think?"

"How did you find that? She was on there two seconds, blink and you'd miss her."

"I made a few calls," said Sasha. "But that's got to be it, right? He's finding them on TV. Well, apart from Rayna, but if it's Cook, that makes sense."

"They all admitted they were divorced," said Erin. "And they all made it sound...well, not *good*, exactly, but like it might not be the worst thing in the world. Sandy did that laugh. Alice said she was free."

"Poor Jessica, though. She'd never have said anything, if not for that kid."

"Poor kid, as well. It'll all come out when we catch him, how he picked his marks. Imagine growing up knowing you got your auntie killed."

Sasha made a strangled sound. "I'd rather not," she said. "And as for you—well, I ought to hang up on you. But you've been looking ahead, right? To where he'll strike next?"

"*Yes*." Erin leaned back on her pillows, relief washing over her. "I'm worried about that anchor from Channel 5. She said something this morning, like *if he's after divorcées, who's not in trouble?* And then she said—"

"*My whole book club's divorced,*" said Sasha. "And something about Rottweilers—if he hits her place, he'll be a chew toy. See, we're tripping over each other already. We need to coordinate, split up the load. I'll take Nevada news, you take California stations that broadcast in Pahrump. And check out that morning show, *Breakfast with Tiffany.* Call me if you catch anything, and I'll pass it on."

"Thanks, Sasha." Erin hung up, already diving for her laptop. Her spine tingled, not with dread, but with anticipation. She had him—she could feel it. She'd cracked his code. She'd been two steps behind him, but now she'd get ahead. If Cook slipped the net—if he wasn't Cook at all—she'd still be there waiting when he reared his ugly head.

The Crusader had claimed his last victim. She'd make sure of that if it was the last thing she did.

27

Brody called just after seven, startling Erin from her work.

"I heard what happened," he said. "I want you to know it wasn't my decision."

"But how hard did you fight it?" Erin couldn't hide her resentment. Brody knew as well as she did, it was all about the collar. All about *closure*—that half-drunk relief, coming down from the hunt. That sharp taste of victory, of justice done.

"I fought when I could," he said. "When it was reasonable to do so. But, Erin, you got hurt, and you didn't even slow down. I'm not going to lecture you, but—"

"Okay, I get it." Erin rubbed her aching temples. She'd heard it all from Randy. She didn't need Brody's recap. "Sasha got hold of you, right? About his next victims?"

"She passed on a few names," said Brody. "We've got uniforms on their streets in case Cook's not our man. But I have a good feeling about this one. I think you—hold on."

Erin held on. Brody's radio crackled and muttered, too low to hear. Moments later he was back, voice laced with frustration.

"They thought they had him coming out of the museum, but it was just the janitor. Can't see anything in this rain." Brody's radio squawked and he let out a curse.

"When'd it start raining?"

"Right after we got here. What are the odds? I didn't think it rained here, but it's coming down cats and dogs."

"Climate change, right?" Erin stood up and stretched. Her joints crackled like Rice Krispies. "Where are you anyway? Watching the Lambo?"

"Ready to roll when he makes his move." Brody's radio pipped again. "Speaking of which, I'd better let you go. Rest up, though, okay? And don't worry. We've got this."

"Ten-four," said Erin, but her attention had already drifted back to her laptop, and yet another episode of *Breakfast with Tiffany*.

———

He accelerated down the highway, into the storm. The rain drummed on his windshield, fat, oily drops that spattered like grease. Thunderheads hung like steel wool along the horizon, flicking forked tongues of lightning at the earth below. The road stretched ahead, black and deserted. No taillights pierced the gloom, and when he checked his rearview mirror, he found it clear of travelers.

His hands tingled on the wheel. He breathed deep and smelled ozone, and his arms prickled with gooseflesh. His impatience had reached a bursting point and blossomed into something new, anticipation so piquant he could taste it on his tongue. The mad risk he'd taken had only made it better: the heart-pounding terror of nearly being discovered; the high-flying thrill of realizing he hadn't. He'd known he could do it, but knowing and doing were two different things. He wondered if Agent Hastings had been there, if he'd slipped by her too.

The sky lit up with sheet lighting, noon-bright then dark again. The Crusader counted to three, then the thunder rolled in. He turned the radio up to drown out the storm. Cheerful Christmas music tinkled from the speakers, silver bells and fluting voices. The Crusader sang along, grinning ear to ear.

"Six knives a-flaying! Five faithless wives! Four dirty birds, three wronged men. Two dead doves, and a partridge in a pear tree." He drew his nail across his throat and laughed out loud. When he squeezed the wheel, he could almost imagine a slim, yielding throat. When he breathed in the storm, he fancied he smelled fear. His pulse pounded so hard he felt it behind his eyes, the sky throbbing dark then bright with the beating of his heart.

He'd take his time with this one, he decided. Her house lay down a private lane, set back from the road. She could scream, she could struggle, but no one would hear. He wanted her to understand before he let her go. He wanted her to see him, and he wanted her to repent.

"Make you grovel," he muttered, hardly aware he'd spoken aloud. "Make you *crawl*. Make you piss down your leg, and the last thing you see will be—"

He grinned wider than ever, his own ghostly reflection grinning back at him from the windshield.

———

"They got him," said Sasha.

Erin jerked upright. She banged her elbow on the headboard and shouted in pain.

"Scream in my ear much? What's the matter with you?"

"Funnybone," groaned Erin. She rubbed at her elbow, kneading out pins and needles. "What was that, though? They've arrested Cook?"

"Not arrested him," said Sasha. "But he's on the move. He's in the Lambo, headed east toward Vegas. Here, check your tablet. I sent the GPS feed."

Erin thumbed on her tablet and tapped on the link. A map of Nevada popped up, five dots inching east. One had pulled a couple of miles ahead of the rest. Erin rolled her eyes. "Is that Brody speeding ahead?"

"Nope. That one's Cook. They stuck a tracker on that Lambo the first chance they got."

Erin nodded. She should've guessed. They'd hang back until Cook hit Vegas, let him think he'd got out clean. Then they'd merge in with traffic and nose up on his tail.

"He's going for that news anchor," said Sasha, almost dreamily. "The one with the dogs. I hope they take a bite out of him before Brody swoops in."

Erin smiled at the thought, Cook yipping and dancing, a pack of hungry Rottweilers nipping at his ass. She'd pay to see that—and maybe she *would* get to see it on Brody's body cam. Erin craned back to look over her shoulder. The clock on the nightstand read ten PM. Whatever happened, it would happen by midnight.

"My stomach's in knots," she said. "I can't take this, just watching. It's like—I feel like a mom dropping her kids off at school. Anything could happen, a riot, a shooter, and I can't do jack. The whole school could burn down while I'm...at the spa?"

"What kind of school are you sending your kids to?" Sasha laughed, then swore. "Crap, I got company. Call you in a bit."

Erin hunched over her tablet, watching the GPS blips inch their way across Nevada. The copper taste of adrenaline sat heavy on her tongue. When she touched her tablet, she left humid prints. She rose from the bed, breath hot in her lungs. Her headache was gone, her vision bright and vivid. The hunt had started without her, but her guts didn't know it, or the muscles in her jaw. She paced, ground her teeth, a predator on a leash.

Brody slid into traffic three cars behind Cook and one lane to the right. Cook was bopping to the radio, nodding his head to some catchy beat. Every so often, he'd tap his fingers on the wheel. He hadn't looked back once, hadn't shown the slightest hint of concern. Brody had to admire his confidence—like he hadn't even considered the possibility of pursuit.

"Car two moving ahead," said Wells, from his radio. "Gonna get out in front of him in case he makes a break."

"I don't think he's seen us," said Brody. "But go ahead." He blinked uncomfortably, squinting against the rude Vegas glare. Cook swung onto the Strip, straight into the dazzle, and a thought crossed Brody's mind—*what if it's gambling? What if that's his big secret? If he drives out and hits the tables, and he and Hubert split his wins?* The idea seemed plausible, maybe more so than murder. Cook was a loser in need of a win. Gambling fit with the flashy cars, even his mood swings. He'd win a few hands and feel on top of the world, lose a week's pay and want to lash out.

Cook sat up straighter, stopped nodding to the beat. Brody frowned. Something felt off with him, the way he held himself, the way he gripped the wheel. He cruised past the Bellagio fountains without turning to look, across West Flamingo and past the Cromwell. He was leaning forward now, straining over the wheel, searching for something, or maybe just tense.

When Cook made his break, it happened so suddenly Brody almost missed it. He slowed at a yellow and then hit the gas, squirting through the intersection as the light turned red. Brody came to a squealing stop, nearly rear-ending the car ahead of him. Horns blared at his back. Cook swerved off the Strip without slowing or flashing. Brody's radio squawked.

"Damn. Where's he going? I left him behind."

"I don't know, but don't spook him. Circle the block." Brody eyed his GPS. Cook's blip slowed, hung another right, and rolled to a stop.

"He's stopped down the alley," said Wells. "Behind, uh...Wonderful Sushi Burrito?"

Brody grimaced at the idea of a burrito stuffed with sushi. The light turned green and he sped after Cook, down a wide, gaudy street bustling with tourists. He slowed at the sight of a huge neon burrito, a flashing pink fish poking out of one end.

"Wells, what's your twenty?"

"Coming up on the alley from the far end."

"Okay, but don't let him see you. You got a visual?"

"Not yet," said Wells. Brody swung inward, as though searching for a parking space. He crept past the alley, catching sight of the Lambo just as his radio exploded with profanity. He loosed a quiet curse, himself.

"You seeing what I'm seeing?"

Wells made a disgusted sound. "Door swinging open, driver fled the scene?"

"He can't have gone far," said Brody. "Car three, sweep the neighborhood. Wells, watch his vehicle. Car four, you're with me. We'll canvass on foot."

Brody's radio crackled with rapid-fire acknowledgments. He stepped out of his car into a welter of sounds and smells—the crude shouts of porn slappers, the aquarium reek of Wonderful Sushi Burrito. A wave of tourists surged past him, all noise and polyester. Someone trod on his foot and kept walking, never glancing back.

"I hate Vegas," he said, and plowed into the crowd.

28

Erin jumped when her phone rang. The room did a sick spin, her screen dipping one way while the walls dipped the other. She clutched her head with one hand, grabbed the phone with the other. Her own voice seemed distant as she barked a hello.

"Cook's slipped his tail in Vegas," said Randy, without preamble. "You're on with the whole team."

Erin blinked. "What?"

"Don't play with me, Erin. Sasha's told me everything. We'll get into your insubordination later, but right now, what I need to know is where he might've gone. How are we doing on potential victims?"

Erin swallowed, dry-mouthed. Her eyes wouldn't focus through the spots dotting her vision. She'd spent the last hour watching bad break- fast TV, mostly to distract herself from the chase playing out without her. Her headache had snuck up on her, pressure growing to pain.

"I haven't got anything," she said. "At least, no more than I had four hours ago."

Brody cursed down the line, startling a laugh from Sasha. Randy cleared his throat.

"Yes, it's a mess," he said. "But I need clear heads at the table. Brody, you start us off. How did this happen?"

"He ditched his car down an alley and went up in smoke." He cursed again, barely audible this time. "I'd have sworn I had him ducking into a Starbucks. But it was just some security guard, some—"

"Start at the beginning," said Randy. "From the museum."

Brody huffed down the line, his angry grunt half-drowned in the clamor of the Strip. Erin lay back and closed her eyes. Her head felt full of cotton, itchy and fat. Her focus kept slipping, chasing off like a kitten in pursuit of butterflies. Her new shirt was chafing her, tight under the arms. The bloom of headlights from the street flashed red through her eyelids.

"—thought he was being clever," Brody was saying. "He parked the Lamborghini on the street, five blocks from the museum. There's this big open area heading out of town, a parking lot on one side, empty lots on the other. I think he thought he'd spot us if we set up surveillance. But we had our tracker, so—"

"Got it," said Randy. "You parked a few blocks away. I've got your game plan right here. Who was on the museum?"

"That was the state cops," said Brody. "They've got Cook entering the museum at quarter to seven, Hubert at ten to. The janitor exited at twenty past. They thought *he* was Cook at first, but—"

"Are they sure he wasn't?" Erin blurted her question without thinking, and immediately felt stupid. Brody laughed without humor.

"Unless our man grew a foot and went gray overnight." A door slammed in the background and the sounds of Vegas cut out. "Anyway, Cook exited the museum some time before nine thirty. The cops missed his exit, but the Lambo started moving at nine thirty two."

"Wait—no one saw him leave?" Erin sat up too fast and nearly screamed from the bolt of pain through her temple. She clutched her phone like a lifeline, breathed through the spasm. Brody was saying something, too garbled to hear. "Did *you* see him?" she interrupted. "Did you see his face?"

"What?" Brody was pacing, boots crunching in gravel. "I'm sure I did. I must have. I was three cars behind him all the way up the Strip. You saw him, right, Wells?"

"I saw a man matching his description," said Wells. "Average build, dark hair, Caucasian. But if you asked me to swear to it—I don't know. I cruised by him doing twenty. I never turned to look."

"It *was* him," said Brody. "It had to be. The cops checked the perimeter when the Lambo started moving. They found an open window at the back of the museum. Cook got out that way while their eyes were on the exits."

"We know *how* he got out," said Randy. "But can anyone swear to when?"

No one spoke. Brody made a sound, half growl, half exhale. Erin listened to his footfalls, to the distant wail of sirens. Someone opened a soda with a fizzy hiss.

"All right," said Randy. "Sasha, pull surveillance from every camera you can get—every camera pointed at the museum between six thirty and ten. Brody and Wells, keep up with your search. Erin and Catherine—Catherine, are you on?"

"I'm on," said Catherine.

"You two keep going on victims. Until we know when he walked out, we need to assume Cook could be anywhere. You two are our last, best chance to get out ahead of him."

Catherine said something, but Erin didn't hear her. Her blood was up, rushing, rapids in her ears. She dropped her phone on the bedspread and reached for her laptop.

"You and me, Cook," she whispered. "Where did you go?"

Cook had basic cable, a hundred and sixty channels, plus Hulu Live. That made thirty-eight local newscasts playing over his dinner hour, three Nevada morning shows and four more from California. Then there were national shows filmed in LA, which brought up the total to —Erin had lost count. She'd collected two more possibles, Sharon Rice from Palmdale and Amy Marsh from Santa Clarita. But Sharon was in Canada visiting her mom. Amy was a firefighter, on shift at the station.

Erin glanced at the clock. Midnight had come and gone, crawling into the wee hours. Cook could be anywhere—except he couldn't, not really. He'd be in the one place his sickness had led him. With the one victim he couldn't resist. Someone worth an escape worthy of Houdini. Someone so tempting he couldn't wait one more night.

She cued up the next video, a dismal local talk show mostly devoted to petty crime. A veteran had been victimized by canine porch pirates, possibly trained by his spiteful upstairs neighbor. A shopkeeper had painted over the graffiti on her Dumpster only to discover a fresh crop the next morning. Erin's head throbbed and sang. When her phone blared at her elbow, it was almost a relief.

"Hastings, what's up?"

"Bad news," said Sasha. "Cook snuck out with the janitor, just like you thought."

Erin let her head drop, *thump* on the keyboard. "Seriously? How'd he do it?"

"The janitor stopped by the shed to drop off his cart. When he opened the door, all these tin cans fell out. Everyone looked over and Cook took off running." Sasha laughed dryly. "It was pretty slick, actually. He jumped out the window and ran across the lot. He was in view two seconds, then he ducked behind the trees. They'd only have caught him if they'd known where to look."

"Tin cans," echoed Erin. "Why would he...?"

"We think Cook threw them in there before we arrived. Probably around the same time he parked the Lambo."

"I hate this guy," said Erin. "Okay. I'd better get back to my—"

"Oh, that's not all." Sasha was moving, heels clicking on the tile. "The cops just grabbed Hubert. Randy's questioning him right now."

Erin rubbed her eyes. "Gary Hubert?"

"I think you'd better hear this. Check your tablet."

Erin powered up her tablet, wincing at the glare. A grainy feed popped up, stamped INTERROGATION ROOM 2. Hubert was hunched in the same chair Ben Witt had occupied just days before. He didn't look any happier to be there, throat working furiously as he gulped his coffee.

"He came in half asleep," said Sasha. "Randy's thinking Cook drugged him, but—"

"I don't *know*," said Hubert, his voice a high whine. "I only dozed off two minutes. He was there before that. Whoever you saw—"

"This isn't Allen Cook?" Randy held up his phone. Erin couldn't see what was on it, but Hubert's mouth turned down.

"I mean, that looks like him, but..." He covered a yawn. "Sorry. I was up all day with the shits. We ordered in Thai last night, which, obviously I know better. But Allen can't get enough, so I figured, just this once—"

"Gary, this isn't the first time you've fallen asleep on the job." Randy pushed a piece of paper across the table. "This is a disciplinary report filed the eighth of November. Your supervisor came in early and found Cook on patrol. You were snoring at your monitor. You want to tell me what happened?"

Hubert's brow furrowed. "The eighth, uh...that was a misunderstanding. I wasn't asleep, only resting my eyes. Nickerson came in, and—"

"That's what I thought as well," said Randy. He glanced at the paper, then turned it face-down. "So, a normal shift for you, you'd come in at seven, do your early patrol. You'd watch the monitors until six AM, then patrol again. That sound about right?"

Hubert yawned. Nodded. He rubbed his eyes like a toddler up past his bedtime. Randy leaned forward.

"And your hourly reports, can you tell me about those?"

Hubert licked his lips. "Those are just, uh, at the end of every hour, we write down what happened, and if anything went wrong. Usually it didn't, so we just put down 'clear.'"

Randy nodded slowly, as though deep in thought. "But you didn't write 'clear' that night. You didn't write anything at all. Is it possible you were, in fact, asleep the whole night?"

"*No!* No, of course not." Hubert hugged himself. "The reports, I just...I don't know. Sometimes when it's quiet, I do them all at once. Maybe that's what I did that night?"

"Are you asking me or telling me?"

Hubert said nothing. He picked at his sleeve and stifled another yawn.

"Mr. Hubert?"

"Allen did his reports, right?" Hubert brightened visibly. "He didn't get yelled at, so that means he must've. That means he was *there*."

"Or he filled them in all at once, the way you just said."

Erin scowled at her tablet. "Hey, Sasha?"

"Yeah?"

"Get Randy to ask him if he and Cook ever talked about what was on TV. Especially anything that might've pissed Cook off."

"Hold on," said Sasha. Erin waited impatiently, drumming her nails on her tablet. In the interrogation room, Randy glanced at his phone. He nodded once, set it down, and turned back to Hubert.

"It must be boring sometimes, just you and Cook, not much going on. What do you talk about to pass the time?"

"Cars, mostly," said Hubert. "Allen loves a good sportscar, a Ferrari, a Corvette. He's gonna get one someday, once he's..." His soft features sagged in sudden dismay. "He *was* going to get one when his wife came home. He'd planned this whole road trip, him and the family. He even did a few test drives, but now, I don't know."

"How about TV? You guys watch the same shows?"

"Not really," said Hubert. "I'm into sci-fi, *Star Trek, The Orville*. Allen's more political. I don't think he watches much, besides the news." Hubert frowned, then his eyes lit up. "Oh, he hates that one show, *Breakfast Book Club*. I don't know why he'd watch it. It's mostly for chicks. But Indira—she's on day shift—she left a book

272

yesterday, one of their picks. Allen threw it out, said he was doing her a favor. Said that show corrupts minds."

"*Breakfast Book Club*," said Erin. "Okay, I'm on it."

"I'll keep listening," said Sasha. "Let you know if he comes up with—"

Erin hung up, already reaching for her laptop.

Erin's phone rang again at two on the dot—Randy this time, hoarse with exhaustion.

"How'd it go with *Breakfast Book Club?* Anything there?"

Erin pushed her laptop away. She'd been sleeping, she realized, dreaming with her eyes open. *Hallucinating,* maybe, her overheated brain shorting out at last. "It's a national show," she said. "Films in New York. The host's there—I checked—and the books..." She blinked to clear her vision. "I thought I had something, this one from last week. *Get Knotted,* I think. *Life After Divorce.* But the author's from Tennessee, and the guests were all—"

"Hold on." Randy was typing, keys tapping down the line.

"What are you looking for?"

"Just gimme a minute." His voice had gone reedy, all thin and tense. Erin went to the window and stared at her own reflection. Her hair was a mess, sticking up at the back. Her eyes were black and hollow, like her skin had peeled back to reveal the skull beneath. She was grinding her teeth, and she forced herself to stop.

"Randy? You there?"

273

"The *author's* from Tennessee," said Randy. "But that book's not about her. It's about Andrea Wembley. You know her, right?"

Erin couldn't breathe. Of course she knew Andrea—everyone did. Lancaster's answer to Kim Kardashian—looks, business savvy, the whole shebang. She'd married rich four times over, walked away unrepentant with a fortune to rival Croesus, a fortune that'd financed an epic world tour and a successful product brand. Then she'd hooked some British earl and nearly married him as well, but he'd found a younger bride, and now she was...

"Oh, God. She's *here*." Erin spun on her heel. "I know where to find her. I'm on my way now."

"Erin!" Randy was shouting, bellowing in her ear. Erin thumbed him to silence, grabbed for her coat. She knew just where to go—and maybe, if she hurried, she'd get there in time.

29

"Hastings, stand down. It's not safe for you to drive."

Erin narrowed her eyes. Randy was probably right. The road was a neon dreamscape, lurid trails of taillights streaming across her vision. Her cherry light left its own trail as she wove through traffic, a ribbon of red carving its way through the night.

"Hastings, respond. This isn't a joke."

She grabbed for her radio. "I'm sorry," she said. "If he's here and we wait—" A van pulled in front of her. Erin dropped her radio, swerved right so hard her head struck the window. She pumped the gas, head spinning, and the van clipped her taillight as she roared ahead.

"Erin? What just happened? Erin? *Erin?*"

She leaned forward, not slowing, groped under her seat.

"Listen, Catherine's right behind you, and the cops are on their way. At best, you'll save five minutes, so—"

Her fingers brushed the radio. She scrabbled, hooked the cable, and pulled it into her lap.

"I'm almost there," she snapped. "Passing the golf course right now."

She flew past the green, wishing she could cut through it. Ram through the fence and just...like Eric with the golf cart, that time in tenth grade. He'd pushed it to its limits, clumps of sod flying as he zigzagged down the back nine. He'd probably have gone to juvie, except it'd been winter, and after sunset. Someone had come, a red-faced night watchman with a honk like a goose. He'd shouted *hey, stop,* but it'd come out *honk-honk,* and Eric had jumped from the cart, breathless with laughter. Erin had been waiting, and she'd grabbed him by the sleeve. She'd rushed him along, hustled him to safety past the—

"I see the golf course," said Catherine, over the radio. "I see you too, Hastings. You need to slow down."

Erin killed her siren, killed her light as well. If Catherine could see her, soon Cook would too. She screamed up the avenue, squinting ahead. Somewhere close by, somewhere past the bus stop—

"We don't know he's out there," said Randy. Erin bared her teeth. She knew. She could feel it, Cook's *why* and her instincts converging just up the road. Andrea was made for him, his perfect victim—a serial divorcée with no shame at all. She left broken hearts in her wake like Cook left bodies—four broken husbands, the first of whom might or might not have taken his own life. The bridge had been icy when he'd gone off the side, but who did ninety at midnight in the thick of a storm?

Erin spotted what she was looking for, a slash of darkness between the houses across the street. She swerved across traffic and shot up the narrow lane. She'd come here as a kid, in another life—come here with Eric, up the old, weed-choked lane, to throw rocks at the windows of Frankenstein Manor. All the kids had, probably would to this day, except Andrea had bought the place. Except—

Erin rolled to a stop, heart pounding in her throat. She snatched up her radio with fingers gone numb.

"I got a green Ford up here, Nevada plates." She licked her lips, swallowed. "Hubert drives a green Ford, right? Cook must've swiped it."

"Hastings, hold position. Do not—I repeat, *do not*—"

Erin dropped the radio in its cradle. Her head throbbed and pulsed and the world pulsed with it. Andrea's McMansion shimmered like a heat haze, blinked out to reveal the haunted house beneath.

Dare you to go in, whispered Eric, back in '01 and right at her elbow.

"Can't wait," said Erin. She was out of her car and gliding up the drive. Inky shadows dropped to cover her, the shadows of sycamores or rusted-out cars. An awful sound reached her ears, someone laughing, someone choking, and Erin froze on the porch with her back to the wall. She closed her eyes tight. Had she imagined it, or—

The sound came again, a low, miserable gagging. Erin snapped back to the present and back to herself. Andrea was in there, and she was still alive.

Get him, said Eric. Erin bit her tongue until she tasted blood. Eric wasn't here. No one was, just her. She was Andrea's last hope, and if she couldn't get it together, Cook would win again.

She eased up on the front door, hardly daring to breathe. She could hear Cook inside, grunting like a hog. Grunting and *growling,* forcing words past his lips. Erin strained to hear them, then decided they didn't matter. She reached out, slow and steady, and tried the doorknob. It turned without a sound and the door swung inward. Erin swung with it, and there in the darkness crouched a terrible ogre in the shape of her brother, scooping maggots from a corpse long gone to rot. She blinked and it was Cook, and he was straddling Andrea, stuffing her mouth with some sort of—

"Get off her!" she roared. She went for her weapon and realized she didn't have it. Cook turned in slow motion, a sick, oily grin spreading over his face. He clenched his fist and something crumpled—a page from a book—and he leaned over and crammed it in Andrea's mouth. She gagged weakly, lips blue.

"I said, *get off her.*" Erin clasped her fists together, pointed her fingers at Cook in the shape of a gun. In the dark, maybe—

"Agent Hastings." Cook struggled upright, one hand in the air, the other clutching a blood-spattered rock. "I was just finishing up here. If you'd put that away, I think we could talk. Come to an understanding, like you had with your brother."

Erin held his gaze. "Get away from her. Now." She gestured with her fingergun, away from Andrea. Cook stepped toward her, his grin only widening.

"I'd planned on saving you for later, but what the hell? You're here now." He scratched at his thigh, or maybe his crotch. "I'm going to savor you slow. Hold you nice and close while the light leaves your eyes. I shouldn't take trophies, but your eyes would make—"

Erin laughed to keep from retching. "That's such a cliché," she said. "Besides, you don't have time. My team's right behind me. Any second now, they're going to come up that lane."

Cook glanced over her shoulder. "Funny. I don't see anyone. Maybe they got lost?"

"*You're* lost," said Erin. "Come on, face the wall. Time to end this nonsense."

Cook didn't move. "Nonsense? I don't think so. My eyes are finally open. All those years, I couldn't see it—all those years I cradled a viper to my breast. I cared for that viper. Loved her, protected her, nursed her every day. Then when my milk dried up, didn't she slither off? Didn't she leave me and take her viper-spawn with her?"

Erin glanced at Andrea. She wasn't moving. She needed help, and fast.

"You can still help yourself," said Erin. "Assault a federal agent, we're going to throw the book at you. But stand down right now, and I'll do all I can to keep the death penalty off the table."

"You think that scares me?" Cook burst out laughing. "No one's been executed in California or Nevada since 2006."

Erin cast about for a weapon. She spotted a bust of Beethoven perched on a low table. She took one step toward it and Cook made his move. He flung his rock at her, then flung himself after it. The rock bounced off her shoulder and shattered on the floor—not a rock, but a snow globe, spilling glitter at her feet. Cook plowed into Erin, knocking her on her back. Plinking music filled the atrium, *Holly Jolly Christmas.*

"Get off me." She clawed at his face, screwed her thumb into his eyeball. Cook roared and thrashed, slammed his forehead into hers. Erin howled, seeing stars, and jammed her knee into his groin.

"This is *over,*" she hissed.

"This'll never be over." Cook was panting, red-faced, blood trailing down his cheek. "The world's full of vipers. I'm on a crusade."

Erin almost laughed. He'd bought into his own hype, like a kid dressed as Superman thinking he could fly. "The Crusaders are *gone,*" she said. "Saladin drove them out, or...I don't know, exactly, but you're too late." She got her thumb in his eye again, forced his head back. Cook jerked and spasmed, gnashed his teeth at thin air.

"Don't you get it? I'm a hero. Saving lives, just like you! Men's lives, good men, and I'm—"

Erin got her arm around his neck, threw him off with a grunt. Cook thrashed, but she held him tight, cutting off his air. "I'm no hero," she snarled. "I'm a monster, and so are you."

Cook made a whining sound, high in his throat. He sunfished in her arms, heels drumming on the floor. Erin held him, unyielding. Black dots swarmed her vision and she blinked them away. She flipped Cook on his belly and cuffed his hands behind his back.

You could kick him, said Eric. *Kick his teeth down his throat. No one could say when you did it.*

Erin resisted the impulse. She ran to Andrea instead, dug sodden wads of paper out of her mouth. Andrea didn't react. She lay pale and silent, her blue eyes half open.

"It's okay," said Erin, feeling for her pulse. She found it, faint and thready, racing in her throat. "Breathe for me, yeah? Help's on the way."

"You could do it," said Cook, his voice thick and bloody. "You could finish her off and say it was me."

Erin ignored him. She felt for her phone, but it wasn't in her pocket.

"I know you want to," said Cook. "Somewhere, deep down, you're aching to do it. To feel what he felt, the Lancaster Slasher. It's true what they say, how twins share one soul."

"You'll get my sole up your ass if you don't shut your mouth." Erin could hear them now, tires crunching up the drive. Catherine, probably. She'd been right on her tail.

"I respect him," said Cook. "You know, your brother. He took 'em out young. Crushed those vipers in their nests. He knew what they'd turn into, if they got to grow up."

Andrea moaned. Erin took her hand and held it, and Andrea squeezed back hard.

"You're okay," Erin told her. "I've got the garbage men coming to take out the trash."

Andrea made a broken sound, but her lips quirked up like she was trying to smile.

"We're going to get you some help, get you all patched up. Your snow globe is toast, but, come on. *Holly Jolly Christmas?* When it comes to Christmas music, that's the bottom of the barrel. I'll get you a new one myself. You like *Silver Bells?*"

Andrea didn't answer, but she squeezed Erin's hand again. Cook was still prattling on, but Erin wasn't listening. The hallway flashed blue and crimson, ghostly police lights streaking across the walls. Boots thumped on the steps and Erin sagged with relief.

"Catherine? That you?"

"Erin? What've you got?"

"Suspect restrained, in custody. Victim alive and conscious, but she'll need an ambulance."

"Already on the way." Catherine knelt next to Cook. "Did you read him his rights?"

"No, she didn't," said Cook. "That means I go free."

Catherine snorted. "That means, Allen Cook, you're under arrest for the attempted murder of Andrea Wembley. You have the right to remain silent. Anything you say can and will be used against you in a court of law."

Erin leaned back, head spinning, as the local cops swarmed in. She let the Miranda warning wash over her, music to her ears. Cook was yelling as well, but maybe it was the sirens, maybe it was her concussion—his shouts were just noise, rabid burbling, nothing more. That suited Erin right down to the ground. She closed her eyes and drifted, high on her win. Voices rose and fell, and she let them: *Erin? Hey, Erin? Think we'll need a medic for this one as well.*

What were you thinking? Hasty Hastings strikes again.

Aw, come on. Not now. She's been through enough.

I'm proud of you, said Eric, or maybe that was Dad. *You took him down, made him pay. Gave him what he deserved.*

30

Erin called Catherine from her laptop, from the cave of her hospital room. Dad had pulled down the shades and turned off the lights, and Erin hadn't protested. The darkness felt good, a cool bath for her eyes. The pounding in her head had quieted in the night, and she felt almost lively, as long as she didn't move.

Catherine answered quickly, her video flickering as the camera adjusted to the light. She was in a dark place as well, the children's museum. She set down her tablet and leaned into the camera.

"Hey, Erin. You okay?"

Erin closed her eyes against the glare from the screen. "My eyes are still sensitive, but my head's stopped spinning."

"Lucky you," said Brody, from somewhere offscreen. "I've still got a headache from the lights off the Strip."

"Great. We've all got headaches." Randy pushed in, scowling. "Erin, hello. Thought we'd do a little wrap-up while forensics does their thing."

Erin nodded. "Found anything new?"

"Not yet," said Randy. "We've been through his house, but no evidence there. He had a hidey-hole here, though. They're going over it now." He grabbed a chair and sat down. "Why don't we start with what led you to Cook? Catherine tells me you liked him from the start."

"Not quite from the start," said Erin. She rubbed her temple lightly, where Watt had punched her. "At first, it was just like, the husband always did it. Plus, he fit Mo's profile almost to a tee. But then when I met him...right from that moment, I felt *something* not right." She frowned, fishing for the details.

"He didn't have any pictures," said Brody. "Erin spotted that the first time we met him. He claimed he'd come to Pahrump to make up with his wife, but he didn't have a single picture of her, or Valerie either."

"And he was angry," said Erin. "I didn't see it that first time, but he was like a pot on the stove, about to boil over. He'd hide it a while, try to mask it with grief, but it always came out, these flashes of rage. And then there was Valerie. She never fit the pattern. Rayna didn't either, once we figured out how he picked his victims. She was never on TV, so why her? Why start there? The killer had to know her. Had to hate her enough to do what he did. It had to be Cook. No one else had the motive."

"I thought Watt did," said Brody.

"For Valerie," said Randy. "But, I don't know. I never liked him for the rest. Valerie would've been, for him, a crime of passion. The rest were cold-blooded, planned out in advance. The killer had maturity. Impulse control. Watt never had any of that."

"That girl on campus, though, *she* mentioned Cook." Catherine made a face. "She said Valerie would go see him and come back all stressed. We might've connected the dots from that, if the call hadn't come in on Watt."

"So, a lot of little red flags." Randy stroked his chin.

"That was the problem," said Erin. "We had all these little tipoffs, but Cook's alibi was solid. How was he getting to the crime scenes when his car never left the museum? When *Hubert* never left, and why would he lie for Cook?"

Brody rolled his eyes. "We're still waiting on blood results, but Hubert's coffee mug came back positive for Ambien. Cook was dosing him all along, ducking out while he slept."

Erin considered that for a moment. "So the night we got him—last night—"

"He thought he'd make fools of us," said Randy. "Thought he was clever. Though, I don't know how he expected it to work. He'd send us to Vegas, chasing some patsy in the Lambo, then what? Call it in stolen, with the FBI as witness? And how did he expect to sneak back into the museum? He thought we'd just leave when the driver wasn't him? Like, *okay, stolen vehicle, guess Cook's not our guy?*"

"He's no rocket scientist," said Brody. "But then, these guys never are. They think they're these criminal masterminds, but they're just common scum."

Erin leaned forward. "Who *was* driving the Lambo? Did you ever find out?"

"Some guy off Craigslist, thought Cook was pulling a fast one on his insurance." Randy snorted. "We got him on camera snarfing sushi burritos. It took about five seconds to track him down."

"I want to know who came up with that, sushi burritos." Brody stuck out his tongue. "It's like chefs get together, all...what's the worst combo we could make, and folks would still eat it? Clams and tomatoes. Pineapple on pizza. I ask you, what's next? Tripe candy canes?"

Erin fought back laughter. "What even *is* tripe?"

"I don't know," said Brody. "But what I do know is—"

"Excuse me?" A shadow climbed the wall, towering over Randy. He got to his feet.

"What is it?"

"We've found something in the basement. You'd better come see."

"Take me with you," said Erin.

Catherine scooped up her tablet and carried Erin along, the picture bouncing and joggling as she headed down the stairs.

"Erin, can you see this?" Catherine held up her tablet. For a moment, the screen went black. Then the camera adjusted, and Erin caught her breath. A tiny nook lay before her, nestled behind the furnace and halfway bricked off. Someone had set up a rickety desk along one wall, stacked haphazardly with papers—a few newspaper clippings and what looked like legal documents, California and Nevada state seals stamped on the letterheads.

"Divorce records?"

The tablet bobbed up and down, maybe from Catherine nodding. "He's got that book too, *Life After Divorce.*"

Erin swallowed hard. She'd spotted it already, a thin paperback with a cheery yellow cover. Andrea was no saint, but what Cook had done to her made Erin's stomach churn.

"You saved her," said Randy. "You got there in time."

Erin hummed her acknowledgment, but she was no longer listening. Catherine had turned her tablet to reveal a ghastly mural: portraits of

Cook's victims pinned to the wall, four with angry black crosses slashed over their faces. Valerie wasn't there. Andrea was, posing in her bikini on some bone-white beach. Catherine zoomed in and Erin picked out her name scrawled underneath, along with her address, her place of employment.

"Check out these calendars," came Brody's voice. Catherine swung her tablet again. Erin's head spun with vertigo. She didn't want to look, but she did. Cook had taped a line of calendars to the side of the furnace. Each was marked up with one victim's routines—when she went to work, when she came home. Who her friends were, when she saw them and where. Where she ate, where she drank, what she did for fun.

Erin coughed. "Where'd he get all that?"

"Don't know," said Brody. "But my money's on social media. Sasha has his computer, so we'll know by tonight."

Randy turned the tablet his way. His expression was grim. Erin's stomach did a somersault.

"Randy, what's wrong?"

He held up a pocket-sized leather notebook in one gloved hand. "I've found his diary, though it's more like a kill list."

Erin cocked a brow. "Isn't that a good thing? With evidence like that, he'll be locked up for life."

Randy stared at the notebook, not speaking, then passed it to Brody. Brody leafed through it and his complexion turned ashen.

"Oh, that's not..."

"What?"

"Later," he said. He dropped the book in an evidence bag, wrinkling his nose like he'd touched a dead mouse.

"Not later," said Erin. "Tell me now, what's so bad?"

Brody glanced at Randy. He cleared his throat. "You were next," he said. "He'd already started mapping your routine."

"Me." A cold wave passed through her, snowmelt down her spine. She laughed to hide her shiver, but it came out thin and brittle. "I don't fit his victim pattern. Guess I'm just *that* annoying."

Randy sighed in exasperation, but his expression lightened a little. "You annoy me," he said. "But this guy pisses me off. I'm going to bury him so deep—so deep he'll strike oil."

"I've got another call coming in," said Catherine. "It's the Nevada state police. Call you back when we're through?"

"I'm not going anywhere," said Erin, and shot her the thumbs-up. The screen went blank, and Erin fell back on her pillows. Her eyes swam with tears, and for once, she let them flow. A taut band had let go inside her, and she could breathe at last. Cook was done. She was free. Seventy-two hours from now, she'd be home in her own bed, her own personal hell fading in her rearview mirror. She just had one thing to do before she put this nightmare behind her once and for all.

Eric was sitting up in bed, sipping bubble tea through a straw. He brightened when he saw her, and held up his cup.

"You ever had this stuff?"

"What, bubble tea?" Erin laughed. "Don't tell me you hadn't."

"I hadn't," said Eric. He sucked up a pearl and chewed it with relish. "I guess this is my first and last, at least for a while. I'm cleared for release tomorrow. Back to my cell."

"Sorry," said Erin. She sat down beside him, at the edge of his bed. "I'm leaving as well. Back to Atlanta."

"I heard you got your killer. I knew you would." Eric stared out the window, past the barren gray tarmac to the blue sky beyond. "Could you send me a picture of that?"

"Of the parking lot?"

"Of the sky. It doesn't have to be a big one, just a little square of blue. A postcard would work. A Polaroid, even."

Erin chuckled. "Polaroids aren't a thing. Haven't been in years."

"You know what I mean, though."

"I'll write you. I promise. And, yeah, I'll send pics." She fished out her phone and snapped a shot of the sky. It came out pretty good, a wide stretch of blue dotted with powder puff clouds. She held it up for Eric to see, and he nodded his approval.

"I was never one of those people who saw pictures in clouds," he said. "No imagination, I guess. I look at clouds drifting by, and you know what I think of? I think of fried eggs, with the sun for the yolk. The clouds are the whites, the way they crinkle at the edges and go all like lace. I look up and get *hungry*. How's that for boring?"

"Boring's good," said Erin. "Boring's a relief. I've had enough interesting to last my whole life."

"I'll believe *that* when I see it." Eric leaned back and stretched, and for a while they just sat, Eric watching the clouds, Erin watching him. She became conscious of the cop standing guard outside the door, the creak of his belt, the waft of his cologne.

"I can't stay," she said. "My boss'll have my head if he catches me not resting. I just came to give you something before I head out."

"Give me something?" Erik's eyes sparked with interest.

"Nothing big. Just this."

She leaned in and hugged her brother before she could change her mind.

Erin was back in her dark room, slipping between the sheets, when Catherine called back. Catherine squinted into the camera, eyes narrowed with suspicion.

"Why are your cheeks all flushed? Were you wandering around?"

"Just went to the bathroom," said Erin. "You'd rather I pee the bed?"

"I'd rather you take care of yourself," said Catherine. "But I've got some good news. The ballistics came back from the Coyote Springs shooting."

Erin twitched at the memory. She still woke with a start sometimes, lunging for her weapon. But this was good news, so she composed her face into a smile. "Hayes, right?"

"Got it in one." Catherine started to say something else, but Brody squeezed in behind her, brimming with glee.

"They're charging him with attempted murder. He'll plead down, of course, but it's not going to matter. The list of charges he's got, he's not getting out until he qualifies for senior discounts. Maybe not even then."

"Couldn't happen to a nicer person." Erin smirked. "Hey, did you talk to Hannady? She must be over the moon."

"I wouldn't go that far," said Catherine. Behind her, Brody scowled. "She's pleased we got Cook, but she gave us a whole lecture about all the skels going unpunished while we chased red herrings."

"She actually said *skels?*" Erin pulled a face. "You know who she reminds me of? One of those old-timey hanging judges, like from a Clint Eastwood western. *Hang 'Em High.* Or what was that one where he shoots the guy off the gallows, shoots through the rope? I guess it doesn't matter. You know what I mean."

"She's pretty hardline," agreed Brody. "But enough about her. What are you going to do until it's time to head back?"

Erin grinned. "I don't know about you, but I think I've earned a nap."

Brody let out a snort. "You'd earned one weeks ago, but okay. You do you."

Erin hung up and smiled. She *would* take a nap, she thought. The sleep of the just.

He'd been so close. He'd felt the life draining out of her, her body going limp. He'd watched her surrender, succumb to the inevitable. Then that *bitch* came along, that crazy-eyes bitch. She'd snatched his victory, taken it for herself. She'd stolen his kill, and now he couldn't breathe.

He gasped for air, tasted hate. It tasted of dust, of spiders and mold. That was the thing with hate: it thrived in dank places, in basements and sewers. In cells much like this one, and in his heart. She was infected as well, Agent Erin Hastings. He'd smelled it on her when she'd pinned him to the floor. It had practically *poured* from her when she'd stood over him in the dark. He'd half expected her to lift her boot and smash his skull like an egg. She'd half-blinded him as it was, squelched his right eyeball like an overripe grape.

He touched his face and it throbbed, a dull pain that radiated from his eye socket and crackled through his jaw. She'd taken something from him, something he'd never get back.

"Bitch," he said. The word felt good in his mouth, so he said it again. A bitch was what she was, a dirty she-dog sniffing after bones. She was no different from the others, when you really got down to it. She saw what she wanted and she took it, even when it wasn't hers. He'd *earned* that kill, and she'd snapped it right up like a nasty Milk Bone.

He closed his good eye and lay back on his cot. His cell had a draft and he tilted his face to it. Only hours ago, he'd been speeding through the night, straight through the storm with the thunder in his ears. He stretched out his hands to grip a phantom wheel. It was all still so close, the world he'd left behind, fast cars and open road, the ecstasy of the kill. With his eye squeezed tight shut he could almost believe he'd dreamed his arrest. That he'd sit up and stretch and the sun would be streaming in his window, a whole world of vengeance waiting on the other side.

He opened his eye and saw cracks spidering across decaying concrete. He'd miscalculated, was all. He'd expected Hastings to chase him, not circle ahead and catch him in the act. She'd got in his head somehow, dug through his secret thoughts and turned up Andrea. He thought of her eyes, cold as sea glass, and seethed with hate.

"Agent Erin Hastings." He held up his hand and saw it was shaking. He clenched it into a fist and pulled it back to his side. He needed his drug back, the high of the kill. If he couldn't get it through murder, he'd have to find another way.

He unclenched his fists as the guard walked by.

This wasn't over. Not by a long shot.

31

The whole team met for lunch their last day in Lancaster, an Italian feast with all the trimmings. Dad had set it up, called in a favor with an old friend from work—a friend who'd gone into the restaurant business ten years before. He'd yet to earn his first Michelin star, but his Yelp reviews were good, and the smell that rose from the takeout bags was close to divine.

"This smells amazing," said Brody. He plopped down in Dad's easy chair and pulled a greasy bag toward him. "Oh, god, yes. Garlic bread. Can I dive in face first?"

"I'd rather you didn't," said Randy. "Not until I've had a slice."

"There's plenty for everyone," said Dad. He passed around paper plates, and napkins to go with them. "I wish I could stay, but you know. Work."

"I'll be here when you get back," said Erin. "We'll have dessert and catch up."

Dad leaned down and kissed her on the top of her head. His cologne tickled her nose, and for a moment, Erin was fourteen again, settling in for Christmas pizza after Dad burned the turkey. She smiled up at him, eyes swimming, and then he was gone.

"Okay, no elbows," said Randy. "I'll pass each dish around, and you take what you want. No hogging the sauces, no snaking last bites until everyone's had their share."

"Sir, yes sir." Catherine sketched a mock-salute, and then the food was moving, trays of zitti and ravioli and chicken carbonara making the rounds. Erin loaded her plate and dug in, savoring the rich taste of marinara on her tongue. Brody attacked the garlic bread, dipping it shamelessly in his pasta alfredo. Randy ate neatly, with a knife and fork. Catherine used her fingers, wiped her mouth with her hand. No one said anything, not until their first plates were empty and they were reaching for seconds.

"I needed this," said Catherine. "I feel human again for the first time in weeks. Which is a good thing, because we need to wrap up Cook's interrogation before we file charges. We're almost at the end of our forty-eight-hour window."

Randy hummed his agreement through a mouthful of zitti. He looked up at Erin. "I suppose you'll want to sit in on that."

Erin pictured herself sitting down to interrogate Cook. Pictured his dull eyes, his greasy brown hair. All she felt was contempt, and a touch of disgust. Her lust for the chase had burned out, leaving, in its place, a strange sense of peace. "I'm still pretty drained," she said. "I think I'll hang out with Dad tonight, then I might just sleep over. I need to get some rest before the flight back."

Randy studied her. "Good idea. Your color's better today, but you're still a bit pale. I'll fill you in on anything interesting on the flight home."

Lunch wrapped up late, almost spilling into dinner. The sun hung low over the horizon when the team got up to go.

"Tell your dad thanks from us," said Randy. "That was really a treat."

"I'll tell him," said Erin. She waved to Randy and Catherine as they headed down the drive, but when Brody went to follow, she caught him by the arm. "Hey. Stay a minute?"

"Something wrong?"

"Come sit down." She led him back to the couch and sat down. He hovered a moment, then sat next to her.

"What's so important it can't wait until we get back to Atlanta?"

Erin reached for her soda and took a long swig. She felt parched all of a sudden, her tongue too big for her mouth. "I know you've been dying to yell at me," she said. "For, y'know..."

"Fingerguns?" He pointed his finger at her head and pulled an imaginary trigger. "You'd hit your head. You were out of your mind. But, Jesus, Erin. What if he'd had a real gun?"

"I'd be dead," she said. "And so would Andrea, and it would all have been for nothing." She looked down at her knees, at a tomato stain on her jeans. "I was writing my reports today. Thinking over my actions, those last twelve hours. The doctor said no screens. I was on 'em all day. He said sleep, and I didn't. He said 'rest your head.' I did exactly the opposite, and ignored orders as well. I'd like to blame my concussion, or..." She made a vague gesture, waving toward the window. "I'd like to say I just lost it, coming here, seeing Eric. But that was only part of it. Truth is, I *wanted* Cook. I couldn't pass up the hunt."

Brody let out a long breath. "I know that," he said.

"It's not enough to say sorry. I know that, but...I want to say, too, don't blame yourself. You're a good leader. It's not your fault I keep doing this, and—"

"That's where you're wrong."

"Brody—"

"No, stop. Shut up." He planted his hands on his knees. "I *am* your team leader. That makes it all my fault, if I can't see it coming when you step over that line. And the truth is, I did see it, but I wanted him too. I should've sent you home weeks ago, but I knew you'd get him. I knew. You've got that killer instinct, so I kept you where I needed you and promised myself—promised Randy I'd grab you if you went too far."

Erin stared at him, dry-mouthed, dizzy with guilt. "You got me to the hospital," she said. "When I puked on my shoes."

"And I should've kept you there. Made sure you didn't move." He hunched over, a stray strand of hair dangling in his face. "This can't happen again," he said. "Going forward, every case we work, we'll be joined at the hip. I'm going to be your shoulder-angel until you grow one of your own."

Erin opened her mouth, then shut it. She didn't know what to say.

"I accept your apology," said Brody. "But Catherine and Randy deserve one as well. Sasha too, after the scolding she got for going in on your madness."

Erin winced. "I was going to talk to her tonight. Who knew she'd catch the first flight back to Atlanta?"

Brody huffed a half-laugh. "Yeah, well, that's what phones are for." He gave Erin a gentle noogie, rubbing his knuckles on her scalp. "I should head out," he said. "Have a good night with your dad, and try not to get lost on the way back to the hotel." Brody flipped her a V for victory on his way out the door. Erin watched him go, a relieved smile playing about her lips. In a while, she'd have to get up and clear away their plates, pack up the leftovers for Dad to enjoy. But for now, she was full of pasta, the last of the sunset warm at her back. She owed herself an apology, as well—or at least a minute to feel at peace. To feel at home, for the first time in years.

32

E rin dropped by the office her third day back in Atlanta, partly to grab some things, mostly to check in with her team. She arrived around lunchtime and stayed to eat some fruitcake Catherine's kids had baked. The cake was mediocre, but the company was good. She was just settling in when Brody poked his head out.

"Hey, Erin. Good to see you. Randy says drop by his office before you head out."

"All right," she said. "I'll go do that now. I ought to get out before those fluorescents trigger a migraine."

"You still getting those?" Catherine touched her forehead. "You feel kind of warm. Maybe you're coming down with something."

"I don't think so," said Erin. "I talked to the doc, and he says it's just my brain telling me it still needs to rest. Two thumps in the head like that, I guess I can't blame it."

"That's right," said Brody. "Give it a vacation. This is your brain in the Bahamas."

Erin snorted laughter. She waved goodbye to Brody and Catherine and made her way to Randy's office. He saw her coming and motioned her inside.

"Erin, take a seat."

She did as he said. She knew what was coming—the talk he'd promised back in Lancaster, about her insubordination. Still, she met his eye with a smile. "Brody said you needed to see me?"

He nodded. "I'm sure it comes as no surprise to you that you're being placed on medical leave."

"Not really. How long?"

"Until a doctor clears you," said Randy. He folded his hands on his blotter, a sure sign he meant business. "Between now and then, you are not to set foot in this office. Understand?"

Erin looked away, chastened. She'd apologized to Randy, but she knew it would take time to rebuild the trust between them. Still, he'd hoped he'd let her ride a desk until she got her feet under her. "I understand," she said. "I'll stay out of trouble."

Randy fixed her with a stern gaze, but then he relented. "If you're worried about your job, don't be. This is just a time-out. A chance to recover, and to think about your future." Randy's eyes narrowed. "You can't ignore direct orders, regardless of the circumstances. If you'd come to *me* that last night, instead of running to Sasha, I could've got a team together to go over that footage. You might not have thought so, but it didn't have to be you."

"I know that now," said Erin. "And I really am sorry."

Randy waved her off, impatient. "You've said that already. And I'm giving you a pass *this time* because I'm positive your head injury compromised your judgment. But, Erin, you're a good agent with the potential to be a great one. I see a great future for you—but only if you don't manage to get yourself fired. And make no mistake, you *will* be fired if you cross that line again."

Erin nodded meekly. "Yes, sir. I understand."

"Good, then." Randy clapped his hands together. "That's it for the riot act. Now, what do you plan to do with all your time off?"

Erin leaned back in her chair. "I'm not sure," she said. "Dad wanted me to fly back out, but..." She looked away. Dad had showed up at the airport the night she flew out. He'd pulled her aside and repeated Eric's assertion that he'd killed four women, not six.

"I believe him," he'd said. "I don't know why, but I do."

"It wouldn't change his sentence," said Erin. "That's still four murders, four he *did* do."

"But what about the killer? The other one? What kind of justice is that, if he's still out there with their blood on his hands?"

Erin had promised to do what she could, but she wasn't sure that amounted to anything. Eric's case wasn't just cold. It was closed and done with, a win for the books. Digging into it now would only get her in trouble.

"But...?" Randy prodded.

"My family's a lot," she said. "More than most." Still, Dad had said one more thing, as she'd turned to go. *Don't be a stranger,* he'd said, and his face had contorted, showing his age. *My door's always open for my little girl. Come visit or don't come—just, whatever you do, make sure you stay safe.*

Those words had stuck with her, the offer of a safe haven. A place she could come to, no matter what. She'd never had that, or never known she did. Her relationship with Dad had been strained for years. But now she knew they still had one, and that was a start. Maybe, with

300

time, they'd build up to something better. Something strong, something loving. The dream felt far off, but at least she dared to dream it.

"I think I might hit the spa," she said, returning her attention to Randy. "Get some pampering, a manicure, one of those seaweed wraps. Do you eat those, or...?"

"You do *not*," said Randy. He stared at her, eyes searching, until she shifted in her seat. Then he reached for a file. "Listen, I shouldn't give you this, but this is a dossier on a man named Dion Finney. I think you should take a look at it while you're on leave. Off the record, of course—and only once you *can* read without getting dizzy."

Erin took the file. It felt heavy in her hands, and a thrill walked down her spine. "Thank you," she said. She got up to leave, then another thought struck her. "I don't suppose you'd want to let me see what you've got on my brother?"

Randy studied her, his expression regretful. "Erin, it's been fifteen years. I'm not sure what you'd gain from that, besides a whole lot of heartache."

"I know," she said. "But he's still my brother."

Randy smiled, faint but kind. "I'll take a look around, see what I can find. But Erin, don't hold your breath. You know chances are slim I'll turn up anything new." He wagged his finger at her. "And don't go stepping on any toes or getting into any trouble. You got us Cook, so you've earned a little grace. But you start making a nuisance of yourself—well, I've seen promising agents let go for less."

Erin bobbed her head. "Understood. I'll focus on getting better. And on getting to the bottom of that seaweed wrap mystery."

"Sounds like a plan." Randy waved her off and Erin drifted out of the building. She tried to let her mind go blank, to keep the wheels from spinning, but the Finney file called to her. Begged her to take a peek.

"Not today," she said. "But soon." She climbed into her car and dropped the file on the passenger seat. It sat fat and heavy, promising new adventures. In her head, she heard hunting horns calling her to the chase.

This medical leave had just become a lot more interesting.

END OF WHAT YOU DESERVE
FBI AGENT ERIN HASTINGS BOOK ONE

PS: Do you enjoy crime fiction? Then keep reading for an exclusive extract from *Mother's Don't Lie.*

ABOUT ALICIA LAWSON

Loved this book? Share it with a friend!

To be notified of the next book release please sign up for Alicia's mailing list, at
www.relaypub.com/alicia-lawson-mailinglist

Alicia Lawson first delved into the world of serial killers when she watched true crime documentaries with her grandmother. Alicia was so intrigued by how the detectives would solve the case that she would read stacks of crime fiction and as much forensic non-fiction as her worried mother would allow.

Now a full-time writer, she lives in her native California with her husband and two dogs. Returning to her roots, she draws inspiration from real case studies, genre staples, and research for her own stories. Her books feature strong female characters who face their pasts head-on, using their driven nature to dig into the evidence and catch the killer.

To learn more about her books visit:

BLURB

The perfect life becomes the perfect lie.

Molly Burke has it all. With the help of medication to control her borderline personality disorder, she's become a successful real estate agent with a loving husband who treats her four-year-old son as if he were his own. The emotional highs and lows from childhood trauma have smoothed out but are still best concealed with little white lies to protect loved ones from her troubled history. Until Molly's past returns to shatter her idyllic life.

Molly's son is discovered injured and covered in his grandfather's blood—and her father-in-law is nowhere to be found. The police suspect foul play. Longstanding bitterness erupts between Molly and her mother-in-law, exacerbating Molly's feelings of inadequacy and triggering fierce reactions that can no longer be contained.

A hallucination of her missing father-in-law only increases Molly's paranoia over the sins of the past. Deceit lies around every corner and embroils everyone in the growing madness. Someone knows what she did. And someone is trying to expose the truth.

And if the truth is kept hidden, her family will pay the price.

**Grab your copy of *Mother's Don't Lie* from
www.jocrow.com/books**

EXCERPT

Chapter One

My palms were clammy. Beneath them, the steering wheel felt cold and heavy. I was driving too fast. Every now and then, the car jittered and threatened to swerve into a dark crevice at the side of the road. And with it, my heart hammered hard against my rib cage. I wanted to stop, to turn around and slide back into the life I was living yesterday. Before I made the decision to run. Before I realized that everything was not *okay*.

Yesterday, the promise of a happy future had still glimmered on the horizon. If I'd stayed, in just a few months, I'd have had the money to clear my debts and start fresh; scrub out all the mistakes from my past and focus on truly turning things around. But now, in the dead of the night, with the inky sky squeezing the sides of my battered old Civic as it hurtled down the freeway, I knew I couldn't go back.

In the rearview mirror, headlights appeared in the distance. At first, they were just pin pricks—a good way behind me on the road—but as I watched, they drew closer. In the dark, I couldn't tell what kind of car they were attached to, but whoever was driving was moving quickly, catching up with me, closing the gap between us. I pressed my foot on the accelerator, but the Civic groaned and refused to go any faster.

I shuffled in my seat, shaking my head so that my long red hair fell back from my face, I tried to keep looking ahead. On the passenger seat, my phone began to ring, and my body jolted as if it were a police siren cutting through the silence. The ringing filled the car. Behind me, the headlights were drawing nearer. I swiped the phone into the footwell, and it clattered hard, but whoever was trying to call me hadn't stopped. The glow of the incoming call was leaking out from its facedown screen. Finally, it went quiet.

I looked up. The headlights were so close and bright that their reflection made me wince and narrow my eyes. I was holding my breath. The car behind me beeped its horn, and then it swung out of its lane. It was pulling up next to me, driving alongside me. Still beeping.

I tried not to look at it. I didn't know whether to slow down and stop or keep going. It was still level with me, too close, trying to make me pull over. Finally, I turned my head, expecting to see Tracy's desperate and bruised face screaming at me not to leave.

But it wasn't her.

It was a middle-aged guy with thick shoulders and a long, wiry beard and, even though I didn't know what Tracy's partner, Andy, looked like, I knew that this man was not him. "Speed up or get off the fucking road! Stupid bitch!" he yelled through his open car window.

Tears started to roll down my cheeks. Relieved tears, scared tears. He slammed his fist on his horn a few more times, raised his middle finger at me, then sped off, his tires screeching as he accelerated away.

A hot wave of nausea flooded my limbs. My breath was coming quick and shallow, warning signs that a panic attack was about to take hold of me. *Calm down, Molly, it's not good for the baby. Think of the baby. Think of the baby.*

Eventually, I saw the exit I needed. As I pulled off the freeway, the wide empty road I'd been traveling on began to narrow; I was nearing the beach. By the time I stopped the car, my legs were trembling, and my arms felt like they were made of lead. I tried to slow my breathing. *Five, four, three, two, one,* the way Carol had taught me to when we were hiding beneath the stairs and praying our foster parents didn't find us. I closed my eyes and counted until my breath returned to normal.

The spot I'd arrived at was somewhere I'd been many times before. It was the place I retreated to when I needed to be alone with my thoughts. The place I came to after my parents died, after Jack died, when I dropped out of college, and when I discovered that I was pregnant. That day, the day I saw those two fateful blue lines at the end of a white plastic stick, all I felt was panic. But all these months later, for the first time, I felt the way expectant mothers are supposed to feel— like the little person growing inside me was the most important thing in the world. Like I'd rather die than let anything happen to him. And that was how I knew I was doing the right thing by getting him away from Tracy and Andy.

Even if they hunted me down. Even if they found me, hired fancy lawyers, made me do what I'd promised. At least I'd know I'd tried to be a good mom. The best mom. The kind of mom who takes care of her kid.

I breathed out slowly and turned off the engine. Pressing my palms against my stomach, I leaned down and whispered, "You have nothing to be afraid of. I'll never let anyone hurt you. I'm your mom." The words caught in my throat, and I blinked back my tears. "I'm your mom, and no one will ever, *ever*, take you away from me. It's just you and me now, little buddy. You and me. Forever."

As I spoke, I felt a tiny flutter beneath my hands.

"Oh," I said. "There you are."

I smiled a shaky smile and tried to tell myself that it would be hours before anyone noticed I was gone. It was the middle of the night. I wasn't due to see Tracy until the weekend and, by the time she realized what had happened, I'd be miles away. My phone had stopped ringing. We were alone. Just me and my son.

There were two dusky orange streetlights over towards the steps that led to the beach. But nothing else. No one else. I reached over to the glove compartment and flicked it open. I took out the handful of papers that I'd wedged in there weeks ago. Papers that promised my baby to another couple. Papers that would have given us both an entirely different life.

I took the matches I'd shoved into my purse, got out of the car, and strode down to the water. Letting the cool waves bite my toes, I lit a match. Then I held it beneath the neatly typed contract and let the flame engulf it.

When it was nothing but a fiery torch clenched in my fist with the heat scalding my skin, I dropped it into the water. And I let the ocean carry it away.

Taking one last look at my faithful old car, I slung my bag over my shoulder and walked away. Away from the life I thought I'd be living. Away from Portland. Away from the promises I'd made.

I took the unborn child I was never supposed to keep, and I left.

Grab your copy of *Mother's Don't Lie* from
www.jocrow.com/books